I Was Not Alone

Other titles from Scottish Cultural Press

Roots in a Northern Landscape: Celebrations of Childhood in the NE of Scotland
W Gordon Lawrence
1 898218 79 X

In My Small Corner: Memoirs of an Orcadian Childhood
Margaret Aitken
1 84017 002 6

Discover Scotland's History
A D Cameron
1 898218 76 5

I Was Not Alone

Robert Dick

SCOTTISH CULTURAL PRESS
EDINBURGH

First Published 1997 by
Scottish Cultural Press
Unit 14, Leith Walk Business Centre
130 Leith Walk
Edinburgh EH6 5DT
Tel: 0131 555 5950 • Fax: 0131 555 5018
e-mail: scp@sol.co.uk

British Library Cataloguing in Publication Data
A catalogue record for this book is available from the British Library

ISBN: 1 84017 006 9

Printed and bound by
Cromwell Press, Melksham, Wiltshire

Editor's Note

The spellings of place names reflects regional variations, anglicised
translations and changes in spellings over time and this should be taken
into account.

FOREWORD

It was a sense of duty, not a labour of love, that moved me to write about my early life. What became an irresistible urge stemmed from a belief that not enough writing emanated – to use the Army definition – 'from the rank and file'. It was my appreciation of the many I travelled with in the echelon which gave me reason to take this view. I found that they had much to impart, but for reasons best known to themselves, nothing came of it. In the end they gave way to the dictate of their lineage; they were content to withdraw into themselves and allow memory find a way to express itself in the silence of their own isolation. To amend for their silence, and to break with my own, I feel that in some way, I have been given a directive, to give an account of that past. After all, it was an era of great significance for those of us who lived through it and, regrettably, for the many who did not survive. For our offspring and later ones, it remains for them to try and comprehend the *difference* and take care with what they now have.

In putting together this work, I have had the assistance of a good memory plus memorabilia and notes that I have kept all this time. In retrospect, I find it rather strange that in my early life the other self was so much of a 'magpie', and the purpose for this has only now come to light.

I have tried to avoid the lures of hindsight by relying on the seeds of thought that found root in those early days and sprouted in later years. To many I give thanks for pointing the way and for the quality of the many memories they left with me.

Robert Dick
Forres
May 1997

1

After an absence of many years I was back visiting the twin villages of Garmouth and Kingston, in Northeast Scotland, where I had spent most of my boyhood.

The first place I made for at the start of my nostalgic tour was the village school. As I made my way to the school brae, I was aware that much of what had registered in my young mind had lain dormant over many years, but now it had come alive. It was this reaction, and seeing again the familiar setting, that decided me where my story would begin – here in the North East, the area that had always been very much a part of me.

As I reached the school gate, I discovered much to my surprise that the school building, now a private dwelling, had lost none of its character, its structure was unchanged and it still had that formidable look. Its position on high ground made it visible for miles around, while access from Garmouth was by way of the school brae and from the Kingston side by a winding footpath over the hill. The entrance, a grille gate, had stood the test of time and still looked the part – a symbol of authority on entering and an opening to freedom at the end of the school day.

The layout of the school grounds were still discernible – shelters, playgrounds and garden. The front playground was where the girls played hopscotch, peaver and skipping; to the rear of the building was the boys' area where we played marbles, conkers and football; the latter was the most popular even though the 'ball of the day' was sometimes just a round object of material tied with string; it was great when we had a real rubber ball.

However, it was football that revealed the hidden danger of the boys' playground, part of which sloped down to a retaining wall that enclosed the toilets – at one end, the retaining wall was only two to three feet above the surface of the playground. One winter's day, a boy slipped on an icy patch, collided with the retaining wall and disappeared head first into the toilet below, a drop of approximately twelve feet. The injury he sustained kept him off school for a long time and he never played football again. It was an incident that served notice to us all to keep away from the wall; when I left school the danger still existed; nothing had been done about it. This was the sort of thing that went on outside the classroom, but the authorities did not go out of their way to extend a protective hand. A by-word often quoted, 'look after yourself as no one else will' was most appropriate.

During playtimes, restricted space decreed the number of games played and this gave the 'bully' the opportunity to flex his muscles; for others, it was a time to show, in a furtive way, the streak of cruelty that most children have – stone throwing by hand, sling, and catapult was a constant danger and as a result, a number had scars to show; but no preventive action was taken to stop this behaviour. It all took place in an 'arena' where little compassion was shown. In particular, I remember a boy with one leg and how the others picked on him. They kicked the simple wooden crutch from under him and he in turn would bravely respond, but the odds against him were too much. A lot of the time when there was rough and tumbles it would develop into fisti-cuffs. This was something that I always tried to avoid, but when pressed, I had to respond.

During playtime and lunch-break when weather was bad, we took refuge in the open-fronted shelters. This kept us from getting wet, but gave us no protection against the cold biting winds. At lunch time we ate our piece (sandwiches), the contents of which varied according to family well being; the make up was usually of a simple nature, a spread of butter, jams, cheese or egg with some having to be content with a sprinkling of sugar over a mar-garine spread. As there were no school meals, the envy of all were those who lived near to the school, as they could go home at lunch time. Whatever the day merited, 9 a.m. to 4 p.m. was a long day for everyone, but for most of us, the thought of a warm dinner as we made our way home made up for every-thing.

The hedge and fence that separated the garden from the playground were missing, but the garden remained intact and in use. It was the same garden where boys, twelve years and over, were taught the fundamentals of garden-ing – I never forgot the simple, but important use of spade and Dutch-hoe. There was also – once a week – a period of cooking for girls and boys of the twelve and upward age group. Both subjects were a relief from the continual grind of what we knew as the three 'Rs'.

There was no school transport, it was left to parents to see that their chil-dren got off on time, but in the end the onus was on the children not to be late. The sound of the school bell demanded instinctive response, everyone knew that seldom was an excuse good enough to allow for late attendance. Distance did not come in to it, a walk of three miles or more was not a matter of consideration. The walk to school in winter months very often had its side effects. It was unpleasant to sit in a classroom with wet feet or have a gar-ment on which required drying out. During frosty weather, it was never easy to avoid hacks on knees or hands. As boys always wore shorts, unprotected knees suffered a lot, but despite the dangers, anyone who had his hose pulled over his knees was called a 'cissy'. On leaving school long trousers were then worn, a distinction which showed that you were of age for the labour market.

Looking at the outside of the building, I knew by the windows the different classrooms where I was taught, and this in turn reminded me of the teachers – Miss Mackay, Miss Sellars, Miss Adam and the Headmaster Mr Fordyce. All were respected for their knowledge and position of authority. The measures used in the running of the school kept us all on our toes.

Apart from the dreaded tawse, there were other effective forms of punish-ment – extra lessons were meted out, which had either to be done in classroom after school hours or taken away and done at home. Outside of school grounds, whenever or wherever a boy passed a teacher, he had to show respect by giving a military style salute. Both boys and girls were also expected to show respect towards their elders. This was instilled by teachers with approval of parents. The general attitude towards children was a form of containment, which smothered any chance of children becoming too much the centre of attraction. The maxim was not to give children a sense of their own importance too early in life. That was something which had to be worked at and in the process, one had to know one's place, a condition which overlapped into the period of apprenticeship.

Once the school day was over, the journey home in good weather was usually delayed and this aroused greater hunger; the answer to this was to be found in the nearest field. The choice was – to split a turnip using a fence post, extract a handful of peas from a crop of tare or pull a few sooricks from the embankment. Sometimes there was the emergency of being caught short by the call of nature and the only toiletry available was a tuft of grass. One soon discovered to avoid the sharp-edged type – it could be hurtful.

The homeward journey gave the 'bully' time to show of his prowess. Whoever he picked on, usually had the choice to stand up and fight or make a run for it. Sometimes the 'bully' came off second best and when that happened, it gave much satisfaction to those who stood by and to the victor, a new status. Some boys had other things in mind, they directed their attention to the girls – a mixture of curiosity and pleasure, which fuelled the growing-up process. During the school year four events took place – concert, Christmas party, summer picnic and the end of term prize-giving day. For those who had a part in the concert, rehearsals were more than just practice, it was a period away from work in the classroom. The venue for the big occasion was the local drill hall and it attracted capacity crowds. It was a two night performance and to have any chance of a seat near to the stage, parents had to arrive early. Seat reservation was only for those who were considered dignitaries for the night.

The Christmas party and Summer picnic were two events which created much excitement and expectancy. There were prizes to be won at the picnic and Christmas gifts for all at the party; at both events there was the usual bag of 'goodies' to be washed down with lemonade or tea. The picnic was held in the recreation park, except for one summer, when we went by train to Straithlein near Cullen. For many this was their first train journey so this was one picnic, that gave a greater degree of excitement.

Such events called for best attire to be worn, which sometimes brought about the need for parents to buy something new. Purchase of clothes only happened once in a while, but when it did, it gave a great up-lift to the recipient. Small things meant a lot to the young mind; for example, a hip pocket on your new shorts, a new belt instead of braces or an addition of fastening straps to summer sandals.

The end of term Prize-Giving day was the main event of the school year –

successful ones received their awards and the 'Leavers' rejoiced in the knowledge that they would now have to earn a living and discard their shorts for long trousers. For the ones who would return to school, it was the start of summer holidays. A time remembered for its freedom, days of sunshine, backed up with the rustle of wheat crops, swish of long grass, response of tree to wind, noise of insects in flight and birds in song. Time seemed to be an understanding friend, one only lived with the present. The instinctive reaction to warmth and plenty of space to move in, was to doff footwear and go barefoot, not always with parents' consent. At night one was wrapped in blissful sleep, induced by the knowledge that there was no school the following morning. It was a time when one wished that time would stand still.

In retrospect, I look on school discipline of the era, as a reflection of the moral standards set and expected of society as a whole. It was a society, which, in the main, came from the unenviable side of the 'divide', living a life that was all they had ever known. Paradoxically, parents' contribution had in lots of ways prepared us for what was yet to come.

As I took a last look round what used to be the school compound, I was reminded that it was from here that I returned each school day to the love and protection of home. It was also the same place I finally left from, to go out into a world which turned out to be rather rough at times.

> Innocent thoughts was childhood's lot,
> A 'cloister', a transient spot,
> Then came man's inhuman way
> Which made, for many, a shortened stay.

2

I turned from the school entrance and walked a few yards to the breast of the hill. What lay below and beyond lived up to the mental image I had carried with me all these years. There it was, the familiar stretch of coast-line with its number of small fishing ports. Inland were the spreads of a village or two, several farm steadings and here and there an isolated dwelling. All were set down on a ground carpet coloured in brown, green and gold. Towering over everything was the Bin Hill while down below, mid nature's tapestry, was the River Spey threading its way northwards to Spey Bay and the Moray Firth beyond. For a time I stood there, taking in the beauty of it all and aware that never before had it looked so good.

On my way down to the main street I stopped at the first back garden, one which, as I remember, featured in a youthful escapade, a classic of its time. One winter's night, assisted by a shadowed moon, several of the young men of the village removed the dry lavatory from its position in the garden and placed it in the centre of the adjoining field. They then returned to a concealed position within easy viewing distance of the garden, to wait the outcome. It wasn't long before the night silence was broken by a loud utterance of surprise and anger. At this, the deviants with shouts of delight scampered off into the night leaving the poor unfortunate to find a way out of his plight.

The incident was reported to the village 'Bobby' who, on the following day, began his enquiries. As a good upholder of the law, he had his own mental dossier on who were the 'likely', but this got him nowhere. Despite all his efforts, the culprits were never discovered and with no damage done to the lavatory and once back in its rightful place, the whole affair was soon forgotten. Many no doubt are still around who can remember the inclemency and indignity associated with the sentry box style structure. In its passing went the vegetable gardens valued source of nourishment!

Youth, as in all generations, has its share of high spirited pranks. But it was a time as I recall, when there was never any physical hurt intended. The 'crime-count' was usually misdeeds such as cycling without lights, under-age smoking – which was to a limited extent as there wasn't the money – and pilfering fruit from gardens. The most prevalent, by the younger element, was stone throwing and the usual targets were the insulator cups on the telephone poles. Drink-related crime and breach-of-the-peace did not occur that often, and theft was usually when need had turned to despair.

The village policeman treated everything, from the petty to the serious, in the same conscientious manner. There was no allowance for steam to be let off whatever the age, and when children were involved, he had his own way of sorting things out – a cuff round the ear, in which case you dare not tell your parents for fear of further punishment. The most effective deterrent on juveniles was the threat of the birch, and for adults, having to do hard labour if sent to prison. It was a time when the law made sure it held its position in a community. By its actions it preserved 'benefits' for those who did not tangle with it. Times have changed, now those benefits are being eroded because the law, instead of being respected, is being flouted.

On reaching the main street, I turned right and made my way up to the Cross. Here an open area of space is formed by the two main streets of the village merging into one and it is here where the annual fete, known as Maggie Fair, is held. The history of Maggie Fair goes back centuries and in its continuity it has kept its popularity. As I remember, it was not only the attraction of the stalls which drew the crowds, but curiosity as to who might attend. It served as a meeting place for friends and in many instances it renewed old acquaintances. Takings for the day enriched local activities and amenities. It's still an annual event and its objectives, I expect, remain the same.

The Cross was also a favourite meeting-place for the young people of the village, more so on the Sundays than at other times. It was on Sundays when groups would walk to and fro from one end of the village to the other. En-route, each group would stop at the Cross and exchange banter before continuing their separate ways. It was an occasion for everyone to dress in their Sunday Best.

The code of conduct expected on the Sabbath allowed no leeway for the exuberance of youth. Walking was looked on as a permissible activity, a letting of energy, which did not slight the reverence of the Sabbath. The energy spent during the course of the day was sustained, between meals, by the delights of a poc (bag) of sweets bought at the local newsagent.

Sunday was an exceptional day in many ways; it was considered disrespectful to whistle, play games or make a noise out-of-doors – children had to be on their best behaviour. Some households were known to cook the Sunday dinner the night before. To hang out washing to dry or to do any form of gardening was left for another day. For those who did not conform, it was thought by the devout that they would have to answer for it in some way. It was a time when the Church influenced most peoples lives, but it was not always the comforter it purported to be. Instead of the expected uplift, it was more likely to leave a legacy that had to be grappled with in later life. For many this only sowed seeds of disenchantment.

Although the Church in the course of time has become more condescending, more in line with a Loving Father, there still remains many who distance themselves from it. This is a disregard which stems not so much from the past, but from the emergence of an affluent society. A society with a selfish desire to be in on the monopoly of wealth, irrespective of the imbalance it creates. On the other hand, there is a gallant twinge of conscience which it demonstrates with its vogue about caring – it throws a life line, but with it there is a greater dimension to what is a net of hypocrisy.

Sunday in my boyhood was not only set aside for Church and Sunday School, it was also a day for visiting relatives and friends. Visits to my Grandparents involved a walk of some six miles each way, it seemed to go on and on, but as I grew older it became less irksome. I take from those visits the memory of having to remain seated in the living room until conversation veered to something children should not hear, and of then being ushered outside to play in the garden. At tea-time it was a second sitting for us children, this was the usual arrangement when there were visitors to cope with. It took care of sitting space and allowed for the limited cooking facilities. While it inflicted on children an exercise in patience, it also gave them a greater appreciation of what was eventually set-down.

Before leaving the Cross, I made my way over to the War Memorial. I looked down at the list of the Second World War dead, at each one I paused, the face I remembered and its link with the past. Some shared my boyhood, others were of an older age group. As I paid my respects, for a moment the gaiety of their young lives shone through the reality that was before me. It reminded me, not for the first time, that in their distant far off silence, they and others like them, had a message for ones like me – 'Try to keep in mind, that you have been granted a bonus and don't let time have its way, and forget'.

As I continued my nostalgic tour, I was at times jolted out of my reverie by passers-by. They were of a different generation, it would be a surprise to them, if they could only but know what was passing through my mind. I was in a different world with the company of a phantom assemblage of contemporaries, characters and others. A strange phenomenon was at work; I was seeing faces again which I had long forgotten about. Three appeared as I approached the local Post Office, they were the three postmen who served the community. The one most remembered of the three was Davey Vass, he was a veteran of the First World War and was disabled as a result of having suffered trench-feet. He wore the uniform of the day – dark blue trousers and jacket with red piping, shako styled hat minus the plume. He walked the road for many years, his tactful manner and highland humour made him a favourite with the public.

The Star Inn, the local pub, only a short distance from the Post Office, was where Davey spent quite a lot of his leisure time. The effect showed as he made his way back to his lodgings, his swaying gait was like that of a sailor, treading the deck in a heavy swell. Christmas and New Year was when the public showed their appreciation. Sometimes he was given too many drams and, when that happened, he would fumble, drop letters and often had to retrace his steps to effect delivery. Whatever happened, he knew that he would not be let down, there was always someone around to help him out.

The local pub, no longer known as the Star Inn, has stood the test of time, its white-washed exterior has not changed. A glance at the entrance to the pub reminded me of another character who many times passed in and out in his pursuit of convivial company. Alex Geddes was a ships' engineer, who on return from spells at sea made up for lost time. On occasions, he would call at our house after one of his 'sessions', and Mother would revive him with a hot cup of tea and something to eat – the talk would then flow. It was interesting to hear him talk of his experiences at sea and of his times spent in the many ports of call. It fed my imagination and I would go off to bed with the vision of sailing to some far away place. I did not have too long to wait for the reality!

Like all small communities, nothing escaped the prying eyes of gossip carriers. Alex Geddes was one who had their attention because of his frequent visits to the local and the difficulty he had in avoiding the unprotected ditch which ran along the back of his house. An account was always circulated when he had to be recovered from the ditch by his ever attentive wife.

I walked beyond the pub and roughly about a quarter of a mile on, there among several new houses stood the house where I spent some of my boyhood years. As luck would have it, someone was busy in the front garden and my interest was rewarded by being invited in and shown round. It had been modernised, but the change and my absence of over fifty years had not let me down – I felt again the comfort of those years which the place had given me. Although the garden had been altered, I was still mindful of the plentiful yield from the few apple trees we had and how in our world of make believe, the out-house was our frontier post.

It was the only house during my boyhood where we had the luxury of in-side water and a sink. The day it was installed was memorable and exciting – it may seem a trivial memory, but not for those of us who had the inconven-ience of having to carry water from an outside source. We had not yet reached the time when values were created by means of whimsical adverts, and deemed necessities as well as rated popular demand.

Across from the house, I could see the derelict remains of the railway sta-tion. In its operational days, it was a tidy and gaily painted structure and to the community, an important place, a link with the outside world. Apart from the arrivals and departures, the steam locomotive was always a focus of inter-est. A closer look at the mechanism and shining parts could be seen when it came to a halt. As it started up again, there was the crescendo of escaping steam and the metallic sound of slipping wheels, which boasted its degree of power – an imposing sight for a country lad! The driver or fireman, as he leaned out from the cabin, always had time to exchange a wave for someone. They were men who always seemed well turned out, just like the engines they controlled. It was a sad day for the community when they closed the line down.

It was time for me to return to the foot of Garmouth village, and from there make my way to its twin village of Kingston. Before driving the short dis-tance which separated both villages, I made a stop at the Garmouth Drill Hall. This was the place where nearly all local functions took place. The most popular of the time was the Saturday Night Dance, but in keeping with the sanctity of Sunday, the last dance had to finish before the midnight hour.

The Drill Hall was originally built for the soldiery and, therefore, they had prior claim over others wishing to use it. During the winter months the local Territorial Unit, under the watchful eye of the Sergeant-Major, held training sessions in musketry, drill, PT and boxing. In summer the unit attended the .303 Firing Range, which was set up just a short distance along the coast from the village of Kingston. The annual camp was held in August and it was then when Companies from the various districts came together to form the battal-ion – the camp as a rule was at Barry Angus. 'Fireside Soldiering', as it was then sometimes called, was not only a great source of interest for the young men of the district, but it was a tradition which had gone on for a very long time. Many from its ranks went on to join the Regular Services.

I remember as a boy climbing on to the window of the Drill Hall and gaz-ing inward in wonder at the activities of the soldiery. The scene impressed me, but little did I know that it was a setting which was to have some bearing on my life and in my subsequent thinking.

At the time, I was too young to be concerned with social conditions and other factors, all of which created the climate for 'service' tradition to flour-ish. There was also at that time an atmosphere of hesitance, a generation waiting for something to happen. Eventually it did, but it was not the hopeful long awaited *eureka*. Earlier in the century our fathers had experienced a similar situation which was again in incubation just biding time. The 'new' had to take over from where the 'old' had left off and, again, a War Effort was asked for.

Every generation, whatever the nationality, has its aggression and it is always ready to meet the demands of the manipulators who stand on the sidelines. With their hypocrisy, sham and vanity, they exploit the young man's Achilles' heel – his warring instincts, sense of adventure and the so-called glory associated with war. Its ranked as a mark of proven manhood, an ego boost which the authorities are quick to seize on. They pull the strings and we like puppets respond.

After wars come speculation, but for the survivor there is only his 'take-away', a mental record of the reality which for him remains a 'live-file'. It's the same for all, whatever side of the line you are on.

For those who talk of war as something they would not have missed for anything, seems to indicate that time has favoured them or that they have never been long enough or near enough to its dangers. There are also those who have found it to be a relief from the humdrum and shackles of domesticity. Whatever the variance it throws up, it has to be borne in mind that no two individuals have the same war. My appreciation is levelled at those whose lot it was to be in at the deep end. They know how costly a premium it can be to reach the objective.

I had stayed long enough at the Drill Hall, it was time to move on – a change of view brought a change of thought. Behind the hall I found the spot where once stood another of the houses I had known as home, now all that remained was the broken concrete foundation. Looking out from an imaginary front door to the fields and now defunct railway line beyond, I tried to recapture the scene of that on-rush of water. The River Spey, some distance upstream, had broken its banks and a mass of water was moving towards our home. Because of the open country, we were able to see the progress of the water and this gave my parents time to remove much of the furnishings upstairs. I cannot remember how long the flooding lasted, but I do know it was fun for us children and a trying time for our parents. Both ground floor rooms had at least two foot of water and once the level went down, there was a slimy residue to be cleared and walls and floor to be dried out. The threat of future flooding was the reason for our move, which came shortly after, to the house at the top end of the village.

Across from the rear of the Drill Hall stands another hall, known in the past as the Old Church Hall. It was here where Sunday School was held, and for church services I took my place in the church at the top end of the village. Paraffin heaters were placed at intervals along the aisle of the church and church hall. To this day paraffin fumes remind me of my introduction to religion and the subsequent quest it created. A quest, which over the years has been thwarted by the constant vie with reality. In this direction, I have found, that you wax and wane, but the aim is always there to be pursued!

As I made my way out of Garmouth heading for Kingston, I passed on my left, the recreation park and tennis court and on my right, the golf course. The recreation park was where the local junior football team played its home fixtures. They had good support and even some members of the team had star status without the monetary rewards. Adjacent to the football pitch was the putting green, it was a popular place in the summer evenings at a cost of two (old) pence a round. The golf and tennis were more restricted sport because of the cost, but it to had an enthusiastic following.

At the time of my boyhood, all these activities were in their infancy. I can remember the opening of the golf-course and how previously it had been waste-land covered in whins (gorse). Looking at those same locations today showed how well they had been taken care of and supported.

The golf-course was a place where money could be made – boys were taken on as caddies and there were lost balls to be found, which earned a few pence when re-sold. Gorse and muddy water-holes were searched but it could be risky – bare feet probed the muddy bottoms and sometimes, instead of finding a ball, all that one had to show for the effort was a cut foot.

One particular water-hole was more than just a place for lost golf balls, it was a favourite bathing place and was good for beginners as it was only three to four feet in depth. The only way to learn was to watch those who could swim, and copy their arm and leg movements. Eventually, like many of my companions, I managed to keep my feet of the bottom and with that basic start, I was later to become a strong swimmer.

The proximity of sea, river, water-holes and the many boats and punts that were around, provided fun and excitement, but for some parents it only provided anxiety. My Mother's means of dissuasion was to speak of the dangers and, as a last resort, hide my swimming trunks. It was, I suppose, a wonder and a blessing, that during those school years, there was only one drowning tragedy.

I drove on, crossed the bridge which spans the Kingston Burn and entered the village. I stopped opposite Dunfermline House – the one prominent building in the village – and had a look at what had been at one time a well known corner shop. It was in a poor state but was in the process of renovation. The shop owner I remember was affectionately known as 'Old Kyle', and was well known in the village. He obtained the nickname from his place of origin, the Kyle of Lochalsh. His house and the corner outside the shop, was a favourite meeting place for the young people of the village.

The shop was a general store and stocked an assortment of goods, which were piled in disarray all over the place. A corridor linked the shop with the living room of the house and because of his open-house attitude, it made it easy for the unprincipled. He lost a leg in the First World War and the squeak from his wooden artificial leg gave warning as to his whereabouts. The method mostly used by those who wanted something without paying, was to enter the shop when no one else was about. He would hear the door-bell ring, but by the time Old Kyle reached the counter from the living room, the expected customer had fled along with some item of goods. For all his losses, it did not deter him from spending a life-time in business and remaining unruffled in his dealings with his fellow man.

A short distance along the street from Kyle's corner shop was another one; it too was no longer in business. As I remember it, George Clarke was the owner and he sold fish, groceries, spirits and tobacco. The usual scene as you entered the shop was to see George, with bonnet on, perched on a stool behind the counter. His stock was so arranged that he had seldom to come off the stool. With the short winter daylight, he had the need for a lighted candle nearby. The flicker of the candle created enough shadows for the imagination to expect witches and warlocks to appear at any moment. In summer George would sometimes sit on the outside sill of the shop window with his Long John Silver-style crutch propped against the wall – it was then when his stump of leg was most noticeable.

Across from the shop was an area of open ground; it was here where, as boys, we played football and there was a small wooden shelter where we gathered. It was now a picnic area with several tables and seats, and I remembered how good a vantage point it was, so I drove in and parked. The view had not changed; in the distance, on the far bank of the river, stood the village of Spey Bay. Between the village and from where I stood was marshland and water-holes, a favourite spot for boyhood exploration.

Spey Bay is where for me it all began – my birth certificate reads: Benview Cottage, Spey Bay, 12 October 1920. The sight of the low roofed cottage turned my thoughts to the earlier part of childhood – the period leading up to when I became a pupil at Garmouth School. It would take a lot to uncover some of those very early years. Apart from what I had gained from family talk, my own input is fairly limited.

3

The first eighteen months of my life was spent in Spey Bay and Garmouth, and from there the family moved to Kilmarnock, Ayrshire. We remained in Kilmarnock for five years and then returned to Northeast Scotland.

My earliest recollection is of seeing my father in the attire of a coal-miner. He wore moleskin trousers which were tied with a piece of string below each knee. On his bonnet was fixed the small brass pit lamp. At another time, while waiting with Mother at the pit-head, I saw pit-ponies being lead out to daylight from the lift-shaft. The significance of those scenes came to light years later – then my father spoke of the fear of black damp and of working waist deep in water to get at the coal seam. For him, it was a transition from one hell to another – the 1914–18 War to the drudgery of the coal-mines. There were many others like him, deprived of what his generation had been promised – 'a land fit for heroes'.

I never knew my father other than in ailing health, but for all his physical struggle, he never avoided employment or shirked the responsibility of family 'bread winner'. The effects of a touch of gas in the war and an attack of double pneumonia in the early twenties, was something he never recovered from. Ever after, for the remainder of his life, he suffered from asthma. It was the morning he suffered the most, his struggle for breath racked the body and it was frightening to see, it was something I never got used to. Treatment came in the form of a herb like substance and was called Hinksman's Asthma Cure. He tipped a small quantity on to a saucer, set it alight and inhaled the smoke. It gave relief for a time, but the uncontrolled smoke found its way throughout the house and the unpleasant smell was forever present.

About the time when my father was ill with pneumonia, I stayed a few days with an aunt and uncle. The occasion reminds me of the type of bed I had to sleep in. Once we children were in over and covered, the rectangle box-like structure with castors at each corner, was pushed under the recess bed and the valance on the recess bed was then drawn across. The darkness and confined space was not conducive to early 'shut-eye'. I suppose it was, perforce, one way in overcoming limited bed space. I discovered later, that it was a method used in the industrial areas of south Scotland.

There is one other memory of those early years, which few, if any ever forgot and that was the first day at school. My eldest sister had to physically drag me through the school gate and due to some anxiety, my sitting position for the day was most uncomfortable.

Our home was in a busy part of town, two of the windows looked out on to the main street. Through the windows one could watch the daily movement of the public. The policemen passed in twos at regular intervals, and across the street, the crowds spilled out through the shoe-factory gate at the end of each working day. Each evening the lamp-lighter with his long pole and attachment, ignited the street gas lights and in the morning snuffed them out.

The one street incident which stands out more than any other, happened on Armistice Day. It was at the time of the two minute silence, when everyone and all vehicles were stock still. Suddenly the silence was broken by shouts and the clatter of a horse and gig. As the vehicle careered down the street its occupant was letting everyone know what he thought of the occasion, to him it was sheer hypocrisy. Intervention by the law soon ended his crusade. Through the eyes of a child it was no more than an incident of excitement, but for the grown ups, it gave them a lot to talk about. Years later, after I had experienced war and had time to ponder the aftermath of both world wars, the action of that man in a Kilmarnock street, conveyed a message which I was able to understand,

In February 1927 my youngest sister was born, and she was to be the last of the line. Mother had kept pace with her generation; she had four sons and two daughters – I was second youngest of the family. Before my sister's arrival, I was shown baby clothes and in the drawer where they were kept was a strong smell of talcum powder. It was a smell that for long after reminded me of the happy event. Sometime later, there was one incident I did not easily forget. While my mother was breast feeding my baby sister, I noticed in her hand what appeared to be a piece of treacle toffee. In response to my curiosity Mother offered me a lick, to my horror it had a most foul taste. I discovered much later, that what looked like toffee turned out to be a substance known as Bitter Aloes. When applied to the mother's nipples it put the baby off breast feeding. It was widely used at the time but I wonder if the mothers of today would approve of the method?

My last memory of Kilmarnock, was hurrying through darkened streets and at the railway station boarding a London-North overnight train. It was the start of our journey back to the Northeast; our destination, the hamlet of Auchenraith, a few miles from my birthplace at Spey Bay.

I must have been six going on seven, too young to understand the reason for our sudden move. As I was to discover later, it was my father's illness which was the decider. He was unable to return to work as a miner and the doctor advised him to find an outdoor job, preferably in the climate of the northeast. Because of his disability, it made it a very lean time for the family, my older brother was the only one contributing. As a result, when the time arrived to leave Kilmarnock, certain action had to be taken to cope with the situation. By subtle means, my parents managed to get the furniture away and by good timing, a late night departure by train, completed the 'Moonlight'. Our experience was a sign of the times; nevertheless, it was a sore point with my Mother, and forever after, she could not bear to talk about it.

4

Our new home in Auchenraith was a thatched cottage, a type of house very different from what we had been used to. Like many country dwellings, it had an ancient look about it and the interior was of its time, its decor looked to have served many different occupants. The low ceiling, small windows and sombre fire-place made the interior dark and dingy – one's eyes took time to focus properly after coming in from outside daylight. It was not only the drabness, but it was also badly in need of repair. What readily comes to mind was how the loose floor boards, when walked on, exposed the darkness beneath, and how childhood fear wondered as to what might emerge from the depth. The room where I slept, had above the bed an uncovered entrance to the loft; it was a menacing dark hole, something I was unable to distract from. The shadows from the flickering candlelight did not help matters any, all I could do to allay fear was to cover my head with the sheet – sleep did not come easy!

The outside dry lavatory was in poor shape, rain and wind had easy entry – the toiletry, old newspaper cut to convenient size and hung on a nail, was sometimes wet with rain. In bad weather, it had to be a last minute dash and once there, a quick performance. Our drinking water had to be carried from a well which was at least half a mile from the house. The equipment used for this chore was a wooden frame and two pails. The frame made it easier for the carrier, it gave balance, kept the pails steady and prevented spillage.

I found our move to the country an easy transition, but I did not take too well to the distance that had to be walked to school. From our home to Bog-moor School was a good three miles each way and it was rough going – the route was by way of cart-track and footpath. The rewarding part of it all was the feeling one had on the homeward journey, particularly in cold weather, knowing that each step was taking you nearer the shelter of home and a hot meal.

Auchenraith, in its isolation, made it a good place for getting to know the ways of country life. Round the corner from where we lived was the farm where I spent many of my playing hours. It was an adventure to explore the farm-steading, follow the ploughman as he ploughed, have a lift on a two wheeled farm-cart and on the rare occasion, ride bare-back on a Clydesdale horse. To accompany the life of the farm and its surrounds were various smells, the accumulation of which, was carried around in the tweed of the farm-workers clothes. At times, the smoke of the black twist bogie roll to-bacco from the worker's pipe, added to that already piquant quality of smell.

Hay making and harvest were always pleasant and exciting times. It was a time when nature seemed to respond to the needs of the farmer. One can only remember an abundance of sunshine and transient hours of darkness. There is the memory of the noise of the rhythmical action of the reaper, laying out rows of cut hay to be turned over later by means of the pitch-fork. After dry-ing, the hay was gathered in and stacked in the farm-yard.

At harvest time, the snort and emphatic step of the pulling horses signified the steady progress of the binder. As it cut and tossed out the sheaves, the farm-hands followed up to collect and stack them in upright bundles of eight. The bundles known as stooks were set down at equal distance within the area of the field. Following a dry period, stooks were carted from the field to the farm-yard and there, off-loaded and built into stacks. The building of a stack required a certain skill, this weather-proofing process created competition between farms, a good symmetrical job caught the eye and gave a seasonal touch to the landscape.

Later came the thrashing of the harvest and this was another important date in the farmers' calendar. The thrashing mill travelled an area, farm to farm and its stay depended on the number of stacks which had to be thrashed. It consisted of two separate machines, the mill itself and the pulling and driving machine which was similar to a steam-roller with wheels at the front instead of a roller.

As it puffed and clanged its way towards its destination, the noise itself let everyone in advance know that it was coming. On its arrival in the farmyard, both vehicles were positioned at a set distance from each other and near to the stacks. Once the driving belts were connected to the fly-wheel of the driving machine and the mill, thrashing could then commence.

As the forkers and mill reduced a stack to near ground level, children and domestic animals gathered round for the last layer of sheaves to be lifted. Once the ground was uncovered, the vermin, mostly mice, made a mad scurry to get away, but few made it as there was usually wire netting round the base of the stack. The 'arena' made it easy for them to be pitch-forked or caught by a dog or cat. All those summer operations on the farm were usually punctuated, half way through the morning and afternoon, by the arrival of the women-folk with their basket of eats and container of tea. Children very often had the delight of sharing with the farm-worker.

It was all great fun for us children, but for the farm-worker it was a different story – in time I got to know more about this way of life. Their hours of labour throughout the year, Sundays excluded, were a round of the clock, in winter it was start and finish in darkness. On Sundays there had to be someone around to attend to the animals. Conditions for a single man could differ from farm to farm. He either had the bothy for accommodation and cooked his own meals or had food cooked and served, in which case, he slept in a room adjacent to the farm-kitchen which was known as the chamers. The type of living quarters determined wages. Whatever the accommodation, bothy or chamers, there was one thing which was always at hand, and that was the farm-worker's kist. The kist was a wooden trunk in which the worker kept his belongings, a limited space for what was never a lot!

The type of food for the single man consisted of milk, oatmeal, vegetables and a portion of beef – the frequency and size of portion depended on the goodwill of the farmer. At some farms, tea was a restricted beverage, given only on Sunday; harvest time was the exception, then it was brought out to the men in the fields. By comparison, the married man, although it was tied accommodation, had a home to return to after work.

The farm worker had a stoical attitude towards what was a very hard life, they were a breed apart! In the course of the year, the Feeing Market, which was every six months, was the only break they had from their drudgery. It was only then when the farm-worker was paid for his labour – wages at that time varied from one pound to approx. five pounds a month. At the Market, the worker had the choice, to remain with the same employer, move to another farm or seek other type of employment. Whatever his decision, market day was a time to savour, a few pounds in the pocket, a new suit of clothes and the gaiety of the market town put a new slant on life, albeit that it was only for a short time. Hovering around, ever ready to persuade, was the recruiting sergeant. Many succumbed to the temptation of the King's Shilling rather than return, to another six months of labour and poor reward.

5

For my father and older brother, time in Auchenraith must have been soul-destroying. The Feeing Market was outside their range, so for a long time, they had to put up with the indignity of unemployment – a social malady of the time.

Their daily routine was to leave home early each morning and walk for miles in search of work. Each evening when they returned, Mother was ready with the same question – 'any luck today?' The eagerly awaited good news was long in coming, but when it did everyone was in seventh heaven.

During the period of unemployment, my father was not averse to taking certain action when he deemed it necessary. Returning home one night after a fruitless day's search for work, he and my brother felt sorely in need of a smoke. With only a foreign coin in his pocket, Father entered a small dimly lit shop and asked for a packet of cigarettes. As the cigarettes were placed on the counter, he picked them up and at the same time, with the other hand, passed over the foreign coin. With the one movement complete he turned and made for the shop door. He had barely reached it, when there was a shout from the shop-keeper – at that he made a dash for it. My brother, who was standing outside, followed suit. Once they had covered some distance, they sat down by the roadside and in a haze of smoke, enjoyed the luxury of a Woodbine.

Other means were pressed into service during this period when need over-shadowed the moral issue. One that was beneficial to us all was the visits my father and brother made to the nearby potato-pits. I accompanied them on their first visit, but it was the one and only time – it was a harrowing experience for a child of seven. My instructions were simple – I had to wait at the gate and give warning if I heard anyone coming. In the darkness, shadows played tricks and I was petrified with fear.

I waited, but I was never more glad to see them emerge with their spoils. That night we all returned home without mishap. It did not always work out so well; on one occasion, as they made their way home, they came face to face with the farmer, who's potato-pit they had just raided.

My brother's immediate thought when he saw the farmer approach was to drop the sack and make a run for it, but a few steadying words from my father stopped the panic. Before both parties passed each other, Father and my brother changed the position of their sacks from shoulder to under-arm, physically not an easy thing to do. This was intended to give the farmer the impression that they had been down on the sea-shore collecting driftwood, a necessary chore which we all took a share in. As they passed each other, they exchanged greetings, the farmer commenting on how fine a moonlight night it was. To Father's delight the night could not be better, but was the farmer really fooled, or was it that he appreciated my father's guile?

In the second half of 1928, both my father and brother found employment. My brother, who was a butcher to trade, had to work for a short time in a garden nursery before resuming in his trade, while Father became an estate labourer. For Father, who had worked in Canada and the USA before the First World War, and in this country on the railway and coal mines, found general labouring not easy to come to terms with, but it was a living! His need for an outdoor job, for health reason's, left him no choice and anyhow he had to take what first came his way. As it turned out he remained with 'The Estate', later to become 'Crown Lands' for the rest of his working life. At times the physical aspects of the work got too much for him, but he had good work-mates who helped him out, and that was something he never forgot. In many ways he was a patriarchal figure in their midst and was always helpful as a scribe to those in need. I think that if fate had been kinder, his mental potential, along with his use of the pen, would have seen to it that there was a more fitting niche to his life than having to handle a pick and shovel.

Once the wages started coming in, it was then time to look for more suitable accommodation. During the autumn of 1928 we moved to Garmouth to the house near to the Drill Hall at the foot of the village. It was the house already mentioned, which was eventually to fall foul of the River Spey flooding. With the move came a change of school and as it turned out, it was where I was to complete my education. My time in Garmouth School was from the autumn of 1928 until the end of summer term 1935 by which time I had reached the school leaving age of fourteen.

6

My wait in the picnic area had allowed me enough time to reminisce the period of very early childhood. It was now time to move on, I had a lot more to do and there were other parts of Kingston to visit. Once I had done that I would know if my nostalgic tour had served any useful purpose!

My next stop was a few hundred yards along the street, near to where a rough road leads to the seashore, a one-time favourite meeting place for many of the locals. The thought of those gatherings reminded me of Bob Payne, who had us youngsters spell-bound when he talked of his exploits in the First World War. His favourite gesture whenever he wanted to emphasise a point was to spit into his hands, then smack the palms together. Its strange how the memory can still retain so small a detail. Two other personalities of that ilk were Tom and Alfie, but they had, at that time, the unique distinction of being English and for us children, they had a strange way of talking. Tom sold firewood and his pony and cart, with its big wheels, was often a target of mischievous comment. As he passed we would shout, 'The wheel is coming off,' and his good humoured reply would be, 'Your bloody head is coming off!' To hear his English idiom was our reward. Alfie, on the other hand, was noted for his attention and devotion to his herd of goats. His long white beard was the manifest kindred connection, which was vouched for by his wife's favourite remark whenever a caller enquired as to his whereabouts. She would point to a cluster of goats and explain, 'He is the one with the hat on.'

There were others, different in strain, who ventured into a world that demanded the pioneering spirit. Their choice of the villages as their haven of retirement added a special quality to the place and for what they accomplished, earning them a certain respect. However, it did not always mean that they escaped from being given a nickname. This was something which for different reasons was common practice at the time. Two or three come to mind: there was Stormy Joe, a retired mariner of the windjammer days. We had an understanding with him: for every sizeable eel we caught he would give us a penny. Then there was Tabby King, a retired tea-planter, who got his name because of always having a cigarette stub in his mouth. His nicotine-tarnished white moustache was evidence of his addiction. At the opposite end of the village from where Old Kyle lived, there was Old Willie Mitchell. He had a special status, as his house was surrounded by a stockade which, it was said, was a replica of his living quarters in Africa. To us children, he was a sinister character and as rumour had it, he conversed with his mother who had been dead for many years. He was never given a nickname, perhaps it was because of his so called involvement with the occult. His house was always given a wide berth, but if we had but known, rumour and exaggeration was what created the mystery – he lived a quiet life and bothered no one.

I now left the car and made towards the beach. On the way, I noticed, that the Beach Shelter had been demolished. In its day, it was the favourite place for courting couples and with its demise went the chuckles, subdued talk and the initials and declarations of intent which covered the walls.

The intent was not always words of endearment, some were crude words of desire. We were living at a time when the subject of sex was not openly talked about or even discussed in an informative way. Outwardly, it seemed to be something which nature decreed could not be avoided and of necessity had to happen. The taboo which the subject attracted, caused torment and conflict of conscience, leaving little choice, but to go with the tide of consensus and in the end grapple, particularly in adolescence, with the physical and emotional.

There was however, always the so called exponent, willing to impart his knowledge and of course youthful talk, all of which was far from what was needed. I don't suppose anyone ever thought at that time, that sex would one day be a subject for the school curriculum. A development which has certainly made it less secretive, but has not removed the controversy which continues to surround it. Progress has been made by moving away from past prejudice and fickle thinking but there is the need to turn away from that element of society, which would have us believe that the uncommitted and promiscuous road leads to Valhalla.

The Moray Firth was now peaceful, not a ship in sight, so different from the days when we had a large Navy and the Home Fleet made its appearance in these waters. It was during autumn manoeuvres, when light was fading, that their presence was most impressive. Ships of varied structure silhouetted the skyline, star shells sparkled and filled the sky and the flash and rumble of guns completed an unforgettable spectacle. A number of the really big ships were always part of the assembly, but despite size, as quickly as they appeared they could all just as quickly disappear. Retreat was either into Cromarty Firth or Scapa Flow.

During naval exercises, it was not unusual for sailor hats to be lost overboard. This we knew about and many of us boys searched the shoreline in the hope of finding one. There was an air of competition in our quest – hat bands with names such as *Hood, Rodney, Renown* and *Ramilies* were special value because they were names which held pride of place in naval history.

As a result of all the naval activity, our imagination got the better of us and we created our own naval guns. This consisted of a number of tins (Lyles Golden syrup), each with a hole pierced in its base. Into each tin was placed a few lumps of carbide (its normal use was for cycle lamps) and a drop or two of water. The lid on each tin was then firmly pressed on and the tins were lined up and placed at an angle on the ground. The final action was to put a lighted match or piece of paper to the ignition point, the hole in the base of the tin. There followed a loud woof as the lid of the tin was ejected into the air.

My arrival on the beach revived the boyhood day-dreams which accompanied me, on the many occasions I walked this same stretch of shore-line. The lapping waters and distant horizon was a stimulant to the obsession I had of becoming a soldier and travelling to distant lands. The Army was one of the few gateways to travel, and travel was something of a fascination to me then, and has possessed me ever since. The thought of becoming a soldier was on a par with the common boyhood ambition of becoming a railway engine driver. However, in my case the desire was not given the time to extinguish itself. If it had been, who knows perhaps in the end the outcome would not have been any different.

7

I lingered for a while on the shore-line and then made my way towards Daisy Cottage – the one place which was central to my tour of the villages. After fifty plus years I had come full circle, I was back at the house where I had set out from – it was my home from 1930 until I left in August 1935. It was here where I spent the most formative years of childhood and it's remembered as the most comfortable time of those early years. My parents had turned their backs on the gloomy days of the past. Employment for both my father and brother made all the difference and despite low wages, there was much to be thankful for. However, there was always insecurity, the one thing which bred constant worry and sacrifice for people in my parents' position, there were many, and they had to endure it throughout their lives. This got through to me early in life and in later years, it influenced many a decision I made in my own life.

The sight of our cottage again brought back many memories. House and garden seemed to have diminished in size, an illusion of childhood made into realistic proportion by the adult eye. The garden, once my first real challenge, was no longer a productive spread – the lawn-mower was the only implement now required.

I took over the working of the garden because of my father's poor health. It was quite a task for a twelve year old, but it was work which soon became an interest. The sprouting potatoes and vegetables gave one a sense of achievement and satisfaction came later, when the yield found its way to the dinner plate. The garden also revived another memory. In the corner stood a large wireless pole, the aerial from it stretched to the chimney; and at the junction in the wire, the aerial extended down through a hole in the frame of the living room window to connect up with the wireless set. For the set to function, it required two batteries, one dry and one wet. The wet battery had to be re-charged at intervals and without a stand-by, it meant the set was out of use until the re-charged battery was returned, a wait of two to three days.

When we first got the set, it created much excitement, it seemed a miracle, that words and music from distant places could be heard in our living room. It became very popular to have a wireless set, but to obtain one, most households had to scrimp and save. What I remember most about the wireless were the musical programmes – I had not reached the age when news and other programmes were of interest.

There was a limit to what came through the wavelengths. The media as a whole still had a long way to go in its development and people, at that time, were spared the muck-raking and gory details which today's media gives out. Communications today supply us with a varied and never ending flow, but the notoriety and gory details of it are elements which don't go down well with everyone. It seems that the dictate of the media will always have it over consensus!

The attraction which the wireless created did not interfere with the long established forms of entertainment; for example, the popular whist-drives and dances, or the occasional concert and visit from the travelling cinema. To while away the long winter evenings there were also musical sessions of sorts in many households. It ranged from vocal to instrumental and to the simplest of all, to strum a Jews' Harp or hum into a hair-comb with a piece of tissue paper. My father and brother played the button-keyed melodeon. It was only

Even at the age of 13 the Army Glengarry had its attraction!
Along with my youngest sister, outside our home in Kingston-upon-Spey

when I attempted to play the melodeon that I discovered how much joy music had to offer. I was to bear this in mind ever after, and later in life, as a musician in the Army, I found great satisfaction in fulfilling that role.

The paraffin lamp cast its light over other winter evening activities. As children, there were such games as dominoes, playing cards, ludo and snakes and ladders. There were also scrap-books to be made up and the boys' papers *Adventure* and *Hotspur* to be read, but school home-work had to be completed first. While we got on with our pursuits, Mother most likely would be busy at 'make and mend'. Father as he sat at the fire-side would be at one of three pastimes. His favourite was compiling 'Bullets', a competition all about the meaningful use of words, and run by the magazine *John Bull*. He read a lot; and when the need arose he would set to and knit his own socks, a skill he acquired during his service in the 1914–18 War. His pipe was never out of reach, and he enjoyed a puff of 'Three X Bogie Roll Twist'. He used the open-fire as his spittoon, the sizzle on the grate lasted but a few seconds as did any bacteria there might be. As I grew older, I would drag from him stories about the First World War and of his travels in Canada and the USA. Whenever he got in a nostalgic mood, I was happy to sit quietly and listen.

During the school year, it was the usual procedure to get everything ready on the Sunday night for the week ahead. Around the open-fire clean garments were aired, some had to be patched or stitched and usually hose had to be darned. The zinc bath tub was filled with hot water from a kettle and after a good lather of carbolic or life-buoy soap, one emerged clean and refreshed. To nullify cold draughts from the adjoining rooms, the bath was placed in front of the fireplace – one fire usually heated the whole house.

Mother would sometimes spread an old newspaper on the table and with a fine-toothed nit comb set to work on one's hair. After a few downward strokes of the comb, she would inspect the paper. If any were found, the dreaded beastie was quickly picked up and despatched to the open-fire. When hair required to be cut, Father with comb and scissors did not take long to give a short back and sides. Footwear required periodic attention and Father's repair work stood up well to time and abuse.

When it came to bed-time, little time was lost, especially in winter, in getting under the blankets. Probing feet soon found the hot-water bottle, some of the time it was a hot brick, heated in the oven and wrapped in a flannel – both had our approval, it was comfort.

With the arrival of the summer months, indoor activities ceased, the outdoor beckoned and home became a place to return to for food and bed. The countryside provided a treasure in the form of woodlands, area of open space, river, streams and shore-line. There were dangers and certain activities which caused parents concern. Mention has already been made about those that were water related, but there was another, which I was repeatedly warned about and that was setting fire to gorse. It was something which authorities seemed unconcerned about and we were never aware of any action having been taken to stop this from of arson. Perhaps it would have been different had our 'patch' been other than wasteland near the seashore. I was never one to get involved, for one thing, the smell of burning gorse stuck to the clothing and this was a give away that could spell trouble when you got home.

The highlight of any day was when the time arrived to sit down at the dinner table. Seldom was there any doubt as to the capacity of one's appetite – whatever was laid down was devoured. There was a philosophy at that time – 'if you had one good meal in the day, then you had nothing to complain about'. Likes or dislikes did not come in to it, you had to eat what the rest were having.

Home grown vegetables assisted in the making of the main meal, which frequently consisted of soup made from a marrow bone or a piece of boiling beef. Other bills of fare could either be stewed rabbit, mince, fish, potted-head or corned-beef – potatoes were always part of the dish. We did not always have dessert, but when we did it was usually boiled rice or semolina along with jam, stewed rhubarb or stewed garden apples. Bakers' delicacies and fresh bought fruit were out of reach of many households. A bowl of fruit on the living-room dresser was a luxury, it distinguished the 'haves' from the 'have nots'.

Mother's substantial home baking of scones, pancakes and oatcakes made up for everything. A hot scone straight from the girdle spread with syrup, went down well, as did a slice of hot clootie dumpling. The latter took the place of dessert at dinner or as a delicacy at tea-time. One always knew when Mother had done a baking, as the baked items were spread over a special cover which was placed on top of the recess-bed. Once the baking had cooled, it was wrapped in muslin cloth and placed in the food cupboard.

I suspect that, by today's standards, the repetitive way of eating would be faulted, but it's possible that, in its plain state, our childhood digestive system got off to a good start. A lot of provisions were bought from vans who called at the door, but the main source was the small village shop. There was one door-to-door caller, who even then was one of a limited breed, as she was the fish lady and made her rounds on foot. In the course of a week she must have covered a lot of miles. Her distinctive dress consisted of a mutch, ankle length black dress with shawl, high laced boots – strapped over her back was her fish-creel. During the early nineteen thirties she disappeared from the scene.

Childhood was not always a period of carefree happiness; shadows came and went and some never left. I will never forget seeing what, at the time, was a not unusual way of getting rid of an unwanted pet. The dog was tied to a sack weighed with stones and tossed into the river. For whatever the reason, it was a most callous method and served to show what people at the time were sometimes driven to. Humans had perforce prior concern for themselves and this left the status of the domestic animal never in any doubt. The same cannot be said today, but we all should know that when there is plenty around, the definition of what is a priority tends to become obscure.

It was a time for large families and with limited living space, privacy was hard to come by. The closeness had its drawbacks, as youngsters could not be protected all the time from hearing and seeing things which would have been better not known about. At the same time life was lived with a streak of Puritanism, an influence not easy to contend with during those impressionable years. However, despite possible shortcomings, the wonderment of childhood was not taken away – parents were looked on as being something more than just humans.

Towards the time when school days were coming to an end, I became more aware of the sensitive side to my character. In time I was to develop a strong sense of conscience, which over the years has not been easy to reason with. One thing eludes me: when is a standard good enough? In casting a critical eye over myself, I realise that whatever assessment I arrive at, a lot of the time, the inbreed accounts for what we are. Environment has a hand in shaping the mould, but it is a malleable process and can either de-stabilise or be the means of finding stability!

I was brought up at a time when the text-book do-gooders, or so called experts on child and youth behaviour had not yet arrived on the scene. It was a time when parents were in control and not the child in control of the parents! The overall attitude of those early years is thought by many today as having been too stringent, which leads me to ask the question: 'Will today's attitude be seen in the future as not having been stringent enough?' Regrettably, I fear, this could well be the case; all too often the veto on truth and simple logic, either goes unchallenged, unnoticed or it is conveniently overlooked.

Perhaps an earnest attempt at self-analysis would help get nearer to the answer to this hypothesis, but the failing is that most of us are too content with what we think we are. Assuming that hindsight, after a measure of time, makes us better thinkers, then sooner or later we should come to recognise that there is an element of 'farce' in the way life is lived. It has also to be recognised that hindsight is not infallible, and in trying to span the gulf between past and present there arises the 'grey area' which we have to contend with. But however much one tries to analyse life, in the end, I think there is room to consider the possibility that we are all assigned a 'path' on which to travel.

8

There was no thought about a 'path' that August day in 1935: I was concerned only in getting to the starting line, which was the recruiting office in the Drill Hall, Cooper Park, Elgin. In little more than two months after leaving school, I was there to finalise documents and swear allegiance to King George V and accept the King's Shilling. It didn't take long; I emerged from the building feeling great. I had acquired my ambition, I had been accepted into the ranks of the Queen's Own Cameron Highlanders as a Boy Soldier at the age of 14 years and 10 months.

The events of 23rd August 1935 remain a vivid memory and, today whenever I pass by the same building, I am reminded that it was here that my life's journey began. I particularly remember the anxiety I felt at the time – would Mother, at the very last moment, stop my enlistment? I required both my parents' consent, and Mother told me years later, that as she waited for me outside the building, she was sorely tempted to interrupt proceedings and have me back home. To this day, I often reflect on the one question which at the time, I was insensible to – how did I at such a tender age, manage to get my own way? There were no compelling factors which made it necessary for me to leave home, it was entirely my desire.

Granted there was little opportunity around, but I suppose like many others, I could have found work of a limited kind and fall into line with rural life. Possibly it was my father's experience and more enlightened view of the outside world that swayed the issue in my favour. I have no doubt that my parents only gave in because they could see that, locally, there were not many prospects and it was in my best interest to get away.

On the day of my departure I wore long trousers for the first time. Little did I know that it would be several years before I was back in civilian clothes again – home leave, 1945. Such deprivation had no place in my thoughts that day, I was pre-occupied with the elation I felt at having been accepted into the army. There was no thought or apprehension of what was likely to follow, such as home-sickness, and the lonely battle that had to be fought in order to get over it. Unconsciously, youth seemed at the time to create a useful criteria – 'sufficient unto the day'.

I had an hour or two to share with Mother and my young sister before boarding the train. All the time I felt anxious to get away and yet when the time did come, it was a different matter. As I stood at the open carriage window waving to the receding figures on the platform, I could feel an invisible cord trying to arrest the progress of the moving train. The moment of truth had arrived and as they disappeared out of view I felt, for the first time, very much alone.

An awesome journey lay ahead. Aldershot was a long way off, but I was in luck, as I had for company a mature soldier making the same journey. He was given instructions to see to it that I arrived safely at my destination. He is nameless and the face has gone from memory, but for all that, I still think of him as the Good Samaritan who saw me on my way. He kept my mind free of thoughts of home and talked about the Army in a way that made me feel I was doing the right thing. I remember that, on crossing the Forth Bridge, I responded to tradition (at the time) and tossed a half-penny into the river for luck. In the years since, I consider myself to have had more than a fair share of return on the loss.

On arrival at Oudenarde Barracks, Aldershot, the first thing I had to do was report to the Guard Room. Once I had handed in my documents to establish my identity, I was taken to the boys' quarters and there I was introduced to the NCO in charge of the Boys' Barrack Room. L/Cpl Peter Bell, besides being in charge of Boys, was also leading drummer in the Pipe band. He was a man who impressed me from the outset. My intuition was to prove right, for as a drummer and bugler, I was to owe him a lot for the enthusiasm he instilled and for his excellent tuition. Later in the day I was to meet the man who had overall charge, Drum Major Cameron. As I was to discover, he was the one man who saw to it that discipline was maintained at all times.

Seeing the interior of a Boys' Barrack Room for the first time filled me with amazement. Everything I looked at appeared to be correct in every way, it glistened and the floor reflected like a mirror. On both sides of the room, beds were lined up at a set distance from each other and each bed was made up 'chair' fashion. The bed consisted of a 'three biscuit' mattress and the bedstead was in two parts – the bottom part, when not in use, was slid under the top half.

In order to make up the bed chair fashion, a blanket was wrapped round two biscuits and placed upright to form the back of the chair. The other biscuit was also wrapped in a blanket and laid flat. Remaining blankets, sheets and bolster were fitted in behind the upright biscuits and acted as a support for the back of the chair. The swagger cane was inserted at the front between the blanket and the upright biscuits. From the swagger cane hung the bed-ticket. The bed-ticket was a polished metal plate bearing the Regimental

Badge and below the badge was inscribed number and name. On the reverse side of the plate was inscribed the word 'Duty' and this was shown at the appropriate time.

Behind and above each bed was a wall-locker in which toiletry, under-clothing, shirts, canvas outfit, socks, spats and oddments etc. were kept. Beneath the locker hung dress-kit and equipment – great-coat, kilt, sporran, white-belt, music card-pouch, drum-apron, dirk etc. Under and at front of each bed was arrayed, in line, and pointing outwards, all footwear not in use – cleaned with leather highly polished. Also included were boot-brushes, button-stick and boot polish tin. The Cherry Blossom motif on the lid of the tin was rubbed off and the bare metal was highly polished.

Apart from having to look after kit and belongings, there was also general cleaning to be done in the barrack room. This was carried out on a weekly rota system and was part of daily duties. As I looked round the room on my first day, I could see that stoves and table-trestles were treated with black lead and the area round the foot of each stove was pipe-clayed. Tables and forms and wooden parts of furnishing were scrubbed white and buckets were burnished. All cleaning utensils – brushes, bumper etc. – were laid out in orderly fashion on the floor. Such a display of cleanliness made me wonder what I had got myself in for – it only took a few days more for me to discover how all this was accomplished!

I was to find that the most laborious of all the barrack room chores was the polishing of the floor. Once the polish was dubbed on the floor, the 'bumper' was then brought into use. The bumper had a long handle at the end of which was a heavy cumbersome polishing pad – it was manhandled backwards and forwards until a fine sheen appeared on the floor.

Apart from all the confusion of the first day, there is one visual impression which remains with me to this day, and that is the tree lined Queen's Avenue and its surroundings. How could one ever forget such a hive of military activity and its background – lines of barrack rooms, drill squares, admin. blocks and playing fields. It was a far cry from the rural setting I had left behind, the sudden change was an unforgettable experience.

When I think back to those Army days, especially to the more disciplined period of Boy Service, I have to pinch myself and ask the question – 'Was it really like that?' If this is my reaction, how can I expect the others of today to understand and appreciate the conditions of that time. The yoke of blind obedience prevailed and in Army parlance, you were not to question why, you were there to do or die! It was a dogma which owed its response because attitudes and way of life then were very different to what it is today.

For some it did not matter much if it thwarted mental vigour, while for others it invigorated them to reach for greater mental ability. However there was little on which aspiration could feed on. But in reaching this late analysis, I also recognise that, in many ways, service life turned out to be a gainful experience.

After my talk with the NCO in charge, I was allocated a bed and a locker and one of the more senior boys was assigned to assist me in getting into the run of things. This was the usual procedure which lasted for a few days, afterwards it was a case of getting on with it – keep asking and it was up to you if you didn't know, to find out! Failing that you were likely to be reminded that you were no longer attached to your mother's apron strings!

Within a day or two of arrival, I was fully kitted-out and given the traditional service hair-cut, short back and sides. New recruits to Boy Service did not arrive at a set time of year or in set numbers. There was one who arrived shortly after me, so I was not alone in having to get on par with the rest of the boys. The flow of boys going over to Man Service when they reached eighteen and future requirements for tailor-shop, pipe and military bands determined the number needed to maximise the boy soldier compliment. Several who served on Boy Service came from Military Schools such as Dunblane and the Duke of York's. Those like myself who had no previous connection with the military were initially at a disadvantage, although it made no difference: we were all treated alike. I quickly realised that the sooner you fell into line the better, there was no place for passengers!

In the three years and two months I served in Boy Service, routine remained unchanged. Overseas service had its difference in that there was more emphasis on health and hygiene, and duty hours were aligned according to the dictate of climate.

A normal day's routine began with 6 a.m. reveille, introduced by the sound of the bugle and the bagpipes (Hi Johnny Cope) and the shouts of the NCO i/c, 'Wakie, wakie, rise and shine, get your feet on the floor.' Within half an hour of reveille, cold water ablutions had to be completed, beds made up chair fashion and everyone had to be ready for the first parade of the day. At most times, this was a physical training period, either road walk and run, swimming, exercises on the square or in the gymnasium. The last named venue was a place I dreaded. For me, a small fifteen year old, it wasn't what you would say exhilarating to be physically assisted over the gym-horse and parallel-bars or made to climb the wall bars and from there carry out exercises. The gym-instructor had his way in seeing that you did; it was an ordeal which dissuaded me from ever thinking of becoming a gymnast.

Breakfast was 8 a.m. and as at all meal-times, we had to parade and be marched as a party to the dining-hall. Dress for the occasion was canvas jacket and tartan trousers (home service). Before we were marched off, hands and nails were inspected as well as knife, fork and spoon. This was one of the many additional checks which were in force in Boy Service. At 9 a.m. it was stand-by beds for barrack room inspection. This was one parade which had everyone keyed-up because kit and personal turn-out was under close examination. A big sigh of relief followed when it was all over. However, it was not always a clean slate for some: that well known phrase, 'You are on a charge' was heard by the unfortunate. Preparation for the 9 a.m. inspection was made the night before and completed the following morning. The inspections were usually carried out by the Drum-Major but the Adjutant (rank of Captain) had his periodic visits and these were not always made known in advance.

On Thursday of each week, full kit was laid out on the bed for inspection. There was a set way in which this was done e.g. all underwear, shirts, gym-kit and canvas suits made up two main bundles and were folded in a uniform way. To give a straight edge to the front and both sides of the bundles, a piece of paper was inserted in each garment. Those same bundles were at other times kept in the wall-locker which was open during daily inspection. On the Thursday inspection, as well as the two bundles, there was the remainder of kit down to the smallest items of all – spare boot-laces and the holder known as the 'housewife'. The housewife contained needles, thread, darning wool and spare trouser/shirt buttons. A good display of kit over a period was re-warded by the individual being excused the laying of kit for the next one to four weeks. It was an incentive which encouraged effort and sustained high standards.

There was no such thing as an electric iron to do the pressing, but this was overcome by a method which, today, would seem archaic, but yet at the time was very effective. First of all, the creased edge of the garment (e.g. tartan trousers) was sprinkled with water and then placed under the mattress. A strong piece of cardboard under the garment gave it a firm base and kept it in place. Overnight the heat and weight of the body gave the desired result – a distinct and fine-edged crease.

Following the 9 a.m. inspection, the greater part of the day was taken up in training for those in the tailor shop and practice for boys in the Military and Pipe bands. There was never a week passed without drill sessions on the 'square'. My chosen field was drummer and bugler and then in 1937, I trans-ferred to the Military band as a trombone player. A set standard had to be reached, before it was possible to take your place along side your serviceman counterpart. Once this was attained, as a member of the band (Military or Pipe), you took part in all ceremonials and various other parades. For the bu-gler, he had a duty to perform on the 24-hour Barrack Quarter Guard. This involved having to sound the many bugle calls between the hours of reveille and lights out. During service in Palestine there was an additional 24-hour duty for the bugler and that was at the High Commissioner's residence. In whatever line you had joined-for, progress for various reasons was quicker for some than others. As bugler and drummer it took me roughly six months to reach the required standard; for a musician (bandsman) it took longer.

Other forms of training were slotted in at different times of the day and sometimes only on specific days. A special mention must be given to the drill square; it was here where the bellowed commands of the Drum-Major were turned into movement – march, counter-march, slow march, foot-drill, salut-ing and the handling of the swagger cane. From the outset, it was a part of military training which I found easy to adapt to, as it had a stimulus all of its own. There was always a demand for physical fitness and outer and inner cleanliness, something which for me had a lasting effect. During our periods of schooling, we were taught Regimental history and the main educational subjects. Educational attainment was measured in certificates. The 3rd Class Army Certificate of Education was within the reach of all and had to be gained in the early months following enlistment. 2nd Class took longer, but it was a level necessary for progress in the ranks. Beyond the rank of sergeant a 1st Class was required and this consisted of four advanced subjects – English, Maths, Geography and Map Reading. I passed on two of the subjects and I was reading to sit the other two when war put paid to any likely chance I had of success. As well as educational there was religious instruction, which no doubt was intended to give some meaning and understanding to Sunday Church Parade.

The demands of daily routine were so arranged that it left little time for relaxation, and the word 'bored' was not in our vocabulary. The more enthusiastic and those who knew it was in their best interest, spent time after the evening meal in cleaning up for the needs of the following day. In army parlance, this was known as 'beezing-up'. A lot of spit and polish went in to the cleaning of boots and shoes (highland brogues). The areas concentrated on were the toe-caps and heels. With the use of a piece of cloth, spit and polish was applied in a circular movement until a skin was formed and then it was finished off with a polishing rag. Whenever possible, a little methylated spirits instead of spit made the job much easier and guaranteed an excellent sheen. The same method was used when polishing the leather belt, dirk scabbard, bayonet scabbard and top part of the sporran.

Stand-by beds for roll-call was at 9 p.m. (Boy Service only) and was followed by lights-out at 10.15 p.m.. By the time the sounds of the lone piper had trailed off into the distance, the tired body was on the verge of sleep. At roll-call each Friday (pay day), all personal cleaning material had to be displayed and was inspected – white and green blanco, boot polish, brasso and toiletry. The weekly pay (2/6) was considered to be more than ample to cope with all requisites. After they were paid for it didn't leave a lot, perhaps enough for a daily visit to the canteen (NAAFI) for a tea and cake (wad or sinker). Any money for spending went on foodstuff, youth's appetite demanded it; even the extra 'bread-heels', provided you were not last in the queue at meal-times, were never enough!

Man Service was not reached until the age of eighteen; until then the pay of a boy soldier was one shilling a day; before I finished my term on Boy Service pay was increased by a shilling to eight shillings a week. Every Friday (pay day) after giving a smart salute, two shillings and sixpence was handed out. The remainder of the weekly pay was credited to the individual's account. This money which was put aside assured one that they had something to draw on for furlough and any other need which might arise. The conversion rate overseas made a slight difference to pay: in Palestine and Egypt twenty piastres (equiv. 4/-) was paid out and the remainder was put to your credits. The state of most servicemen's credits were always a concern!

As well as the rigid discipline of an infantry unit there were additional rules for Boy Service. The most notable was having to be indoors (except on late pass) by 9 p.m. roll-call which usually meant being in bed before lights-out at 10.15 p.m. Smoking and drinking alcohol was prohibited and you were supposed to keep company with your fellow contemporary and not with the men soldiers. The latter was difficult, if not impossible, as you mixed with them when on duty and you were all part of the same community.

In such a set-up, there was a constant awareness of control and of the punishment which awaited the wayward. Defaulters, known as 'Jankers' (CB – confined to barracks) was the usual run of punishment. This involved having to report after duty for fatigues, kit inspections, and after tea-time reporting every half hour to the Guard Room in different forms of dress. The last reported time for boys was 9 p.m. and for men 10 p.m. The type of fatigues selected as punishment varied from day to day. There was always work to be found – scrubbing tables, forms and floors, general cleaning, peeling potatoes, attending to garden plots, white washing demarcations such as stones and the burnishing of fire-pails. The provost staff never failed in finding something unpleasant for the defaulters to do.

For what was termed serious offences, the sentence was usually a spell in cells – detention. In Boy Service, the cane – as in civil law the use of the birch – was an additional form of punishment in extreme cases. I only ever knew of one boy having been punished in this way. He had repeatedly failed to reach the required standard and was subsequently discharged from the service. To be discharged in this way did not happen that often, as the Army maxim of make or break seldom failed. It may seem strange, but in those days a stigma was tagged to anyone who was put out of the services. One way which cast no aspersion was to buy oneself out, but at that time, £35 for other ranks without specialist training, was a lot of money and few took the option. For those of us who stayed the course there was always some form of challenge to contend with, a stoical approach to all things was the only answer.

Soon after I arrived in Aldershot, I discovered, as a member of the 2nd battalion, I would be leaving in November on overseas service, three months to the day of my enlistment. This came as a complete surprise, but I was quite happy to have been given the chance of going overseas so early in my service. When my parents heard of this, they were very concerned, but there was nothing they could do about it. Conditions of service taken on oath covered such a contingency. The only way open to my parents was to buy me out, but even if I had wanted them to, they didn't have the money! There only consolation was that they knew of my wish to travel abroad, and that my show of youthful exuberance, made it easier for everyone!

Time seemed to go in quickly during the period of initiation, but not too quickly for the day to arrive for the start of embarkation furlough – two or was it three weeks? It was mid-October 1935 when I arrived home in the full walking out dress of a drummer/bugler. The outfit consisted of tunic with the drum insignia on the arm, kilt, sporran, diced hose and white spats, brogue shoes, white belt, dirk, dress lanyard, glengarry and swagger cane. I felt very proud to be the wearer and a member of a famous Highland Regiment. My father was delighted to see me in the uniform of his old regiment, as he had served in the 2nd battalion in the First World War.

I had joined a large 'family' which was steeped in tradition and history – membership asked for and developed *esprit de corps*, the hallmark of every good regiment. It was early days, but it had already got through to me – camaraderie had a spiritual and comforting influence! It was of great value in those early years and was something, which became a quality trait of one's character.

Enjoying the comforts of Home Embarkation leave, 1935

My leave was spent visiting relatives and friends, and the occasional cinema show, but mostly enjoying the comforts of home. I had been long enough away to fully appreciate that precious element, family life! I was home for Halloween and was persuaded to dress up and take my young sister out to enjoy the fun of the evening. It was a widely recognised event and very popular with young people as well as children. As well as the fun there were the rewards which came in the form of nuts, fruit, sweets or pence. Before rewards were handed out, there were the guessing games as to who was behind the disguise and then each one had to recite, sing or dance. Nearly every home had an open door and the householders enjoyed the fun every bit as much as the participants.

That evening I dressed up as Haile Selassie, Emperor of Abyssinia, and by a quirk of fate, the disguise had a connection with what was to happened later. Some nine months on, I was to come face to face with His Excellency. It happened while I was bugler on duty at the High Commissioner's (Sir Arthur Wauchope) Residency, a building which overlooked the Jordan Valley on the outskirts of Jerusalem. His Excellency was on a courtesy visit and was invited to inspect the guard. By then he had fled his country and was in exile.

All too quickly leave came to an end and ahead lay the long return train journey to Aldershot. My only company for the return journey was a subdued awareness that this time I would be away from home for a very long time. Parting was a bit difficult but thankfully, whatever concern my parents might have had, they kept it to themselves. For me, the uniform I wore helped me put on a brave face and there was something else, due to my youth, I did not really comprehend the commitment I had taken on. One other factor was the anticipation of travel and adventure. But in the end, I did not escape lapses of home-sickness – this had to run its course and then it was over with!

My early call to foreign service was in keeping with how the military system then worked. It was in the days when we had to man far outposts of the Empire. To fulfil this responsibility, apart from support units, infantry regiments had always one battalion overseas and one battalion on home service. After approximately twenty-one years, the role of the battalion changed – the overseas battalion returned home and the home battalion moved overseas. As it turned out for me, I joined at a time when the battalion I was assigned to was about to start its overseas tour of duty.

When a battalion started its overseas tour of duty, every other rank, providing he had sufficient amount of time still to do, was required to serve, without home leave, the maximum period of six years. In time, with normal wastage and replacements, most members of a battalion completed this maximum period of time.

The minimum term of enlistment at that time was seven years with the colours and five years in the reserve. For Boy Service it was different on attaining eighteen years: for the Military and Pipe bands it was nine years with the colours and three years in the reserve – for the trade of tailor, it was eight years with the colours and four years in the reserve. An individual, if he so wished could sign on for a longer term, in which case it was usually for the pensionable period of eighteen years to twenty-one years or more. In the case of long serving men, they usually spent more than one spell abroad, but in peace-time, never at one time did the period go beyond the maximum of six years.

Six years overseas for the rank and file weighed heavy at times, by nature of the location, it could mean a form of isolation. The serving soldier overseas was cocooned in a unique life style. It took the demands of the Second World War to expose this out-dated act of banishment which had gone on for a very long time. As I understand, in 1943 the time span was reduced, but unfortunately for those like myself, the change of heart came to late. I was taken prisoner-of-war in 1942 by which time I had spent nearly seven years overseas; consequently it was near on ten years before I saw home shores again.

For officers and senior NCOs the peace-time situation overseas could be said to be more fluid. The married had their families along with them at most overseas stations. This meant that for a lot of the time they had the comfort of family life. It was not uncommon, particularly among officers, to return to the UK on special courses; and among senior ranks, there was always possible movement because of promotions.

This, as memory serves me, illustrates the basis of the Army as I knew it, in many ways different from the one it is today. I make the comparison because in terms of military history, its been a transformation which has come about in a comparatively short period of time. No doubt due to a changed map of the world, technology and in large measure, attitude. But for others to appreciate the significance in all of this, I must continue with *my* days of soldiering!

9

It was now the second week of November and preparation for our departure to Palestine (Israel) was well under way. Already an advanced party to deal with heavy baggage was at Southampton, our port of embarkation. Back in barracks, much of the time was now spent in getting ready for the big day. It varied from the issue and fitting out of tropical kit, to having inoculations and vaccinations – while the packing of kit had to be done in a way that gave ready access to whatever was required in transit. Time had come to get rid of certain items of private property – I had not been long enough in to have much to dispose of. My only two items were a suitcase and a thermos-flask, both of which I was not readily to forget! When I posted them home, I just put the thermos-flask inside the suitcase and without any packing, it arrived back home broken in several places – inexperience has its price!

The day arrived for our departure: it was 23rd November 1935, three months exactly to the day I enlisted. Reveille that morning was very early. In darkness we were marched to the neighbouring unit where we had breakfast. That morning it was hard boiled eggs, and to cope with the long day ahead, we were issued with haversack rations.

At first light we marched off in battalion order and our first halt was at Farnborough Railway Station where we entrained for Southampton. I do not remember much about the journey, except it did not seem long before we were making our way over the many railway tracks which criss-crossed the Southampton dock lands. The train finally came to a stop near to the ship which was to be our home for the next eleven days – it was HMT *Neuralia*.

As I looked up from the quayside, I was impressed by its size: this was my first sight of an ocean going vessel. It turned out to be the first of eight different ships I was to sail on. I made a second voyage on the HMT *Neuralia* in 1939 when I took passage from India to Egypt.

Once the battalion had detrained, everyone collected up their personal travelling kit and in Company order filed up the gangway. Immediately we got onboard, mess-decks were allocated and this allowed us to remove our webbing equipment and stow it. We were then free to go on the main deck and watch from above the happenings on the quayside below. Bands were playing, the embarkation staff were buzzing around and the end details were making their way onboard. The married men of the battalion, in parting from their families, were leaving it to the very last before ascending the gangway. Apparently, there was no recognised Army Married Quarters in Palestine and because of this, families were not re-united again until we moved to Egypt in December 1936.

The turn of the tide decided the hour of our departure. To the strains of 'Will Ye No Come Back Again', HMT *Neuralia* slipped her moorings and slowly edged her way into Southampton Waters and finally down the Solent, onwards into the open sea. All who were free to do so remained on deck, long enough to see The Needles recede and dip below the horizon.

The last sighting of home shores gave me a strange sense of loneliness even though there were many people around. How many others were restraining that lump in the throat feeling? Even though I was the youngest on board, perhaps I was as adept as they were at covering up. It was something I was to discover early on, that a soldier's emotions were not to be shared or exposed. Being away for years made home a place which they knew, and although loved ones remained loved ones, the longer the absence went on, the more distant the tie with home became.

As it was to turn out, many who stood on deck that day were seeing home shores for the last time. For the fortunate ones who returned, many of us had to wait a long time. In the course of that waiting, we had come to know the significance of the common expression – 'it's the way the cookie crumbles'.

On the day of our departure there was no thought of foreboding as to the future. It was a time to enjoy the excitement of the occasion, and to look forward to the expected venture which foreign service was known to offer. By nightfall, the ship's motion made it known that we were well under way and in the open sea.

After the evening meal, hammocks had to be drawn and slung within the allotted space of each mess-deck. Throughout the voyage, hammocks could only be slung at a certain hour in the evening. It was a new experience for most of us and I had my doubts about its comfort – there was no need, it turned out to be all right. Later I followed the example of several others, and spread the hammock on the open deck; the hard surface did not deter sleep. To do this one had to move quickly to find a space. It became preferable to the mess-deck because of the stuffy conditions below. It got worse the further east the ship sailed. Without stabilisers, the heaving of the ship was felt more down below than on the main deck. There was one other discomfort in mess-deck living and that was the mixture of smells from the galley and from what was usually a liberal spread of disinfectant around the ablutions.

The ventilation system was not the air-conditioning as we know it today. It consisted of a circular shaft of canvas (sail-cloth) which extended down each hold. The upper end was rigged to catch the wind flow and this enabled a continuous down draught of air to reach the areas below the main deck. Chutes could also be fitted to the portholes. When inserted they directed a current of air into the mess-deck and other areas. It was not always practical for the chutes to be used – weather, mood of sea and distance between port-holes and waterline decided when.

It was in the Bay of Biscay that I first experienced sea-sickness, but fortu-nately out of all the sea voyages I was eventually to make, it was the one and only time I had to go through such an ordeal. While it lasted, there was no wish to eat, but one had to get something down in order to put something up. At meal-time, the sight of a greasy dish immediately turned the stomach and with the hand covering the mouth, it was a quick dash to the nearest latrine. For the able and hungry they gladly accepted the extra food. One mess-mate who sat next to me at meals – he shall remain nameless – found it amusing to dangle a piece of bacon or fatty meat before my eyes. There was little in the way of sympathy: more often than not, seasickness was the butt for humour and laughter.

A good example was when one mess-mate, taken suddenly with sickness, made for the nearest porthole. As he wrenched open the cover and stuck out his head, he was met with an inrush of water. Covered in salt water and vomit he quickly withdrew, and to the chorus of banter made for the refuge of the ablutions to tidy himself up.

For those prone to bouts of sickness – while they lasted – the end of the voyage could not come quick enough. I know, because much of the time, that is how I felt. Regrettably for one member of the battalion, he did not finish the voyage; two days out from Malta he died from internal haemorrhage and was buried at sea. It was rumoured that his illness began with seasickness, but we were never to know just what happened. The service and burial was a moving experience – most of the battalion attended. The ship stopped only long enough for the canvas-wrapped body to be slipped over the side and committed to the deep.

Routine on board was for obvious reasons restricted, but there was always plenty to keep us occupied – lifeboat drill, physical training, lectures, stowing of hammocks, mess-deck inspections and checks on equipment. For enter-tainment, we had performances by both military and pipe band. Several con-certs were held during the voyage and it was then when hidden talent came to the fore. There were no rehearsals, it was mostly based on who would get up and have a go, and there was always plenty of good hearted banter and sup-port for those who dared.

The one popular song at the time was 'Red Sails In The Sunset', and to this day whenever I hear it, I associate it with those evening concerts on board ship. The singer who captivated the audience on those occasions was Pte. Ramage of D Company. Although there were no 'Red Sails', it was a setting for the song – a Mediterranean sunset, that feeling of isolation with horizon all around and the ship's never ending movement in parting the waters. Inter-company boxing was another item on the entertainment's list and, of course, the popular game of Housey Housey, known today as bingo. In a league of its own was the illegal gambling game of Crown and Anchor run by members of the ships crew. Our Provost Staff (Regimental Police) were for ever itching for a kill, but the crew's look-out was too quick at raising the alarm and gathering up the evidence and clearing off.

On the Sunday an open air Church Service was held on the main deck. I remember being strangely moved by the service, and aware that the surroundings gave an extra dimension to worship. We were close to *His* work, an alien void below, buoyancy which kept us above it, space above and all around. The only distraction was the vibration from the engine room, reminding us of the continuous movement which was taking us ever nearer our destination.

On St Andrew's Day (30th November) 1935, we entered the Grand Harbour of Valletta, Malta. It was our first port of call since leaving Southampton. Up till then, the only other sight of land was in the straits of Gibraltar when the prominence of the Rock caught the eye. There was plenty of interest to make our short stay of three hours quickly pass. Naval vessels of varying size filled the harbour and on the dockside there was much activity. No sooner had our ship dropped anchor than bumboats with their wares converged on us from all directions. Others, in boats of similar size, dived for coins which were thrown from the ship.

To sell their wares from the bumboats, the vendor would throw up a double rope for his client on the main-deck to catch and hold on to. A basket was then tied to the rope and by hand movement at both ends, the basket was pulled up by the client. The client would then place the money in the basket and lower it to the bumboat. On receipt of the money, the vendor put the goods in the basket and they were then hauled up. It was at this stage when things began to get risky. As the goods were on there way up, a hand would sometimes shoot out from a porthole below and take hold of the rope and basket and grab the contents. It was soon realised, that to prevent this happening, the rope had to be kept beyond the porthole as far as possible. A lesson on how you must not under-estimate the so called 'old soldier'!

With Malta astern we were now on the last lap of the voyage. From the beginning, we were informed daily of the distance travelled during the previous twenty-four hours. The final total was reached on 3rd December 1935 when we tied-up in Alexandria Harbour, Egypt. I was relieved that my first sea voyage was over, simply because I never found my 'sea-legs', though it was to be the only time.

Towards mid-morning, as I was preparing for disembarkation, I was told there was a visitor to see me. To my complete surprise it was my brother, who had joined the Navy the previous year – unknown to me, his ship HMS *Valiant* was on a visit to Alexandria and was berthed just over from where HMT *Neuralia* had tied up. He heard of our arrival and had immediately applied for permission to come on board. We didn't have long together but it was very pleasant while it lasted. Some months later, I again had the pleasure of his company; this time he stayed for a few days at our barracks in Jerusalem. It was to be the last I was to see of him until after the war.

Movement from ship to train was carried out in the customary military fashion, lots of activity, order and counter order, but in the end everything was completed in time. Once in the train however, we were at the mercy of the Egyptian railway, travel on which was a unique experience. I do remember that there were hold-ups but I don't know to what extent it delayed our arrival in Jerusalem.

Our first train journey overseas convinced us that train travel back home was not all that bad – this was one of many discomforts which turned us away from triviality! Train travel in the Middle East always produced the same discomfort: wooden seats, dust, flies and in summer months stifling heat. For the civilian passenger it was extreme overcrowding – clinging on the outside of carriages to windows and doors and sitting on the roof. At every railway station vendors plied their wares and whenever troops were onboard they had their adroit way of doing things. If you were not careful, just as the train was about to leave, their tentative attempt would leave them with the money and you without the goods – goods which ranged from eggs (hard boiled) and bread, to fruit and mineral drinks.

After leaving Alexandria, the rail track stretched through part of the Nile delta, the fertile area of Egypt, through places like Tanta and Zagazig and on to the Suez Canal at Kantara. It was here, if I remember correctly, where there was an interruption – we crossed by ferry and linked up with another train on the Palestine side of the Suez Canal. By the time the train reached the vicinity of the canal the greenery of the delta was left behind and in its place was desert sands. It was November and the desert was in dull mood – in the years ahead I was to discover its many moods. I was to know it in extremes of cold and heat; a place of infinite space; a reflection in colour like that from a furnace and the Khamsin from April to May, and as always the sandstorm. It tantalised with its creation of mirages, and night expressed an uncanny silence. It was an unkind environment which baited man to challenge!

Once we had made the transfer at Kantara, we continued our journey. The railroad skirted the Sinai Desert and kept for some distance to the coastal strip. Two place names come to mind, El Arish and Lydda Junction; it was after passing through the El Arish area, that there was a change in the passing scenery. In the midst of sand there started to appear scattered communal settlements with their orange groves and patches of greenery. Unknown to us at the time, what we were seeing was the beginning of a development which was to turn areas of arid land into productive land. A spread which was eventually to become the heartland of the future state of Israel.

As we neared Jerusalem the ground texture changed, and I have the memory of seeing a surface of weathered limestone, interspersed with stone and rock. Apart from patches of greenery, Jerusalem stood on what appeared to be a somewhat barren landscape.

As Duty Bugler mounting guard, Jerusalem 1936 (x mark is the author)

10

Our train reached Jerusalem in the forenoon of 4th December 1935. On the platform to welcome our arrival was a reception party, headed by the High Commissioner of Palestine, General Sir Arthur Wauchope. Once the preliminaries were over with, our column moved off headed by the Pipes and Drums and Military band. Our line of march took us through an area of Jerusalem which kept us visually aware that on our left was the Old City. One landmark on our right, St Andrew's Church, was a place which many of us were to frequent several times during our stay.

A mile or two on, after passing the Church, we reached our destination – Talavera Barracks. It was a location which gave a commanding view of the surrounding countryside. To the east one could see in the far distance what appeared to be a convolution of high ground, and somewhere in the midst was part of the Rift Valley. Over in the same direction stretched the Jordan Valley and contained in its basin was the Dead Sea. North and north east of the barracks there was more for the eye to feast on – Jerusalem with its white and sandy grey buildings, domes and minarets. There was also the partial view of the old walled city with the prominence of David's Tower; to the right the Mount of Olives and to the south, out of sight from the barracks, were the towns of Bethany and Bethlehem – history was all around.

After the restrictions of sea voyage and the discomfort and frustration of train travel, our arrival in barracks was a somewhat welcome relief. For many of us, it was our first experience of this new environment, but we were to discover that Palestine was a good place to start from. It was an environment which gradually absorbed us into how to deal with difference of climate and ways of the east. There was something to be said for the old soldier's adage, and by the time we moved on from Palestine, we did have our knees brown!

There was no shortage of places of interest to be visited, but one was limited by time and at a later date by the Arab uprising which resulted in all places being placed out of bounds to off-duty troops. However, I did take what opportunity there was, and visited Bethlehem (Church of the Nativity), Bethany, Rachel's Tomb, Shepherd's Fields, David's Tower, Garden of Gethsemane and in the old city walked part of the Via Dolorosa (Way of The Cross). At another time I had the memorable experience of bathing in the Dead Sea. The buoyancy was so great that one could recline on the surface without having to move a limb, but the intensity of salt made it a severe irritant to the eye. Where the River Jordan entered the sea, one could see from a distance, high banks of salt just like snow drifts. The road from Jerusalem down to the Dead Sea was, and is, a twisting decent of some 2000 feet, most spectacular and at times hair-raising. It was the people at the Mission Hut (Church of Scotland), down the road from the barracks, who arranged some of the tours. They in their own way helped us to understand more about the Holy Land. In the frequent visits we made to their Hut, their hospitality, which included tea and cakes, never waned and it was nice to be treated in a homely way. Our only other outside contact was with the YMCA which was housed in an impressive building in town, next to the King David's Hotel. The main attraction there was the use of the swimming pool. On one occasion, a number of us were invited by the Jewish community to an accordion band concert in the town. The other form of entertainment was the occasional cinema show in the NAAFI – in the part of the canteen where beer was sold and consumed, known as the wet canteen, it had its own special brand of entertainment. There, as the evening wore on, there were solo efforts and singsongs, some bawdy, some nostalgic (Burns' songs found favour).

Our first Christmas abroad was soon upon us, and for me it was my first

Pipe Band 'Beating Retreat', Jerusalem 1936 (x mark is the author)

**Boy Soldiers of the Cameron Highlanders along with
Boy Soldiers of the Loyal Regiment, Haifa 1936**
(author front row, 4th from left)

away from home. In the traditional way of the Army, at the Dinner we were waited on by Officers and senior NCOs. This gave rise to a great deal of good humoured satisfaction for other ranks. As youngest member of the battalion, I had to do my Santa Claus act by handing out Xmas Tree novelty gifts to the Officers present. The relaxed feeling of the festive season was an unusual aspect of service life and was enjoyed by all.

During the early part of 1936 our 1st battalion completed its overseas tour and returned to its home posting – Catterick Yorkshire. On the homeward journey from Khartoum Sudan, it dropped off a draft at Suez who then joined us in Jerusalem. They were members who had still time to do within the six years ruling and perhaps there were a number who had volunteered.

On a personal note, my progress as a drummer and bugler was not that long in being recognised. Within six months of my arrival in Jerusalem I was playing in the Pipe band and carrying out Bugle duties. On the 24 hours'-Barrack (Quarter) Guard as Bugler, one had to sound the regular standard calls – reveille, advance, retreat, first and last post and in between, requested and Company calls; and the most unwelcome of all calls – Defaulters. The other bugle duty was along with the Guard at the High Commissioner's residence. By comparison this was a leisurely duty with very few calls to sound-off. One was only there to sound the General Salute whenever His Excellency appeared. His residency was approximately two miles from barracks and the Guard Party, which changed every 24 hours, covered the two miles distance on foot. At the Guard Room there was a resident cook (Pte. D. Hume) and with only eight at a time to cater for, we were assured of a first class meal – it was a treat the way meals were cooked and served up. For the bugler, duties alternated between Barrack (Quarter) Guard and High Commissioner's Guard, roughly every ten days.

Once I was considered good enough to be a member of the Pipe band, it meant taking part in all parades when the band was required – ceremonial and non-ceremonial. One regular duty every Sunday was to head the march to St Andrew's Church in down town Jerusalem. The Church was situated on a knoll overlooking the Old City. On occasions, religious worship took the form of a Drum-Head service and was held on the barrack square.

During our time in Palestine, two events stand out in my memory. The first was the commemorative parade on the death of HM King George V. The period of mourning lasted a week, during which time the second top button on our tunic was covered with a black piece of cloth and Officers wore a black arm-band. The second event was when I attended my first Armistice Day service at the War Cemetery on the Mount of Olives. Its unique position overlooking the Holy City gave the row upon row of head stones an affirmed association with that other 'Great Sacrifice'. For their sacrifice, Palestine was liberated from the Turks followed by the Balfour Declaration. Ironically, some nineteen years on, during our stay, the Declaration brought about a renewal of trouble which sadly, has plagued that part of the world ever since.

It started in the April/May of 1936 and because of the Arabs' aggressive activities, the battalion from that time on until its departure, was engaged in suppressing the revolt. This took the form of guarding vulnerable and key locations, patrols, anti-intimidation and escort work. There was of course a price to pay in all this and the battalion suffered several casualties. A few were maimed and of the others, they recovered to fight again – there was no loss of life although other units were not so lucky. Acts of bravery were recognised, but as always, tradition demanded the ultimate in the performance of duty. For our part in the operations of 1936, each member of the battalion was awarded the General Service Medal and clasp (Palestine). It was not until early 1940 that the award was made official and then we were allowed to wear the ribbon – the issue of the medal itself was not until after the war.

As Boy Soldiers we were not of age to take a combatant's part in the operations, but as drummer boys we continued to do our bugle duties and routine remained the same. There were isolated incidents when shots were fired in the vicinity of the barracks. The High Commissioner's residence was a more likely place to be attacked, but any time I was on bugle duty there, the nearest gunfire I ever heard was from the surrounding valleys.

For a short time, we Boys moved to Haifa and were attached to the Loyal Regiment and shared activity and accommodation with the Loyal Boys. It was a fine break: in Army terms, it was known as a change of air exercise, but it also served to get us out of the way in to what was hoped a less dangerous area. It nearly did not work out that way. Part of our stay was spent under canvas at a place on the seashore between Haifa and Acre. The location had a conspicuous landmark dating back to the time of the Crusades – a ruined fort jutting out into the sea.

Apart from the usual chores of camp life, we had for a change a lot of leisure time, and the nearby Mediterranean afforded us good swimming. However, our pleasures did not last for long. They came to an abrupt end when we got word that an armed band of Arabs were in the vicinity. With little in the way of arms, we hurriedly packed up. We were warned that on the journey back to Haifa by motor transport we could be in trouble and might have to take some form of evasive action. By good luck nothing happened and we returned safely to barracks.

While in camp, we got used to the appearance of convicts from the prison at Acre which was just along the coast from Haifa. It was obvious from the way they were treated, that they were controlled by a very severe regime. They wore brown canvas jacket, trousers and pill-box cap, all marked with black arrow-heads and their feet were manacled with chains – it was a revealing sight!

Apart from our escape from the armed band, we enjoyed what Haifa had to offer. Swimming facilities were very good and while there, our ability was tested. We had to complete 100 yards of the baths within a certain time. I was a bit apprehensive; after all, I was self taught which raised within me doubt as to my credibility. As I hesitated at the deep end, the officer in charge asked if I could swim. I replied that I was not sure! It was an answer to invite an active response from the officer. As he pushed me in, he remarked, 'We will soon know'! I completed the test successfully.

While in Haifa we visited Sherman's Factory; it manufactured an assortment of soaps and toiletry of all kinds. What especially reminds me of the visit was the absence of any gesture of goodwill, such as giving a small sample of their wares to each of us. Our response was some indication of just how we felt. As we made our way out, we noticed that there were several open boxes which looked to contain tubes of shaving soap and toothpaste. It was our chance – as we filed out towards the outside door, we grabbed what we could. On return to barracks we discovered that the tubes were nothing more than exhibits, dummies filled with cotton wool. Was the 'enticement' simply intended as a subtle form of rebuke ?

After three weeks in Haifa, we returned to the battalion to pick up where we had left off. The Duty Companies were as busy as ever in dealing with the 'troubles'. Their response showed how well good training, efficiency and fitness paid off. After all, it had been a sudden transition from peace-time soldiering to active service conditions.

For people like the Commanding Officer and a number of senior Officers and senior NCO, active service was nothing new, as they had seen service in the First World War. All but one or two of the dutymen were undergoing their 'Baptism of Fire'. I got to know many of the dutymen while on bugle duties. This contact, in many ways, gave dimension to our apprenticeship as Boy Soldiers. Many of the dutymen had diverse and interesting backgrounds, and there were those who did not hide their attraction to deviate from the 'straight and narrow'. Yet this was the same type I found, time and time again, who 'balanced the scales' with their unconscious acts of Christianity in a practical way. No doubt, before and after, many were recognised in civilian life as being very ordinary and of little significance, destined never to rise above that status. Yet in uniform, they were the same men who exhibited the 'stuff' that ensured this island its freedom! I made good friends with many in those early days in Palestine and Egypt and that friendship lasted. Today when I look back, I still cherish the privilege of having known them.

Palestine, in comparison to other areas of the Middle East, had a fairly moderate and healthy climate. But like in all foreign stations, more precautions had to be taken in respect of health and fitness. What was very important was to respect the summer sun and not under estimate its dangers. The consequence of over-exposure, and render oneself unfit for duty was unthinkable!

Malaria was one illness which cropped up a lot and because of it, strict precautions were universally applied. After sunset, mosquito nets had to be down and tucked in round the bed, and arms and legs had to be covered between sunset and sunrise. As fruits of all kind were obtainable, one had to exercise a limit of caution for fear of gippy-tummy or, worst of all, dysentery. Certain measures had also to be taken to avoid the dangers associated with scorpion, centipede, termite – and rabies, in the case of the pye-dog (wild dog). In contrast, however, there was interest to be found in watching the behaviour of certain species of ants, and the changing colours of the chameleon.

In overseas stations there were the additional chores known as 'debugging'. Wednesday of each week was set aside for the task – a thorough cleaning which could be called a weekly spring clean. Bedding and bedsteads were the main targets of the operation. Blankets were given a good airing; it was necessary to strip down the bedstead and give it a thorough cleaning, a blow-lamp did a quick job on any vermin. The extent of elbow grease and involvement varied from station to station. One station which stood out above all others was the Citadel Barracks, Cairo. It was here where the blow-lamp was in greatest demand, so much so that it was jokingly remarked that, 'If the bugs walked out, the Citadel Barracks would collapse!' It was a messy business getting rid of the bugs without a blow-lamp. Whenever the human blood intake was squashed out, the remains gave off a putrid smell. That apart, the most disturbing aspect were their nightly activities, which put paid to a restful sleep – truly a 'bugbear'!

Apart from a soldier's fire-arms, bedding was a most important part of his belongings. For that reason, every Sunday bedding was laid out for inspection – mattress (biscuits), four blankets (one u/s), two sheets and one head-bolster. The one known as the u/s blanket was distinguished from the others by a cut off piece at the corner. It was the base blanket and was subject to more rough treatment than the other three.

To mention bedding reminds me of two pranks which I am sure many servicemen will remember. One was known as the 'French bed' and could only be set-up when the bed was made down. The top sheet was removed and folded in half and then placed under the blankets so that the top part of the bottom sheet was covered. The upper part of the folded sheet was then turned over the top blanket to make it look that nothing had been interfered with. It was only when you got in to bed that you discovered you could only get half way down the bed – it had to be re-made!

The other prank was a jarring experience and could only be carried out with the push-in style of bed. This was the type of bed which when fully pulled out locked on to a ratchet. You could over-ride the ratchet by extending the bottom of the bedstead on to a fine edge of the ratchet. Once it was in this position, all that was needed for the *coup de grace* was the body weight of the poor unfortunate – success meant that a resounding clatter ensued!

While kit inspections included all articles, there were additional ones which concentrated on specific items such as the check of bedding. Most items of kit had a laid down life span and providing they lasted out, clothing allowance took care of that which had to be replaced. However, in the case of loss and neglect (in peace-time), it had to be paid for by the individual. In looking after kit there was always the finicky job of sewing and darning.

While overseas, we had standard service uniform as well as tropical kit, but most of the time we wore the latter. The complete tropical outfit consisted of shorts, shirts, long trousers, tunics, all of which was of khaki-drill (KD) material and head-gear, the well known pith-helmet, the topee. Members of the Pipe/Military bands had in addition a white lightweight tunic for ceremonial occasions.

Khaki-drill was a type of uniform which was easily soiled, mainly because of perspiration and had therefore to be regularly cleaned and starched. The 'Dobbie Wallah' (laundryman) had a technique all of his own. Before ironing the KD, he would take a mouthful of a mixture of starch and water and with a contortion of the mouth, spray the garment.

As the year 1936 was drawing to a close, we were told that we were moving to Egypt. Since the start of the Arab uprising, a substantial number of reinforcements had moved in to the troubled land. One such contingent was our near neighbour (county wise) back home in Scotland – the Seaforth Highlanders, who were on detachment to Nablus. Part of their duties was escort work between Nablus and Jerusalem. One escort party to reach our barracks in Jerusalem consisted of three men who I knew back home when I was still at school – they were Alex Duncan, Walter McCurrach and Jim Watt. The three coming from the home village made the meeting such a surprise and something special – even Seaforths and Camerons could sometimes find common ground!

Overall our stay in Palestine had been interesting and eventful, but in a country so much steeped in history, I could have done with having been allowed to see more of it.

11

Just over a year to the day, our stay in Palestine came to an end – on 13th December 1936, we left Jerusalem for our new destination Cairo, Egypt. The route some of the way was similar to that taken the previous year. At Kantara on the Suez Canal, it was the same procedure, a change of train. Once we were on the Egyptian side of the canal, the train took us via Zagazig and from there we branched to Benha, then on to Cairo. On 14th December 1936 we marched into the Citadel Barracks, Cairo and took over from the Seaforth Highlanders, most of whom were by then on their way to the Far East.

For the last half mile of our approach march our eyes were filled with all the characteristics that one would expect of a citadel. Along the ramparts, at roughly equal distance, were spaces where, at one time, cannons had been housed; just visible above the ramparts were several flat-roofed buildings. Two buildings towered above all else: one was the water-tower and the other the Mohammed Ali Mosque. The Mosque with its high dome and twin minarets held everyone's initial attention. We were to discover that it was an entity in its own right, having its own surrounding wall. As a place of worship, it was at the time out of bounds to members of the British Forces.

The citadel was a structural outcrop which overlooked Cairo and dominated the landscape for miles around. Its only rival as a vantage point was the nearby Napoleon's Fort on the Mokattam Heights, an escarpment which stretched for some miles in an easterly direction. The sandstone face of the escarpment appeared as if it had been dug out with a huge spade. It was noticeable from a distance that there were several dug-out positions on the face of the escarpment. These turned out to be ammunition and explosive dumps. The battalion supplied a guard for this area and sometime during 1937 the Egyptian Army took over. The Guard Commander on the day that the hand over took place was a Cpl. McWilliam of A Company.

Not far from the foot of the escarpment was an area known as the Dead City, a name arrived at because of the many scattered graves, alleyways and shanty dwellings. It was a place to be avoided! From the ramparts of the citadel, one had a wonderful view of Cairo; among the mass of buildings and streets were the many distinctive structures of minarets and domes. The combined content of the metropolis extended outward and beyond, to the boundary where sand and sky met and where the hue and heat haze filmed the distant Gizeh Pyramids. To stand on this vantage point, one was treated to a setting that was something special – the allure of the East was truly at our doorstep!

As well as living quarters, there were within the citadel other establishments – Glass House (Army jail), hospital, married quarters, stables and several derelict buildings and dungeons; the latter were treated as a 'no-go' area. The square, where drill and parades took place, covered a large area; around its perimeter were situated Admin. Offices, stores, NAAFI, dining hall and most of the barrack room accommodation. The lay-out of the citadel was connected up by arches and a road system which lead to both front and rear main entrances.

A, B, C, and D Companies occupied the barrack rooms which skirted the large square, while HQ Company was housed in a building situated between the married quarters and Officers' Mess. The complement of HQ Company consisted of both Pipe and Military bands, Pioneer Platoon, employed men, transport mounted and unmounted, Main Admin. and Boy Soldiers.

Accommodation in the citadel was not the usual type, each building consisting of several rooms, each varying in shape and size. We Boys were housed in four small rooms, two of which were adjacent to the ramparts. All four rooms had one similarity to the barrack room back in Aldershot and that was a polished floor, so once again we had to take our turn on the 'Bumper'.

A walled space between HQ barrack block and the gym was where the boxing ring was erected. It was where several inter-company and inter-unit contests took place. The location afforded plenty of room for what was always a very supportive audience. Along with football, both sports had a big following, made greater by the competition and achievements of the battalion during its stay in Egypt. The football ground was outside the walls of the citadel and it was there where I recall seeing a number of excellent games, particularly the ones played against visiting Egyptian teams. It was encouraged among those of us on Boy Service and I was one of the eleven who won the Cavalry and Cairo Brigade Enlisted Boys Football Challenge Cup. When we moved from Cairo, there was never again the same opportunity to play the game because of location and lack of opposition. One or two of the Boys continued to play when they entered Man Service, but for me the Cairo achievement was my limit. However, there was plenty of sport to choose from and it was a prominent feature of activity in the battalion.

Cairo was different in many ways from our previous station, particularly in climate – Palestine was warm, but did not match the high temperatures of Egypt plus its infernal sand and flies. It has to be said, however, that Egypt was not the only place where one had to put up with the wretched winged pest, but it was the one place that had more than its share. Another winged intruder was the Kite Hawk (the services had another rhyming name for it); its exploits caused problems for the unwary. To walk over an open space carrying anything in the food-line required protection, otherwise the Kite Hawk would swoop and be off with it.

Much has been written about Cairo, especially during the period of the Second World War, but in 1936 it was a place known to a limited number, mostly servicemen. The many overseas stations at that time, from Middle East to Far East, were policed by British servicemen. Their roll was to exert authority whenever necessary and in turn the people had to yield having no alternative and having known nothing better. While it lasted, it served to maintain a level of stability. But since the demise of our influence and their so-called liberation, certain parts of our previous domain seem to have suffered more than was reputed during the days of the Empire.

The ordinary serviceman at that time was not concerned with the 'why and wherefore' of the situation; he did what was asked of him. He served in countries where there was a distinct imbalance of living standards – the minority lived well and for the majority it was poverty and life was cheap. It was a situation which was looked on by those of us who were there, as a way of life which had gone on for a very long time, and that we were nothing more than witnesses to its extension. Nonetheless, there was much of interest and the East had a legacy all of its own to offer, for those who were receptive enough to accept! This compensated for the filth, smell, disease and – in places like Cairo – the all prevailing trade in vice. The latter started with the young and along with begging, featured very much in everyday life. Consequently, it was a breeding ground for venereal disease and this was common knowledge to us all. There was one place in Cairo, the Museum of Hygiene which exhibited, in a chilling way, what could be the outcome for such folly!

The authorities acted in a stern way towards any serviceman who was unfortunate enough to become a victim of the disease. As I learned from others, treatment in hospital was harsh for what was considered avoidable. There was no sympathy for rendering oneself unfit. Pay was reduced to the basic and in order to regain lost pay, it was necessary, after leaving hospital, to complete

A visit to the Pyramids, Egypt 1937 (x mark is the author)

Boy Soldiers Football Team. Runners-up British Forces in Egypt 1937
(x mark is the author)

and pass ability and fitness tests. It was no easy task and involved pack drill, one form of punishment despised by the erring!

Like many overseas stations, Cairo had its controlled 'red light' area and was there for the British servicemen. Its occupants had regular medical examinations which, at least, gave a possible measure of safety. Elsewhere, wherever troops went, there was always the alluring and beckoning hand of temptation. Some found it was asking a lot of a young man to remain chaste for such a protracted period of time.

Our arrival in the citadel near to Christmas, seemed to favour the settling in process. The Festive season was a time which was looked forward to, it was a time when the hand of discipline was less weighty and when the efforts of the Sergeant/Cook and his men were appreciated – there were no complaints that day for the Orderly Officer!

We had two Festive seasons 1936–37 in the citadel and this turned out to be the only time when the whole battalion celebrated under the same roof – the citadel barracks had one large dining hall. The New Year's celebrations too seemed more convivial, something which could only be put down to the close positioning of our accommodation; Companies were within easy reach of each other. During the two periods of festivities, we Boys, much to our surprise, had little supervision and this gave some of the men the opportunity to treat us to a dram. I never knew this to happen before or after; anyhow my first taste of alcohol convinced me I was not missing much. To me, this made sense of my belief that there was no need to feel deprived at not being allowed to drink or smoke under the age of eighteen!

Early in 1937 the first draft of reinforcements from home arrived – replacement of personnel took place from time to time. The draft included a number of Boys, replacing the ones who had or were about to reach Man Service. If I remember correctly, the battalion had a compliment of roughly twenty five to thirty Boys at any one time. With the arrival of a new lot of Boys, I was no longer the youngest member of the battalion; I had moved up the seniority list. While seniority was a factor in the promotion race, for Boys there was little incentive in that direction. There was only one step up and that was to what was known as Senior Boy. Usually there were only two in a battalion and the badge of rank was a straight chevron worn on the bottom of the tunic sleeve – overseas it was also worn on the short sleeve of the shirt. During most of my time on Boy Service, the position was not filled and then in the last two or three months of my service it was filled. I was satisfied to know that had I had longer to do, I would have been one of the two to have filled the posts.

Not long after the 'new faces' arrived in the battalion, we moved out for a period of desert training which lasted two months. Our return to barracks was in mid-March 1937. Camp was located at a place – or should I say a map reference, as all that was there was sand and more sand – called Beni Yusef, six miles south of the Gizeh Pyramids. During the two months, we Boys had our own schedule of training while the battalion practised tactics in the outer spaces of the desert and completed their training at a place called Hilwan.

Those of us who were Drummer Boys did the same bugle duties as we did in barracks. Dress was different, a field outfit was worn known as FSMO (field service marching order) and ceremonial dress was left behind in barracks. This meant that there was not the same cleaning to be done and inspections were not carried out in the usual meticulous way.

The difference in Boys' kit from that of the men was that Boys had no steel helmet, large pack, ammunition pouches, scabbard, bayonet or rifle. Those items were issued once a boy reached the age of eighteen and went over to Man Service. At Beni Yusef Camp the duty bugler's dress was tunic with brown leather belt, single cord to sling bugle, kilt and apron, headgear (in this instance glengarry), boots, khaki hose, red flashes and short putties. The latter (leg dress) was worn at all times when in shorts. In barracks or at camp and whatever the dress, after sunset (retreat), arms and legs had to be covered.

Apart from the different routine at camp there was also the discomfort of the desert. From this early experience, we learned that, by comparison, the barrack room was a five star hotel! I was to discover later, that a good night's sleep in the desert was possible, providing you picked a soft spot which enabled you to scoop out a space for ground sheet and blanket. Under canvas, such as at Beni Yusef, space was limited; it was measured by the joints in the canvas of the bell tent with everyone lying with feet to the central pole. It was an arrangement which did not allow blankets to be free from sand, a discomfort which had continually to be put up with. At meal-times, as well as flies, the intrusion of sand took away much of the enjoyment of a meal.

The sanitation in camp was an open-air make-shift structure, easy to set-up. It consisted of a canvas screen, inside of which were several large buckets with wooden toilet seats and there was the urinal. The urinal was a metal trough sloping towards an improvised sump and all items within were doused with a creosote smelling disinfectant. Back in barracks the toilet was the only place where one found privacy, whereas in camp it was a different matter. It was a shared experience, where it was either an exchange of conversation or a facial expression which said it all! In the open desert, sanitation was easily taken care of, all that one had to do was to pick up a shovel and take a walk. If I remember correctly, the Sikh (Indian) soldier had in addition a small tin of water.

The other place which none of us could have done without was the Field-Kitchen; camp cooking was done by the use of burners which, to the layman, looked like large blow-lamps. They were set into a covered section which had openings on top into which the dixies fitted. All cooking was done in the dixie. In some camps the Field Kitchen had also an improvised field-oven.

It was early days but we were learning how to adapt to the desert way of life! One thing which did not take us long to realise was the importance of a water supply. All we had was the water truck and as a source it could not be considered fully reliable. It was just one facet of life in the desert which called for self-discipline – an element of character which in time was to stand us all in good stead! Little did we know at the time, that many of us would have a long association with the desert. An association which eventually was to make us aware and respectful of the desert's sometimes bizarre behaviour.

With the last remaining grains of sand shaken from our kit and being, we returned to barracks to walk again on firm ground. The next big occasion of the year (1937) was the King George VI Coronation Parade which took place on 12th May in the grounds of Gezira Sporting Club. It was a show piece of Army ceremonial precision of which the battalion was fully capable of carrying out. About much the same time King Farouk of Egypt ascended the throne. This was one occasion which the battalion was not called upon to take part. It was also an occasion which placed Cairo out-of-bounds to British servicemen; it was feared that certain factions might exploit the event and therefore it was thought better that we keep our distance!

It was while stationed in Cairo that my career took a change of direction. I transferred to the Military band and took up the trombone. It was a big step, as by this time I was well established as a drummer and bugler. For some time it had been my ambition to become a member of the Military band. It was not easy, as transfer between bands was not encouraged and was seldom approved

Progress in the Military band took time and, in order to acquire the necessary standard, it called for dedication. I had a lot to catch up on as nearly all of my band colleagues had been at music from an early age. Initially tuition was of a personal nature and then I moved on to practice with the band. It was to take me nearly a year before I was playing out as a regular member. This was considered good progress but I had still much to learn. I found it absorbing and satisfying and much more demanding than the side-drum and bugle.

Because of limited pocket money – as a Boy Soldier, one saluted for 20 piastres a week – visits to Cairo were made only when one had reached a reasonable state of solvency. The cinema and restaurant were where one usually headed for and also the interesting places like museums, pyramids and sphinx. To have one's photograph taken at the pyramids was a must! Like others, I crossed over the Nile at Kasr-El-Nil Bridge many times but only once sailed up the river. I don't think we ever gave much thought to the importance and distance of its flow. I suppose after a time, one became accustomed to travel and developed a nonchalant attitude to change and surroundings. However, one could not detract from the fact that Cairo was one place which had all the treasures and less treasureable aspects of the East. It offered a cost-free dimension to an enquiring mind!

At the height of the summer of 1937, all Boys were granted a fortnight's leave which we spent under canvas in Alexandria. The camp was a well established change-of-air location and was open throughout the summer months; it was a popular place for many servicemen. It was situated away from the city, on the seaward side of the esplanade. A pedestrian way under the esplanade connected the camp with Mustapha Barracks. At the time a battalion of the Coldstream Guard occupied these barracks. Incidentally, it was one of the rules of the day that no Guards regiment served east of Suez. I never discovered why this peace-time restriction applied only to the Foot-Guards – perhaps it had something to do with their various Royal duties?

The esplanade was a prominent feature of Alexandria as was its harbour, a large establishment which at the time, supported a busy British Naval presence. I visited the Catacombs and the off-shore location reputed to be where the famous Pharos Lighthouse once shone its guiding beacon. There were also pleasant gardens to stroll through. The sea breezes from the Mediterranean were a pleasant change from the stifling heat of Cairo, and bathing completed what was one very acceptable luxury. Like Cairo it had its bazaars and souvenir shops in plenty, and it was from there I sent home presents to my parents and sisters. Alexandria was where I first took up roller skating which I enjoyed, but the opportunity only lasted while I was there.

The camp had good facilities – marquee tents (by comparison a luxury to the bell-tents used in training) which afforded ample space, comfortable bedding and running water. It was a time free from the drill square and barrack routine, plus the delight of not having to respond to the reveille call. All that was asked of us was to be on time for breakfast – one attendance that was never missed! What gave us the most satisfaction was the use of money which had accumulated to our credit over a period of time.

From camp we had a short distance to walk to the tram terminus at Sidi Bish a suburb of the city. It was a speedy ride from there to the city centre and, like all public transport in Egypt, it was conspicuous for its lack of restrictions on the number of passengers carried at any one time. Passengers clambered on to the roof and hung on to the side of the moving vehicle.

All too soon the fortnight came to an end, and refreshed, we returned to Cairo. As it was to turn out, it was not the last I was to see of Alexandria.

12

Our next move came in January 1938. On the fourteenth we arrived in Moascar and took over the barracks in Nelson Lines from the Manchester Regiment. They moved out to go further east. We were now part of a garrison which manned a strategic position on the Suez Canal. Some distance from the barracks, south of Lake Timsha, on the Egyptian side of the Canal, stood a large commemorative column for the dead of the First World War. It was a sober reminder of what a previous generation had to pay for the defence of this artery of the Middle East.

The other infantry battalion in the garrison was the Royal Sussex, along with supporting units from the Medical Corps, Engineers, Transport etc.

Within the compound were married quarters, hospital, church, church Army centre, cinema and school for both service personnel and servicemen's children. Further along the way, but separate from our establishment was the RAF station. Their activities were kept more or less to themselves. During the years prior to the Second World War, co-operation between the three services was not so much in evidence – combined effort came later. The RAF station had a conspicuous landmark, a high mooring mast which as I understand, was specially built for the ill-fated airship R101.

It was loose desert sand between the barrack blocks in Nelson Lines. The only firm footing was on the paved pathways, the gravel covering on the drill-square and sports area and the tarmac road running through the barracks. Apart from the greenery of Ismailia and the fringe areas around Lake Timsah and the Great Bitter Lake, desert was all around. We hadn't far to go to watch the shipping passing through the Suez Canal. From a distance the ships gave the strange illusion that they were travelling through desert.

Another canal, insignificant by comparison, called the 'Sweet Water Canal', ran close by the barracks and the town of Ismailia. Where it got its name from, I never discovered, but we all knew that it was far from being sweet. It was filthy and, it was said, that if you were unlucky enough to fall in, you would require to undergo a course of injections!

The nearby town of Ismailia had, apart from its gardens, not that much to offer and my visits were few. Within the garrison there was always activities of one kind or another – cinema, indoor recreation such as billiards, a fine library – one facility which was not in every station – and of course there was the sport of your choice. Close by was Lake Timsah, a favourite spot for those who could afford yachting; and for everyone there was swimming. It was here that I did a Life Saving course and gained the Life Saving Bronze Medallion.

Not long after we arrived in Moascar, in February, we moved out to spend a month under canvas at Fayid. During our time there, the battalion carried out desert training at company, battalion and brigade level. Fayid was a desert location south of Ismailia, inland from the Great Bitter Lake and was overlooked by two conspicuous elevations, known to servicemen at that time as the 'Big Flea' and the 'Wee Flea' (I don't know why!). It was this area of desert which in the Second World War became the main base Depot for the Middle East Forces. By that time a much larger area of desert was taken over and out of it were borne the legendary names of Kabrit, Fayid, and Genefa – a 'cross-roads' for many of those who served in that theatre of war. At Fayid, camp life was similar to that of the previous year at Beni Yusef, except for me, as I no longer had bugle duties to carry out. Now as a member of the military band, I had in addition to be trained in First Aid. In war, one of our functions as bandsmen was that of stretcher-bearer.

After our second experience of life in the desert, we were pleased to return to the comfort of the barrack room. Shortly after our return, on 6th April, the battalion Games were held. The event was small in comparison to the previous year's gathering when it had been spread over a period of five days. This time it was only for the one day, but in the track and field events competition between companies was every bit as keen. The day finished with combined bands – Military and Pipe – playing Retreat.

During April I became ill with malaria; on the day I was one of three in the battalion to be hospitalised for the same malady. Because of the nearby swampland, adjacent to the lakes, large mosquitoes proliferated the area. Despite all possible precautions, several of the battalion fell victim. My own experience was very unpleasant and for the first ten days it was a period of high temperature, fever, severe headache, with no appetite, but a desire only to drink. To a great extent the treatment contributed to the misery. It was liquid quinine which was given under supervision three times a day for the first ten days. The supervision was perhaps necessary as the liquid was unpalatable – bitter to the extreme with side effects which stained the teeth and dulled the hearing. By the time the ten days' treatment was over, I had regained my appetite and was on the road to recovery. To help me on my way, for a number of days, I was given a daily bottle of milk stout to replace lost weight – in all, I was three weeks in hospital.

Military Band of the Cameron Highlanders, and Fife and Drums of the Coldstream Guards, Trooping the Colours, Alexandria, June 1938 (x mark is the author)

By now I had reached a standard on the trombone to allow me to play out with the band. Apart from daily practice, nearly all 'turn-outs' were for battalion ceremonial and church parades. There was, in addition, beating retreat with the pipe band and occasional attendance at the Officers' Club in Ismailia. Some members of the band made up a dance band which usually played at functions after duty hours.

In May 1938 a call came for the military band to proceed to Alexandria to take part in the Trooping of the Colours with the Coldstream Guards. Our services for the occasion were required because on this occasion they only had a Drum and Fife band with them. Military bands of the various Guard regiments did not go overseas with their Regiment but remained back home, controlled under a 'pool' system within the Brigade of Guards. It is likely that it was expedience that found us there, but we also had the reputation to fill the role!

To be one of the Boys selected for the Trooping was an uplift to one's position in the band. Not only was it the participation, but there was a certain relief at getting away from the Boy Service regime for a time. What's more, it was an opportunity to enter another domain and assert oneself among men. It was for me a trial-run, as I had only another five months of Boy Service to do.

The band was attached to the Coldstream Guards at Mustapha Barracks for roughly six weeks. A lot of the time was spent on the parade ground rehearsing, during which time the RSM played a prominent part. If I remember correctly, its the only parade where the RSM draws his sword. It seems that over the years the procedure of Trooping the Colours has not changed any.

By the time the day arrived for the parade, we had every movement off by heart. It was a spectacle with an unprecedented variation – the swing of the kilt! Our ceremonial dress for the occasion was: kilt, sporran, diced hose, flashes, white spats, brogues, white tunic, white belt with dirk and, slung over the left shoulder, the white music card-bag showing the Cameron Badge against a background of a circle of red cloth. For head dress, we had a special issue of a white topee (with white hackle/plume) for the occasion.

On the day, with the Guard's Fife and Drum band taking up our immediate rear, we headed the battalion of Coldstream Guards through the streets of Alexandria to the grounds where the Trooping took place. By the time we arrived at the grounds, a large crowd had assembled, most of whom were British and Egyptian notables. Following the Trooping, there was a march-past, and the salute was taken by the British Ambassador, Sir Miles Lampson. After the parade, we returned to Mustapha Barracks in the same formation and by the same outward route. It had been a long day and by the time we were dismissed, we were all glad that our task was over.

During our attachment to the Coldstream Guards, we had a certain amount of leisure time, and when our period of attachment was over, we were granted a few days furlough to spend in Alexandria. It was my second sojourn in the city so I was no stranger to the place. This time however it was different, for being along with our men colleagues afforded us Boys a greater freedom – the 'door was ajar', inviting us to push on it!

I went out on a few occasions with band colleagues, and one particular time stands out. It was when we visited what appeared to be a bona fide café but it turned out to be a front for an illicit liquor den. As we entered the café, instead of being allowed to sit down at a table, we were invited to go through a back door and down a flight of steps. At the bottom of the stairs was a room where a variety of liquor was for sale at very low cost. No sooner had we got settled when an agitated assistant appeared, who instructed us to get up and go. Apparently a police raid had started in the front premises and, for our own good, we had to make a hurried exit through a side door. This led into a dark side alley; once there, we made a dash for the obscurity of the nearest busy street.

One or two incidents during our time in Alexandria made me think that some of the restrictions imposed on us while on Boy Service did serve a purpose. I found it imbued in me a disciplined approach to many things, and I was less likely to take a chance, although this could sometimes be difficult. It could be, however, that it was not only discipline, but my 'make-up' that made me obligatory to the code of conduct asked for. I was later to think about this period – a period when one was in the process of growing up without the aid of someone to 'lean on'. As a result, I have become more understanding of the well known expression – 'Oh, there but for the grace of God go I'. Thankfully for me I stopped short!

A lot of my off-duty time was spent roller-skating, a pastime I first took up during my previous visit to Alexandria. I attended as often as I could, as there would be no chance of continuing once I rejoined the battalion. It was an activity where there was mixed company, and this kept aspirations alive albeit to no fruitful end! All too often being in uniform was more a hindrance than a help. For the ordinary peace-time serviceman overseas, there was not much chance of mingling with civilians of the right type. It didn't help matters when remarks were circulated – such as 'Beware of the men with the V-shaped necks' – reference to the V-shape the sun-tan left; at the time PR was very lax!

After nearly two months of detachment, it was with some reluctance that we took leave of Alexandria. We arrived back in the battalion after a few hours' train journey. It must have been a Wednesday when we got back, for the following morning it was the Adjutant's inspection, and this always occurred on a Thursday. It was a sobering return for me, for during the inspection I was congratulated on my turn-out but asked, where did I have my shorts laundered? I replied that, 'I had them done at the Flying Dobbie'. This by the way was a quick service in addition to the normal laundering facilities. The Adjutant's response to my answer was to turn to the Drum-Major and utter those dreaded words – 'Put him on a charge'. I was taken aback; what wrong had I done?

It turned out that, at the time I had left for Alexandria, an order had come out prohibiting Boys the use of the Flying Dobbie because it incurred extra expense for the individual, and it was considered we could not afford the extra with our limited money. It was only when I was placed on the charge that I knew about the new order. This was how I answered to the charge when I appeared before the Adjutant the following morning. It had also occurred to me that, by admitting to having used the extra facility, it would convince him of my innocence. My explanation cut no ice; he inferred that I was using my period away from the battalion as an excuse. My punishment was to be confined to barracks for three days (defaulters). Inwardly I felt I had been harshly dealt with. The incident is as clear in my mind today as it has ever been, simply because it was the one and only time I was up on a charge during the

The author in uniform for Trooping the Colours, Alexandria 1938

whole of the time I served on Boy Service. It would have been fine to have left Boy Service with a clean sheet, but I suppose to have only one charge in three years and two months, in a regime such as it was, perhaps warrants a credit mark!

The only other time I appeared before the Adjutant was shortly before I entered Man Service. On that occasion I was told that, on my eighteenth birthday, I had the option of either going with the battalion to India or returning home. Apparently the minimum age for serving on Man Service overseas was nineteen. It was one ruling that we were never forewarned about and it was one that was never discussed or explained. Now for the first time I was made aware of its definition. It was put to me that, if I decided to join the home battalion, I would only remain with it until I reached my nineteenth birthday, then I would be sent overseas to serve a further six-year period. On the other hand, if I volunteered to remain with the battalion, my Boy-Service overseas would count towards the six-year period. Once that was completed I would be posted to the home battalion. At the time I thought it rather strange that, while on Boy Service it was all right to serve overseas, but on Man Service you had to be nineteen. Now I had to make a choice – from what I was told there was only one way for me, and that was to remain with the battalion and nourish the thought that I would be back home in three years' time.

But it wasn't to work out that way and, in retrospect, I think that during the interview things could have been better explained; even some advice would have helped, but none was given. The Adjutant was an Officer of some standing, and in 1938 he must have had a good understanding of the situation in Europe and the imminence of war. For me, I was immature in many ways, and like my contemporaries didn't have concern for current affairs nor the time for serious thought. Even a hint in the right direction might have spared me the lengthy period away from home: our 'number' had a more subtle interpretation to it! – we were just a number! However, having said that, perhaps there are times when we can be thankful to fate and this, as it was to turn out, was possibly such a time!

On 12th October 1938 I turned my back on Boy Service and entered Man Service. There was no graduation service or fuss; it was a change which many before and many after me experienced. I did not have far to go. I had two hundred yards to carry my bedding and equipment to the Military Band Barrack Room. After I was allocated bed and locker space, I had to report to the Quartermaster's store for additional items of equipment. They included rifle, bayonet, steel helmet, gas-mask and gas-cape, webbing ammunition pouches, bayonet holder and large pack – now I was fully kitted out. As an ex-Boy I was no stranger to service life as a whole, therefore there was no recognised transition period for my kind. You were expected to adapt quickly to the extra requirements Man Service called for.

The military band had a compliment of some thirty odd and, apart from the NCOs, there were only twenty one appointed bandsmen, the remainder were ranked as Privates. Six months into Man Service and I was appointed bandsman. As well as being musicians, we were required to be able to fulfil the role of the dutyman, which meant that we had to know how to handle weapons and that included rifle drill.

During my first year on Man Service, apart from field training, band commitment took up most of our time – weaponry and first-aid were part of our training schedule, but it was on a limited scale. Nevertheless, it was a schedule which kept us well informed and we all prided ourselves in being able to function in all three 'cylinders' – i.e. musician, dutyman and stretcher-bearer. Having to be able to give a three-fold performance made no difference to our pay. Pay scales were the same as the dutyman and, like the dutyman, progression was over a period of time.

When I entered Man Service my pay doubled immediately; for the first year it was fourteen shillings a week. The second year it went up to twenty-one shillings a week, and the third year it increased to twenty-three shillings and four pence a week. After three years were completed, the maximum was reached – twenty-nine shillings and nine-pence a week (4/3 a day). This was the basic pay structure of the infantryman of that time: on promotion different scales operated according to rank.

For those of us who had served as Boys, the one big change in entering Man Service was the increase in pay and the lifting of restrictions. No longer did one have the many kit inspections or the need to stand-by beds for roll-call at 9 p.m. each evening. Smoking and the use of the wet canteen (where beer was sold) was no longer prohibited and above all else, there was greater freedom!

Just over a month after I entered Man Service our stay in Egypt came to an end – our next move was India. This was one part of the world which, to a serviceman, had a certain aura about it – it gave him the old soldier's status tag! Tales about East of Suez, the Raj and all that geared us up for our new posting.

The last memorable parade before leaving Egypt took place on 13th November 1938. It was the dedication of the Regimental Window, which the battalion presented to the Garrison Church of St George Moascar. Nine days later, we boarded HMT *Somersetshire* at Port Said for our new horizon – India.

13

As we sailed through the Suez Canal, we could see from the ship our previous abode Moascar Barracks and the nearby town of Ismailia. At one particular spot on the canal bank, a large crowd had gathered to wave us on our way. Some time later, while still on passage through the canal, we passed an Italian troopship heavily laden with servicemen on their way home from

Abyssinia. We were told in advance that, if we wished to remain on the main deck while the ships passed, we would have to keep to the far side of our ship. It was to prevent shouts of abuse being directed at the Italians. At the time there was bad feeling between us because of their war with Abyssinia and the alleged atrocities that had been inflicted on the natives of the country by the Italian troops.

We did what was asked of us and this no doubt avoided an international slanging match! Little did we know at the time that some of those very same belligerents would, in a matter of seventeen months, be facing us in combat across the battlefields of North Africa and the mountains of Abyssinia.

In the Red Sea, we stopped at Port Sudan to take on more troops – they turned out to be The Royal Welsh Fusiliers. Although it was a time of year when the sun was not at its hottest, it was still warm enough for a little exertion to cause sweat. In all the eight times I sailed the Red Sea, I never knew it to be anything other than a place of extreme heat. It was also a place where one particular torment thrived and that was a body rash known as prickly heat. It was said that to have prickly heat was a sign that you were in a healthy state. The prognosis of the state of one's health did not make it any more comforting for the afflicted!

Before entering the Arabian Sea, we stopped for a few hours in Aden. It's a place I will always remember for two reasons – its barren setting and for the number of sharks that surrounded our ship while at anchor. Darkness and the reaction of the phosphorus in the sea to their every move made their presence visible. Their back fins created luminous lines which showed up their size and their milling behaviour.

Escorted by dolphin, porpoise and flying fish, we made our way through the Arabian Sea to reach Bombay, our port of disembarkation, on 5th December 1938. After a two hundred mile train journey via Poona and ascending some 2000 feet above sea level on the Deccan Plateau, we arrived at our final destination – Ahmednagar. Headed by the Military and Pipe bands, the battalion marched in company order from the railway station to our new home, Sandhurst Barracks, passing on the way the one and only prominent landmark in the area – Ahmednagar Fort. At Sandhurst Barracks, we relieved the 2nd battalion The York and Lancaster Regiment. Their move was to North India but I can't remember the exact location.

Ahmednagar was our fourth overseas station, so by now we had become adept at packing and moving on. However, soldiering in India was a bit different which meant a few adjustments had to be made.

We were now in the Indian Army, part of the 11th Infantry Brigade of the 4th Indian Division, a formation which we were part of throughout our time in India and during the years of war. A division at that time consisted of three Infantry Brigades and supporting units of artillery, service corps and sappers and miners. In each brigade there were three infantry battalions – one British and two Indian. Our brigade at the start consisted of the 5th Royal Mahratta Light Infantry, the 4/7 Rajput Regiment, and ourselves. Some months later, the 1/6 Rajputana Rifles replaced the 5th Royal Mahratta Light Infantry. The insignia of the division was the Kite Hawk (we had another rhyming name for it) coloured in red with a dark background. The battalion's number in the formation was 218 and, when added up, corresponded to the number of our brigade – in time it proved to be an emblem to be proud of!

All Indian divisions had what was commonly known as 'camp followers,' an additional complement to British units serving in India. They were Indian civilians under contract to serve as batmen to Officers, cooks (bobigees), tailors (durzi), sanitation wallahs and canteen staff. These men were the traditional type, their fathers before them had served in peace and war along with British units. Of the ones who joined us when we arrived in India, a few had served along side British units in the First World War. Some of our bobigees were to remain with us during the Second World War, most of whom were eventually to finish up as prisoners of war. Not all of them were as venturesome, like canteen staff for example: the farthest afield they went was to attend to our needs while on manoeuvres. In barracks, in addition to attending to our needs in the canteen, they came round each barrack room, forenoon and afternoon, selling cakes and tea (contained in a copper char-urn). We also had similar visits from the Fruit Wallah with his basket of various fruits – mango, banana, pomegranate, dates etc. As I understand, the men who did most of the selling round the barrack rooms came from the NW province of India. Another service we enjoyed was provided by the Milk Wallah. He positioned himself each morning at breakfast time outside the entrance to the dining hall, from where he sold milk and cream and, with a small stove he fried eggs. An egg or two always found space, providing one was solvent enough. Such extras I suppose, in terms of luxury, were second rate, but in the circumstances were in a strange way fawned over!

Our barrack rooms were ground floor level, stone built and appeared to have been there a very long time. Each barrack room had a veranda to front and rear, with four double doors at front and back leading on to both verandas. Although we could have done with a cooler breeze many a time, we found that the many doors helped to make it more bearable. A punka mat hung from the frame above each bed. The frame itself extended the length of both sides of the room where, at one end, a small machine was located. The purpose of this was to drive both sets of frames along with the mats backwards and forwards. This was never put to use because we realised that the noise from the machine and the frames would disturb our sleep much more than the heat of a summer night. The frame section, however, was put to another use – to support our mosquito nets. An adjacent empty barrack room was where we did our band practice. It was handy and it suited the enthusiasts as it could be used at any time when the band itself was not in practice. I for one spent many off-duty hours there!

We were fortunate in more ways than one in having our barrack room and nearby wash-house on the edge of the compound. Because of its isolation, the wash-house was used by the 'gamblers' for their sessions of pontoon and brag. These were usually played in the evening of pay-day, when there was enough around to make up a 'school'. Depending on the fortunes of the game, sessions could sometimes go on till long after lights-out. When this happened, they had to put the lights out and use candles. In order to conceal and confine the light to within the circle, the players draped blankets over their heads. It was a crime in the Services to gamble for money but this did not deter some of my band colleagues.

They continued their wash-house escapade and while it lasted they were never caught out. I suppose, in a place like Ahmednagar, where there was nothing much to offer in the way of deviation from the routine of service life, it was one way of killing time! Traditionally, we also had those who did not see very far beyond the conviviality of the wet canteen. A schooner or two had them on the crest of a wave while next morning's activities soon got rid (in perspiration) of the previous night's intake.

Ahmednagar was a small town with a bazaar which filled most of the main street, a hospital, a fort and an entertainment's hall where occasional functions were held. The latter went by the name, if I remember correctly, of 'Billy Murrays'. The town could best be described as being suitable for the main feature in a scene from the 'Back Woods'. I made very few down town visits and I think that went for all of us.

It was in Ahmednagar Bazaar where I had my first and only tattoo. I had it done to give me that tag of having served east of Suez – keeping up, not with, the Jones's, but with my contemporaries! However, one was enough for me, not like many I knew who evidently made it an on-going habit. Their bodies were adorned with the figures of royalty, peacocks, snakes and daggers. The odd one or two went for the extremes, like a tattoo on the buttocks and lower back – the pack of hounds and the disappearing fox – or an eye tattooed on the buttock. One member of the pipe band, a drummer, had the whole of his back covered with royalty, from the time of Queen Victoria onwards. India at the time was well known for its expertise in the art of tattooing, particularly in the colouring. The one I had done on my leg is as distinct today as it ever was.

Poona and Bombay were the nearest places of any size, and several of the battalion spent leave there. We were only long enough in India for one leave period. When my turn came in May 1939, I opted to have leave in barracks. I was not long enough on Man Service to have saved enough money to meet the demands of the city lights. Permission to sleep in barracks while on furlough was a good arrangement for those who, for one reason or another, could not get away. For the person who took this type of furlough he could come and go as he wished and there was no restriction on the length of time spent in bed. The latter was what gave one the greatest satisfaction – repetitive early rising was put aside for two weeks. Casual wear was allowed to be worn, but as it was my first year on Man Service, I had no civilian clothes. For the fourteen days of leave, I bought a pair of sandals, two short-sleeved shirts and with my service KD trousers, I was casual to a degree and could put aside my uniform for a short time.

Our uniform was no different from that worn in the Middle East except for the headgear. In place of the slim styled topee, we were issued with the thick rimmed pith helmet, peculiar to India. We were also issued with the 'durrie', one item which anyone who has ever served in India is familiar with. This was a thick type of matting, coloured blue and similar in size to an averaged sized rug. It was used to wrap up bedding while on the move and could be used in place of an under blanket or on top of the ground sheet when sleeping out. We were also issued with additional equipment in the form of a brown leather belt, two ammunition pouches, bayonet frog and brown leather rifle sling.

The care of arms has always been a soldier's priority, but in India extra vigilance was called for and this was something we had to take heed of from the very start. India was noted for a certain class of native (clifty wallah) whose only mission in life was to steal a .303 rifle or its firing bolt. To counter that danger there was a laid down standard procedure. When the rifle was not in use, the firing bolt and magazine were removed. Bolt and magazine were locked up in the heavy reinforced kit box, which in India replaced the usual wall locker. The rifle itself was locked up by means of a chain in the rifle-rack and as further security one man was left in the room while others were out or on duty – he was known as the Room Orderly.

To emphasise the need for all this, we were told that, whenever a rifle or firing bolt was stolen, it nearly always finished up in the hands of a tribesman somewhere on the NW Frontier and the irony of it all was, that it was then used against British or Indian Troops. This was an area of India which for long had been an active service zone. Over the years, different General Service Medals were struck for operations waged against the rebels. The rebels were in the main Afghans and Pathans and were out to gain some form of independence. For the British serviceman in India, the experience of doing a spell in the NW Frontier was always a hopeful possibility.

Shortly after we arrived in India, a lot of our training was to do with mountain warfare – picketing high ground, building and manning sangars, making use of natural resources to camouflage positions and remembering never to use the same route twice. The last mentioned was a precaution against snipers and fixed-lines of fire. It seemed other than coincidental that we should be doing this type of training. As a result, rumours started to circulate and we were soon hooked on the notion that our next move after Ahmednagar was likely to be the NW Frontier. Our future as it turned out was to be a more lengthy and dangerous experience. This training I refer to started at battalion level in January 1939, and for ten days we were camped at Kaudgaon. For three weeks in February we took part in brigade training, this time our camp was at Jamgaon. Both locations were on the Deccan Plateau, an area which offered space and variation, the prime requirements of a good training ground.

It was here on the plains of India where I was introduced to the nitty-gritty of the lot of an Infantryman. I soon discovered the meaning and the reason why we got the name 'foot-sloggers'! Boy Service had taught me all about discipline, the parade ground, barrack and camp life and now I was completing my apprenticeship – the rigours and physical demands on the 'field'. My lasting memories of peace time field training were the long marches with cumbersome equipment, keeping to the rhythm of step, three miles to the hour; after the day's end, being aware of extreme tiredness and the need to get one's head down as soon as it was possible; finding a 'spot' while at the same time being mindful of the hazards of the 'open' – scorpions etc.; and lastly, that upward glance at a starry sky and then the onset of sleep. All too soon morning arrived with its awakening light, but there was a freshness of mouth and a clear head, giving a good start to another day and a repeat of the previous day – press on regardless!

During field operations, we were subjected to regular foot inspections and this occurred most certainly after a long day's march. In those situations, the kilt had to remain on for an hour after completing the day's task. This was a health precaution and was taken because of the thick padding round the top of the kilt. It made the area of the waist line a holding for perspiration. We were made to understand that if the kilt was removed to soon, we would finish up with a chill in the stomach.

For obvious reasons, attention to feet and good fitting footwear was most important. One came up against it with new boots because of the rigidity of the toe-cap and uppers. There was one well known method which helped to soften the leather and that was to coat the uppers and toe-cap with blanco and then allow the boots to dry in the sun. It required a few coatings of blanco before the leather was more pliable and easier to shine. One method which I heard of, but I was never to see practised, was the so-called 'old soldier's' remedy – soak the uppers in urine. The only time likely for that to happen but not for the same purpose, was at camp. If the latrines were some distance from a tent, the lazy or the one who had a few too many in the wet canteen would resort to the use of his boots or someone else's boots as a receptacle!

Of equal importance was the state of one's socks, as they had to be changed as often as possible, and it was wise to check, that darnings were not at a spot where it was likely to irritate. It was difficult, if not impossible, to avoid what we called Chinese rot. This was a type of fungal infection which attacked the soles of the feet, but it was more unsightly than harmful. It looked – to those who know the Scots' *piece de resistance* – like the skin of a clootie dumpling! It was the result of heavy boots and feet in thick socks being confined for long spells in conditions of extreme heat. In such conditions, when socks were eventually taken off, it was often remarked that the socks could stand up for themselves!

Infantry training was all about lasting the pace. It taught self-reliance and there was always the underlying philosophy – 'If you can do it so can I'. Unknown to us at the time, this same development of character was to serve us well in the trying years which lay ahead. Those pre-Second World War days tested the physical and moral fibre of the individual.

Although the Army in India was a highly trained and effective force, it has to be said it was not advanced in the way of equipment and mobility. Horses and mules were very much part of the scene during the training periods of 1939. For example, the Poona Horse were not yet mechanised, and when we left Egypt in 1938 for India, we had to give up most of our motor transport for mule transport.

We first worked with our Indian comrades during brigade training and we quickly became aware of their jovial and sharing disposition they had towards us. What was very noticeable was their religious strength and dedication to duty. The mutual trust and respect which developed between us was to form the kernel of our joint strength in war.

A few weeks after our return from camp at Jamgaon, our brigade Commander, Brigadier McPherson, carried out an inspection of the battalion and in the following month, March 1939, we had a test mobilisation. This last training stint indicated that there were ominous clouds of war around. Away from the training field, we spent the days in barracks on routine activities – parades and band practice filled most of our time.

During the summer months routine was broken by the afternoon siesta. After the tea meal, for at least two hours, physical fitness activities were pursued. Various tests were set and, as I recall, there was a drive to get as many interested in field events: such as discus, shot, javelin and hammer. My efforts did not show the potential they were looking for, but I found an alternative, a place in the band hockey team. The Indian influence made the game of hockey acceptable, and no doubt its popularity would have spread had our stay in India been longer. As it turned out, we were only there long enough to experience the heat of a summer and witness one monsoon. The latter was new to most of us and I remember its onset and effect – growth seemed to shoot up there and then and the cracked baked ground was immediately turned to mud. The temptation was too great for some of my colleagues, their reaction in the humid atmosphere was to step outside and allow themselves to be drenched by the torrential rain.

By this time, my progress as a musician was showing promise and, as a result, I was nominated to appear before a Board of bandmasters at Mhow in central India. This was the initial stage in the selection of prospective students for the Army School of Music at Knellar Hall in the London area. If successful, the study period at Knellar Hall was eighteen months. My preparation involved a lot of extra practice. On the day, I was successful in theory but, at the practical, stage fright stifled my performance. I was not turned down but I was required to appear before a second Board at a later date. A few months later, events deprived me of that second Board, something which was a great disappointment to me. My vision of a career in music was abruptly put to an end. Six years of war was too long to be away from it and like many others – not only musicians – I had to change direction and take up a different career.

I was now on my fourth year abroad and, in a strange way, I was finding separation from home less of an isolation. It seemed more relative now to apply that well known remark: 'Out of sight out of mind'! It has since occurred to me that perhaps there was an element of compensation in taking the plunge at an early age. Initially, it was hurtful, but that was soon over – would it have been different had I been older?

Resting while on field training, Deccan 1939 (x mark is the author)

Camp Kit inspection, Deccan 1939 (x mark is the author)

While in India, I did have an occasion in which to gain a little insight into the different world of service family life. Our bandmaster, Mr Webster, and his wife were invited to attend a social evening in the Officers' Mess, and as a result I was asked to baby-sit. This was the most unexpected duty I was ever called upon to carry out.

I arrived at the house at the appointed time feeling – may I add – apprehensive; but I was glad to know that their baby girl was in her cot and asleep. After being shown the lay-out of the house and told to help myself to food and drink, they left me to get on with it. The little girl turned out to be a gem, my prayers were answered – only a few whimpers and the sound of crickets in the background broke the silence of the night. When mother and father returned sometime after midnight, I was able to report 'no problem' or words to that effect! I was granted a late reveille in the morning and the forenoon off duty.

Our stay in India was hectic and varied, but as a band, our activities were limited to the demands of the battalion. I can only remember once being required elsewhere and that was to play at a military funeral for the burial of a member of the Tank Corps. About the same time, one of our bandsmen contracted typhoid and was admitted to Ahmednagar Hospital. He got over it, but was medically down-graded and in the early part of the war left the battalion. His misfortune is fixed in my mind because of the story he told after his recovery. As he put it, he was a 'doubter' before his illness, but after being turned back at the Pearly Gates, he was no longer one! Incidentally, the hospital I refer to was where Spike Milligan (member of The Goon Show) was born.

Our time in India seemed to pass quickly, and before we knew it, we were into July, a month which none of us was ever likely to forget. Under the code name Force Heron, our brigade, the 11th Indian, was ordered to mobilise in readiness for a move back to the Middle East. The transition from a peace to a wartime footing was an involved operation. However, finally on 1st August 1939, the battalion took leave of Ahmednagar and three days on, it sailed from Bombay onboard the SS *Karanja*. The brigade's destination was Fayid (Egypt) – known to the battalion in previous years – and was reached in fourteen days.

During the setting-up period of mobilisation, I was one of a number, who, for different reasons, had to remain behind in Ahmednagar as a member of a rear-party. In my case, along with one or two others, I had to wait until I had reached the age of nineteen – my birthday was not until October 1939. During my detachment of two months (August and part September) from the battalion, I was for most of the time on work I had never done before. First of all I was in a party detailed to prepare for the arrival of German internees. This involved fencing off several barracks blocks and laying concertina'd barbed wire around the perimeter of the compound. When the internees arrived, we had to supply a guard for them until a company of Somerset Light Infantry (SLI) took over the barracks and the general security of the place.

Once they had taken over, I was fortunate to get a job in the QM stores where I worked for the RQMS on documents relating to supply and issue of stores. It was fine to have a complete change of work and I found it interesting but it did not last for long. Towards the middle of September I was detailed for the first draft to join the battalion. We moved to Bombay on the first stage of our journey, and were accommodated in Collabach Barracks for a period of five days. It was an unexpected respite, much enjoyed, as we were allowed time off to visit the city.

Bombay had much of interest to offer with some very fine specimens of building design; notably the Gateway to India, a large archway which faced the water front. There were also the Taj Mahal Hotel, Prince of Wales Museum and a number of civic buildings. On the other hand, there was the squalor and the unsavoury areas, where sleeping rough on the streets was a common sight. Prostitution was exhibited at its lowest, like in the infamous Sackalagie street, known as the Cages – their plight as humans had reduced them to animal instincts. Service life overseas allowed one to witness the harshness of a world far removed from the world we had left behind. Despite all the harshness and our own torment, there was the 'discovery' that protection leaves one not knowing; while exposure reveals an awareness of what we humans have the potential to become. Perhaps it has its merits, having the comfort of protection, or are those the ones who are missing out?

During our time at Collabach Barracks, one of our party, Private Eadie, contracted malaria – or it could have been a relapse. Anyhow his was an example of the loyalty and camaraderie which existed and was considered to be the mark of a good soldier, albeit in this case a foolish one! In his desperation not to miss re-joining the battalion, and in ignorance of his illness, he tried to cure himself by taking large amounts of aspirin. Instead of killing the disease he nearly killed himself. He was carried off to hospital and it was to be another three months before he re-joined us.

Military Band on line of march, Ahmednagar 1939 (x mark is the author)

68

Shortly after this untimely incident our departure orders came through. On the morning of 24th September 1939 we boarded HMT *Neuralia,* and by late afternoon the coastline of India had dipped below the horizon. We were now in open sea, bound for Egypt, the land which we had left some ten months earlier. It seemed rather strange that the ship that had given me my last glimpse of home shores, was now, four years later, carrying me to war. I think I was one of the few onboard who had previously sailed on her. Because of our number, the voyage this time was a more relaxed experience, but we did come in for the usual ship-board type of fatigues – potato peeling (spud bashing) was high on the list. Travelling with our party were members of the battalion married quarters, enlisted boys and some senior members, such as the bandmaster, RQMS and others, all of whom were bound for the UK.

Irrespective of destination, I don't think any of us had much idea of what was really happening. We heard the radio announcement on 3rd September and shortly afterwards there was the arrival in Ahmednagar of German internees. That apart, it did not seem that the true impact had reached us; India was far removed from the scene of turmoil. I suppose to some extent it gave credibility to the saying that ignorance can sometimes be a blessing.

We were all voyaging into the unknown, unaware of what was to befall any of us. What concerned our party at the time, and marred the reality, was how we were to overcome the period of limbo onboard ship. However, time did seem to speed up and after a good crossing, we docked in Port Suez on the morning of 7th October 1939 – five days before my nineteenth Birthday.

14

Those of us who were to re-join the battalion were soon ashore and on our way to Cairo. At Cairo railway station, we were taken by motor transport to where the battalion was now located – Mena Camp. The camp was astride the Cairo–Alexandria road, some half a mile beyond the Mena House Hotel, and to the rear of the Great Pyramids of Geza.

Back at Port Suez, HMT *Neuralia* remained at anchor for two days before continuing on its way to the UK. This gave the married members of the battalion an unexpected opportunity to travel down to Port Suez and see their families. Some of the officers' wives disembarked at Port Suez as they had decided to remain in Cairo. This meant that while the battalion remained in Mena Camp, their husbands, whenever possible, were allowed to live out – it was a bonus time for the family man!

In a matter of days I was back into the swing of things and it didn't seem I had ever been away. The battalion had moved from Fayid to Mena shortly before our party arrived. I had known Fayid in the past and for those of us who came out with the battalion in 1935, Egypt was familiar ground.

During my absence from the battalion I had missed very little, but within days of my return a rigorous training schedule was under way, all of which was in preparation for what lay ahead. The initial period was taken up with revision of all we were required to know and handle. There were several sessions in the use of rifle and bayonet; this involved in charging around in loose sand, sometimes wearing a gas-mask – it was a gruelling time for all. The use of the Mills hand grenade was practised, and the efficiency of the gas-mask was put to the test in the gas-chamber. To do our course on the firing range, we had to travel to the military establishment in the Abbassia area of Cairo. On the journey over, we had to cross that well known Cairo landmark, the Kasr-El-Nil Bridge. The imposing statues of the two lions at either end of the bridge were the butt of service ribaldry. It was often repeated that if ever a virgin walked over the bridge, the lions would roar!

As well as the actual firing on the range, we had to take our turn at marking. This involved giving the laid down procedure for letting those on the firing positions know the results i.e. signalling up either a bull, inner, magpie, outer or scrubber (miss). It was during a lull in the marking that I got in conversation with a fellow Cameron Highlander on the next target to the one I was on. To my great surprise, he turned out to be Lewis Simpson who had been a pupil at Garmouth School at the same time as myself. It was a chance remark which brought about the discovery. I didn't meet in with him again until long after, during the Battle of Keren. Then he was on his way back to the rear, after having been wounded in the lower arm – I was never to see him again.

The other type of training which kept us busy was mostly mobility of movement over an area of desert. While at Mena Camp, we still wore the kilt on desert manoeuvres, and when 'lying-out' I remember how useful it was when loosened-off. It could then be pulled down to cover the legs to keep them warm. The pleats in the kilt not only provided warmth for the wearer but could also be a haven for unwelcome 'visitors'. An example was the case of a near comrade, who during stand-to one morning, disturbed a scorpion which had nestled in overnight. As a result he was badly stung and, for a long time after, had a very nasty sore on his leg. We had long since come to fully understand the wording of the phrase – 'When the sands of the desert grow cold'!

Routine at Mena Camp was not all combat and desert training, as we still had our instruments and continued to function as a band. There was however one major change – our bandmaster had gone to the UK and the band sergeant was in sole charge. Ceremonials were now a thing of the past and we did not put in the same amount of practice. We played at Sunday Church Services which were held in the Camp Cinema (Shaftos'). On two or three occasions we performed at the Gazira Races. Our last outside engagement before we left for the Western Desert was at General Wavell's residence. What stands out in my memory on that occasion was the thoughtful way both the General and Lady Wavell treated us after we had finished playing. As we took refreshments, they came among us and had a pleasant word to say to us all. What delighted us most was how the General, an ex-Black Watch Officer, made sure that we all had a drop of scotch before we left.

As well as fitting in refresher courses on First Aid, several members of the band were called on to do Camp Quarter Guard – I was one. It was my first Quarter Guard as a duty man and much to my surprise, I was made 'stick man' for the duty period of twenty-four hours. This was a peace-time incentive which ceased after our time at Mena Camp. It was a form of reward for being, in the eyes of the inspecting Officer, the smartest and best turned out member of the Guard. Instead of having to do the usual 24-hours' guard duty, two hours on and four hours off, the stick man was the duty orderly – in other words the general factotum for the day. His duties ceased at sunset, which meant night sleep was undisturbed and next morning normal duty was resumed once the new Guard took over.

It was known by the middle of October 1939 that the Division (4th Indian) was on twelve hours stand-by, and that we of the 11th Infantry Brigade would be moved to the Western Desert should war with Italy be declared. At the time only two Brigades made up the 4th Indian Division: ourselves – the 11th – and the 5th which was at Beni Yusef, some five to six miles from Mena.

The battalion's striking capability was increased with a newly formed Bren Gun Carrier Platoon. The tracked vehicles, along with new motor transport, were taken over while the battalion was at Fayid. The build up to the Middle East Forces was noticeable during the early months of 1940. Aussies and New Zealanders arrived on the scene. The Aussies were outgoing while the New Zealanders were more reserved – both seemed to be well primed by their fathers (experience of the 1914–18 war) about the land of the Pharaohs. For a time at Mena, we had a number of New Zealanders attached to our Mortar Platoon for training on that weapon. Among the party was a certain Sergeant Upham who was later to become famous with the award of a double VC, and surprisingly was to survive the war.

The first of our wartime drafts from UK arrived – included was a number of Reservists, some of whom had been with the battalion during our time in Palestine and Egypt. We were soon to become used to the exigency of a unit on active service: drafts arrived, new faces appeared, old and new disappeared, there was always change. While the battalion was at Mena Camp, word came through that for those of us who had served in Palestine during the troubles, we could now wear on our tunic the ribbon of the Palestine General Service Medal. It had taken over three years for the award to be authorised.

Mena Camp was different from any of the other camps we had attended; this one was set-up for long time use. We had piped water to outdoor ablutions with a wooden bench to support the zinc-basins at each washing-place, and underfoot were duck-boards. Included in our mod cons were screened-off cold showers and there was the usual dry lavatories. Our tents were the small marquee-type and accommodated eight men (or was it ten?). The bed-stead was three wooden planks, supported at either end by two small wooden trestles, enough to elevate the bed a few inches clear of the desert sand – no longer did we have the comfort of bed sheets; that was now a thing of the past. Our tents were not far from the Cairo to Alexandria road which ran through the camp. All around, away from the boundary of the camp, an undulation of sand obscured the emptiness of the desert which lay beyond. In the direction of Cairo the landscape flattened sufficiently to give a limited exposure of the distant greenery. Amid this were the distinct structures of minarets and mosques, giving a prominent and hallowed appearance to cosmopolitan Cairo.

We had ample opportunity to visit Cairo during our time in Mena Camp. It involved a walk to the tram terminus which was to the front of the Mena House Hotel. From there the tram rattled its way along a straight line to the city outskirts and onwards till it reached the area of Esbekiah, where we usually got off.

Our walking-out dress at the time was kilt, tunic, webbing belt with nickel-plated headed entrenching tool handle – a useful weapon to have should the need arise. Head-gear was the glengarry and leg dress was the usual khaki-hose, red flashes, short putties and boots. Before checking out at the guard-tent, each one was made to take a condom and a tube of prophylactic ointment. It was an enforcement which says it all! Cairo had all the attractions to satisfy, and. if one so wished it was there to remove all the frustrations of youth. This I found gave rise to a lingering conflict of emotions which was not easy to cope with at times. Apart from this, there was much to be gleaned from what one saw, and there was the enjoyment of getting away from camp life, including the delights of eating out. For many, a favourite restaurant was the Egyptiana on the corner of Ibrahim Pasha Street, opposite Shepheards Hotel, and there was of course the Esbekiah Services Club. Both gave a service which suited the pocket of the ordinary serviceman, whereas Groppi's, for example, was on the dear side. However, I did eat there once or twice. Another place where money could be spent easily was in the Muski Bazaar. There were also places and areas of the city which were out-of-bounds to members of the Forces and, for whatever the reason, it was wise to comply.

Outings to Cairo remind me of an amusing incident which happened late one night on my return to Camp. In the darkness of the tent I quickly undressed down to the usual night attire – shirt or perhaps it was white vest and blue gym pants. As I went to pull back the blankets to get into bed, to my surprise there was already someone else in it fast asleep. I soon realised what had happened: in the next tent, George White, a band colleague, had his bed in exactly the same position as my own. I did not disturb him: knowing George, he must have spent too long in the wet canteen that night and as a result had lost his bearings. I didn't lose any sleep by having to take George's bed – next morning there was an exchange of banter, we both saw the funny side to it. Here was an exception to the saying, 'If you make your bed you have to lie on it'!

Humour was always a strong ingredient among the lads, and this had its place in the good and not so good times. In the camp, amusement and relaxation was limited to either the wet canteen or the Camp Cinema (Shafto's). In the wet canteen, as the evening wore on, it was not unusual – especially on pay-night – for the noise of a sing-song to penetrate the night air. The 'well knowns' got to their feet – sometimes to lead, sometimes to sing solo – songs like *Hame o' Mine*, *The Star o' Rabbie Burns*, and *Afton Water*. There was singular talent around, but alas, it was enjoyed by only a limited audience.

The Camp Cinema, my choice, was a patchy wicker enclosure of typical Egyptian character. It was filled to capacity most nights. To supplement a show there were for sale the usual edible delights – popcorn, peanuts and oranges. Whenever there was a breakdown in the showing of the film, which could be quite often, the orange peel then came in useful to pelt the screen to the accompaniment of a variation of unprintable comments.

It never crossed our minds that Mena Camp would be the last place where we would be together as one, able to celebrate the Festive season. For those of us who were to live through the 'festivities' to follow, they were spent in scattered situations, in the shadow and dictate of war, when a week – even a day – could seem a life time; it was this reality which was soon to be upon us.

Before we moved from Mena Camp, our brigade was inspected by General Wavell and General Weygand. It was not long after that General Weygand changed his allegiance and backed Vichy France. The inspection of the brigade took place on open ground in the outskirts of the city at El Maza. It was a long drawn out event and in the heat of a June sun, with steel helmet and wearing full field service marching order (FSMO), it turned out to be a gruelling day. Parades of this type sapped the stamina and the only physical movement possible, was to wiggle the toes, which gave relief to the feet and no doubt to some extent the circulation.

After nearly nine months under canvas in Mena, we were left with only a few final adjustments to make before moving out to war. The peace-time service dress we still had, and that included kilt, had to be got rid of as well as band instruments and personal items. All were packed and removed for storage to the Citadel Barracks, Cairo. For many of us this was the last we were to see of our personal items. After the war, all I received were a few photographs and pieces of memorabilia; the things which I could really have done with had mysteriously vanished into thin air! Claim against such loss would have been a waste of time. The 'Back-room Boys' would have seen to that, with their ready answer – 'Loss due to enemy action'!

By the time the battalion was ready for the off, each man's kit, for the sake of mobility, was considerably reduced. Battle attire consisted of KD shirt and shorts (long KD trousers were worn at times), hose without flashes, short putties and boots. The only head-gear, apart from the steel-helmet, was the

Balmoral less the cap badge – all insignias which identified our unit were discarded. Later during the winter period, khaki serge battle dress along with gaiters and angora shirt were worn.

We were to discover that the cardigan and greatcoat were very useful items of kit. The cardigan, when not in use, was rolled-up and strapped at the small of the back, to the webbing waist-belt. After the heat of the day, the greatcoat served to protect us from the chill of the night and early morning. Because of that need, we were to become familiar with the order that meant our time had come – 'Greatcoats off, tailboards down'! It was an order that resounded down the column as transport came to a stop at the nearest point, where contact with the enemy was likely to be made. It was then up to everyone to get clear of the transport and deploy.

There were also the small field items that had to be carried – identity discs, sand-goggles, clasp-knife, and emergency ration in the form of a block of chocolate sealed in a small square tin. The latter was one item not to be tampered with and could only be used when an individual was in dire need. Each man carried a field dressing, while stretcher-bearers had, in addition, shell dressings. Nothing was carried that would give away the identity of your unit, but it was a precaution which we were later to discover, did little in the way of baffling the enemy.

15

War and deprivation disturbs the dormant in man

In early June 1940, we moved out from Mena Camp to join the Western Desert Force under the command of Major General R M O'Conner, DSO, MC. Transport and heavy equipment went by road while we as a battalion, entrained at Cairo, to later alight at a desolate railway siding on the northern fringe of the Western Desert.

The wilderness of desert was soon disturbed by the activities of the 11th Indian Infantry Brigade. Our first task was to construct defensive positions in the area of El Daba, Bagush and Naghamish. By the time we had finished, we knew all about handling a pick and shovel, building with dry stone, sandbagging and the laying of barbed wire. It was a prolonged start to a type of work which, time and time again, we were called upon to do. If such a thing as affinity could have been linked to any of the three defensive positions, then I think, we all would have plumped for Wadi Gerawla (Naghamish) – we put so much into its making! At Wadi Gerawla, we of HQ Company were located in the wadi itself, while the duty companies were dispersed in defensive positions on the escarpment above the wadi. Because of the stony surface, we, in our position, instead of digging-in had to build up – this also happened to others. However, there was plenty of loose stone around and in sangar fashion emplacements were built. When finished, our section sangar clung like a limpet to the side of the wadi, the roof covering held down with sandbags was just below the top of the escarpment. To add luxury to our accommodation, the interior walls were lined with sandbags, and any discarded boxes we had were fixed into the sand-bagged walls. These were used as receptacles for toiletry and odds and ends.

When we had completed its construction, we felt rather proud of our effort, so much so, that one of the lads, Pte. Stewart from Glasgow, known to us all as 'Stew', put his poetic wit to a notice which he fixed to the entrance. It read as follows:

> On the breast o the brae,
> There stands a wee hoose,
> In the Company by far it's the best,
> So great is its fame
> We've had to find it a name,
> So we call it our wee Eagle's Nest.

From our Eagle's Nest we could see a considerable length of the coast line; in parallel ran the coastal road and desert railway, both linking Alexandria in the east and Mersa Matruh in the west. The rail-head was in the vicinity of Mersa Matruh, while the road continued westward across the Egyptian/Libyan Border – Sollum, Halfaya Pass, Bardia, Tobruk, Derna, Benghazi and beyond. Within sight of Wadi Gerawla (Naghamish) were the former known places of El Daba, Bagush, Fuka; while in the background was the shimmering blue of the Mediterranean. Because of its nearness, we made a number of bathing trips to its shore. It was good to swim in nature's attire and feel cool and clean, but it was a feeling which only lasted a short time; the return journey to our position saw to that.

Anyone who has ever journeyed across desert in a three-tonner truck, will know how dirty and uncomfortable an ordeal it is. The churned up sand thrown up at the rear of the vehicle, envelops its occupants and the continual buffeting strains at the individual's innards. In time we were to travel in this way across hundreds of miles of desert. If it had been possible to clock-up the number of miles we covered – in negative and positive incursions – the result would have made interesting reading! Whenever we got onboard, it was second nature to take a tight grip on the canopy frame and, at the same time, fix a covering, usually a handkerchief, over one's mouth and nose. This helped to stave off some of the in-coming sand. The seating was the raised steel interior of the truck and because of such comfort it was sometimes better standing! The journeys were very often interrupted by vehicles becoming stuck in loose sand. When this happened, everyone had to get off the vehicle and dig away enough sand to allow sand-trays to be placed under the bogged-down wheels; it was then up to everyone to join in and push.

Our arrival in the Western Desert was the beginning of a way of life which was not only demanding but unique in its style. No longer had we the social life peculiar to the serving soldier overseas. Most of us as musicians exchanged our instruments for a stretcher. The allocation was four stretcher-bearers to each of the duty companies, and so many to HQ Company, where the medical officer and battalion Aid-Post were located.

In a sense, the battalion had now taken up the life of the nomad: not staying long in any one place, always dispersed, with close contact only at Company, Platoon or Section level. Like any other unit of the line, our part in battle tended to be parochial; our concern was focused first and foremost on our own sphere of involvement. At the same time we did not lose sight of the fact that we were only one part of the many other parts which contributed to the whole.

We soon discovered, that despite all our training, the reality of war released certain challenges which were not to be found in the Manual of Military Training. Perhaps it can be said that central to it all was self-preservation – an intruder – which nearly every soldier found a way to disguise, although some were better at it than others. Due to my youth, this was something which I took time to realise – I was not the only one to know fear! There were situations when this element was swamped by the adrenaline flow which raised the individual to the height of valour. Some, by the nature of their being sought it out, whilst others had valour thrust upon them, leaving the remainder to do their best in response to the 'call' – the word 'hero' was not in our vocabulary! What was considered beyond the call of duty was not always assessed in a precise or consistent manner. A unit's success in war depended on the criteria set by the Commanding Officer, his Officers and NCOs. In our case, it was a standard which we sometimes thought bordered on the impossible – on reflection, it was and is, in any field, not a bad goal to aim for.

The vastness of the desert meant that battle was the culmination of a great deal of movement, parry and thrust. Because of this, the in-between periods to actual battle had all the variables, and crucial was the degree of response to physical endurance and test of soul. It was then when discipline and training revealed its worth.

Many were the trials – for example, having to put up for long periods without food and water – and there was the total exhaustion, mainly due to lack of sleep. At certain times in the year, the hot wind (Khamsin between April/June) blew as did the sandstorms, but the latter had a nature to do so at any time. Both added to the discomfort of the usual daily grind. During the heat of the day, perspiration soaked areas of the shirt and with the effects of sun and blown sand, it created stiff dirty blotches which gave one the feeling that the garment had been starched. It was a discomfort which did not go away with the setting sun. If the shirt was not covered, the desert dew soon settled on it, a coolant which was too late in the day to be appreciated.

What gave concern was the condition of one's feet – a frequent change of socks was a necessity but much of the time depended on opportunity. The grey army socks were a durable item, but they had their limits, the desert saw to that. They stiffened to its demands, and it was then when one yearned to place one's feet in a cool basin of water, so often an unfulfilled longing. A more dire longing was the desire to quench a parched mouth. We had come to know this condition during earlier desert training, but now war demanded greater effort on our part to conserve this life sustaining liquid. The one great trial in self-discipline was in having to wait for permission to drink from your water-bottle. In the heat of the day, the order was sometimes long in coming, in which case one often turned to the old soldier's tip of sucking a small pebble – it did help! When the order was given, it was wise to minimise the amount of what one drank. At the back of the mind there was always the uncertainty of when the bottle would next be replenished. Even during the short desert winter, when battle dress was worn and there was a drop in temperature, with sometimes rain and thunder storms, a strict control on water was still maintained.

All these precautions were necessary because of distance, source and method of supply. At battalion level, our 15 cwt. water trucks plied between the nearest water point and our location. They had often a difficult time in getting through because of aerial strafing and negotiating a route to what was usually scattered positions. Our field-kitchens had panniers in which to store water, and vehicles were able to carry a water chuggle or two. The water chuggle, initially, had to be soaked in water but thereafter, when filled and sprinkled on the outside with sand, was an ideal container for keeping the water cool. It was made from a type of sacking and, I believe, originated in India.

The chlorinated well-water was not always in supply; in some desert areas, the supply was a crudely distilled sea-water. It had an unforgettable taste and gave tea a distinct flavour and at the same time curdled the milk content of the tea. A lot of the time, toiletry and washing of clothes was per force of secondary importance. Despite having to adjust to circumstance, a shave was something not easily overlooked. It was a respectability which had to be carried out whenever it was remotely possible.

To fully understand the water situation, the supply to a section for washing and shaving had for most of the time, to be used in a communal way. If it happened to be that you were one of the last, it became quite a job, parting the scum to find sufficient fluid. The basin was the bottom half of a petrol-can – the jerrican had not yet arrived on the scene. In the desert and on the heights of Keren (Eritrea), water was both friend and foe – I am reminded how reduced we were without it and how some, in their hour of need, resorted to drinking their own urine.

There was another aspect of the desert which everyone had to be careful about and that was how easy in darkness it was to get lost. This could easily happen when moving between a section or company. Without a navigational aid and in such a plight there was only one thing to do: stop there and then and move first light. The other alternative presented itself when companies were linked by field telephone – look and find the over-land line and follow it!

As well as the common physical ailments, there was the parasitic behaviour of the Desert Sore, a dreaded nuisance for many, but I was fortunate in only ever having one. It was a common sight to see bandaged arms and legs covering sores which took a long time to heal and in the process, suppurated profusely. As sand got in to everything, it was considered the major agent to retard healing. Magnesium sulphate, acriflavine and dry dressing were the progressive means of treatment. Once the sores healed, they usually left a mark which could still be seen years later.

Eyes also suffered because of the abrasive action of blown sand and the constant glare of the sun. The goggles which were supplied did help a little, but the sand always found a way through at the perforated shield on either side. Years later I had to have a operation on both eyes. On enquiry as to the cause of my trouble, I was told that I had an eye complaint similar to that found in people of certain regions of the Middle East. It would seem that the fury of the desert sun and sand had left its mark! It took years for the film of skin to grow from the inner side of each eye. When it reached near the iris of each eye, and to prevent blindness, the film of skin on both eyes was then removed.

The isolation and nothingness of the desert had the effect of making our 'world' seem so distant from the one we were fighting for. This was another aspect to add to the fear, noise, dreadful sights, the smell of cordite and death and climatic conditions which the front-line soldier had to put up with. However, there was compensation in the form of comradeship, excitement and triumph and the unforgettable feeling of relief of having survived. And lastly, the transient experience of comfort when that strange quietness descended over the area where not long before, a battle had raged!

In our young lives, the world did not owe us a living; we took the King's Shilling, a payment for loyalty, duty and the Regiment. It had its down moments, but there was always in our midst the element of challenge. In making reference to those of us who joined as regulars, I have not forgotten the ones who volunteered and the ones who were called up for the duration. They, in their turn, showed the same quota of admirable characteristics of their generation. So at the beginning, it was the same for everyone, but as time wore on, even the hardest found war wearisome. All this I was to come to know in the months and years which were to span the campaigns in North and East Africa and even afterwards. To recapture the progression of that experience, I must cease to digress and return to the wartime desert position – Wadi Gerawla (Naghamish).

16

Of our many desert locations, Wadi Gerawla (Naghamish) was were we remained the longest. On several occasions it acted as our base from where to
operate, and it was our location from late summer until our final departure on
21st December 1940. While there, except for aerial reconnaissance and the
occasional bombing, we had a relatively peaceful time. Our near neighbours
in Mersa Matruh were not so fortunate – we could tell by the nightly illumi-
nations and the familiar rumble of exploding bombs. Early on during our stay
at Wadi Gerawla, we had our first grand stand view of aerial combat. As
eleven Italian bombers approached our positions, no doubt intent on giving us
a share of their load, two RAF Hurricanes and two Gladiators appeared on
the scene and immediately engaged the intruders. Within a short time all
eleven bombers were shot down in flames. Amid the exploding bombs and
burning wreckage there was no chance for any of the crew, it was all over
within a very short time. During the confusion of the engagement the two
Gladiators collided into each other in mid-air, but to everyone's delight, both
pilots parachuted to safety.

Once work on our defences was complete, our time was taken up with
various forms of training – perfecting whatever was one's function and just as
important seeing to physical fitness. We also took part in schemes, demon-
strations and Divisional exercises. We were not always convinced that the
latter were intended as exercises. They involved doing forward sallies towards a shimmering unchanging horizon, in what was at the time a vast no-
man's land. At this stage, all we saw of the enemy were distant dust clouds,
an indication that perhaps the enemy did not want to take a chance and get
involved.

As soon as we arrived in the Western Desert, we had to carry out 'stand-to'
procedure – at sunset and sunrise. During the hours of darkness, the area was
manned by sentries and a pass word was in force. This was continued standard procedure when we were in an operational zone. And as the desert offered so much space in which to move, it had the distinction of being one
large operational zone. At every laagering point or static position, security
had to be tight, as we could easily be attacked or outflanked by a raiding
force. Out of battle, those of us of the military band who were stretcher-
bearers, had to take our share of sentry duty and whatever else active service
conditions demanded.

In September 1940 our complement as a Division was brought up to full
strength. The 16th Brigade joined us consisting of the 1st Queens, 2nd
Leicesters and 1st Argyle and Sutherland Highlanders. Throughout our time
with the 4th Indian Division, we of the 11th Brigade and the 5th Brigade re-

mained part of the Division, whereas the other brigade was replaced more than once. Apart from the one British Infantry battalion in each Indian Brigade, there was British Artillery support – 25th Field (25-pounders) and 60th Medium. Our other support included engineers (sapper/miners), supplies, medical and miscellaneous services all of which were Indian.

While at Wadi Gerawla (Naghamish), catering by desert standards was relatively good although somewhat repetitive. The field-kitchens did their best with tinned sausages, bacon, McConachie's stew, sometimes tinned potatoes and always bully beef. The latter was dished up in a variety of ways and this was one item of food which never ceased to find a regular place in our menu. There was cooked dried fruit such as figs and prunes. We had the delicacy of tinned fruit on the odd occasion. Bread supply was possible, but it had to be carefully rationed. It was the one item of food which we missed most of all and after our stay in Wadi Gerawla we went without because we were isolated from what was a limited source.

It was not until we moved out from Wadi Gerawla (Naghamish) into other locations that we realised just how fortunate, in a number of ways, we had been. It got to a stage later, when the monotonous sight of bully beef and hard biscuits made the experience of eating distasteful, and nothing more than a necessity. However, there was one sustenance which never failed us and that was a mug of hot sweet tea (char).

What contributed in our favour at Wadi Gerawla was the fact that we were as near as we were ever to be, to the rail head and supplies. Our Padre at the time, Captain The Rev. Low, made occasional trips back to base and brought back comforts in the form of socks, balaclavas, sweets etc. I recall that some things we had to pay for, which made us wonder whether he could not have been a bit more charitable? He will always remain for me, and no doubt to others, as being quite a character. He came from the Glasgow area and knew all the mannerisms of the so-called hard men, and therefore knew how to handle the hard-bitten Infantryman – he also had a good sense of humour. His famous ritual, whenever he drove in with his shooting brake (estate car) to a Company area, was to open the back doors to exhibit his wares. As a number of the lads crowded round to see what was on offer, it was then that he came into his own by his standard remark – 'Stand wide o' the barrow' – a reference to the Glasgow Barrows. He will be remembered, apart from his offering up a prayer before battle, for how he strengthened his own faith by having the support of a colt .45 extended cowboy fashion from his waist belt. He was also reputed to have said, if his colt failed him, he still had his open razor!

Our front-line baptism of fire came on the night of 22/23 October 1940. We moved out from Wadi Gerawla a few days earlier and travelled some 75 miles over open desert to within striking distance of our objective. This was an enemy-held position some 15 miles east and forward of Sidi Barrani by the name of Maktila. Two Companies, C and D, were given the task to attack while the remainder of the battalion remained in reserve. I joined D Company for the operation as one of its stretcher-bearers. The purpose of the raid was to take prisoners and gain as much information as was possible.

As we moved forward to the starting-line, shells pierced the air overhead, all were coming from our support artillery as they registered on the objective. I remember having to pause for a short time near to where our Commanding Officer and second-in-command were standing and hearing the CO remark to the second-in-command, 'It's just like old times Andy'! No doubt both were reflecting on their earlier experience in the First World War.

After about an hour the barrage lifted and in the surrounding darkness we went forward into the attack – the time was roughly between 11 p.m. and midnight. Up to this time there was no response from the enemy, but this more or less told us what to expect! They allowed us to advance so far and then suddenly everything was let loose – artillery, mortar, machine-gun, small-arms, tracers and an assortment of flares, all of which contributed to turning night into day. The noise was intense and as nearly all the fire was concentrated at knee high level, we were soon halted and pinned down. One type of tracer fire sounded like some form of bolas and got the name of 'stringing onions'. I don't know where the name came from, but I do know its behaviour was most disturbing. Its swishing noise as it revolved through the air gave us every reason to suspect, that it had the power to decapitate.

C Company on our right was more successful, as they exploited a gap in the enemy defences and got far enough in to take prisoners and destroy a number of transport. When it was thought that we had exhausted our effort, the order was given to withdraw. For those of us in D Company, it was difficult to extract ourselves because of the heavy fire from up front and from elements closing in on our left. After some sticky and confusing moments, by 5 a.m. we had reached the safety of our waiting transport and clambered on-board to make a quick get-away.

Our journey back to Wadi Gerawla (Naghamish) was saddened by having to leave behind comrades of D Company who were killed during the action. Although C Company was in and out without casualties, overall it was a costly night. Apart from the operation being the culmination of all our past training, leaving dead comrades behind on the battle field was upsetting – it was something we had to come to terms with. But even as time went on, I don't think we ever did, and because of what was the inevitable, one became more and more fatalistic as to what lay ahead!

Our night's work gained us the distinction of having taken part in what was the first operation of its kind in the Middle East. As a result of the raid, it was discovered that Maktila, the position we attacked, consisted of a force of some 5000 men.

Throughout November 1940 we took part in a number of exercises, and before we knew it St Andrew's Day had come and gone. On the morning of 6th December 1940, we set out from Wadi Gerawla (Naghamish) on what we understood to be another exercise. Throughout the day, we travelled in desert formation (MT) on a compass bearing and laagered up before nightfall. The following morning, we were told the long-awaited news, that we were about to launch a large scale offensive against the enemy – it was given the code name COMPASS. During the day we were briefed on what was to be our initial part in the operation. The Brigade's objective was the defended position of Nibeiwa, a location some twelve miles south of Sidi Barrani.

After briefing there was no further movement that day and in a waiting situation as such, our only concern was: would we have the luck not to be spotted by enemy planes. All movement in open desert and in a static position was likely, day or night, to have the attention of enemy aircraft – we suffered a number of casualties in this way. It was frustrating because it was so one-sided and the desert made it easy for air attack and there wasn't much we could do about it.

We moved from our laager on 8th December to a second rendezvous point and there dispersed and dug-in – on the day, we were spared the attention of enemy air craft. The last part of our approach to the rendezvous point was made in darkness, taking every precaution to avoid making any noise. Our nearness to our objective created a situation which allowed us only limited shut-eye; boots that night had to remain on.

Since leaving Wadi Gerawla (Naghamish), we had travelled a considerable distance – over one hundred miles in a south then in a northerly direction which brought us to a position behind enemy lines. Our attack from their rear was to be our trump card and as it turned out, caught the enemy completely by surprise. When Nibeiwa was finally occupied, it was revealed just how much we had fooled them. Some were in the process of dressing, shaving and getting out of bed, whilst others were in the process of manning tanks and armoured vehicles. Their stand-to procedure was certainly suspect!

It is worthy of recall, that on the night of 8th December as we moved towards our second rendezvous point, our Indian comrades, the Mahrattas broke into their 'war chant'. It was the first time we had heard this incantation, but it was not to be the last. It was an unforgettable experiénce, having the stillness of the desert night broken by the eerie chant and the incessant murmur of moving vehicles.

The morning of 9th December 1940 was the start of the offensive; our zero hour was 7.15 a.m. After a 15 minute's artillery barrage the 'I' tanks moved forward and we followed in three-tonner trucks. At approximately 500 yards from the objective, we de-bussed and deployed and moved forward. Repetition in training made it second nature to maintain a regular five yards' distance between each other, but in battle it was an isolation like no other! The 1/6 Rajputana Rifles went in at the same time as ourselves, and each battalion had its own area of the objective to deal with. Our advance soon came under heavy fire, but despite pockets of stiff resistance, the whole object was in our hands by 11 a.m. Our battalion alone had forty casualties, nine of whom were killed; the enemy on the other hand had considerable loss – the area of battle was littered with their dead. The accuracy and destructive power of our 25-pounder artillery guns, accounted for many of the enemy casualties. Congested positioning of their emplacements had helped to make their fire so effective.

Many years later I was to read in a national newspaper an account, written by an Italian Officer, who was there at the time of the action. He particularly referred to the considerable number of dead that littered the battle-ground and how it was a sight he never forgot – a sentiment no doubt shared by many from both sides!

In the action the commander of the Italian Forces, General Maletti, was killed. A number of Libyan (Senussi) troops were part of their force and it was noticeable that several were very young. One that I remember could have been no more than fifteen, and he came to us for help with a bayonet wound in his stomach. We found that the Libyans usually manned the extreme forward areas (listening posts) of a position.

After our eventful day on the 9th, we dug-in for the night and snatched what sleep we could get. On the morning of 10th December, we were ordered to rendezvous on the Bug Bug–Sidi Barrani road in readiness for an attack on Sidi Barrani. Our call came in the afternoon and our briefing was zero hour 4.15 p.m. – order of battle Queen's Regiment on our right, ourselves on the left and Leicester Regiment in reserve. Both English battalions were from the 16th Brigade which, at the time, was the only non-Indian brigade on a temporary footing with the 4th Indian Division.

We moved by RIASC motor transport to within striking distance of Sidi Barrani and then proceeded on foot. We only encountered limited machine-gun and rifle fire up to a few hundred yards from our objective but, after that, it was different. During our advance forward a sand-storm was blowing and, as we passed through our own artillery, who were busily firing, we asked a gun crew in a joking manner, if they knew what they were aiming at? Obviously they didn't, but we were hoping their OP had everything under control – their answer to our question was in a few well chosen words but not very reassuring!

As we made our way forward, we passed elements of the Argyle and Sutherland Highlanders withdrawing because of heavy casualties. Apparently several were caused by our own supporting artillery dropping short. Unfortunately, incidents like this did happen, usually due to previously-held enemy ground being over-run too quickly by sections or companies of the advancing forces. The feed-back in such a situation was delayed at a cost!

The battalion did what it had to do and we were the first unit to enter Sidi Barrani. By 9 p.m. all objectives were taken and cleared. During the five hours of action, we suffered a total of twelve casualties which included four dead – three other ranks and one Officer died of wounds. We attended to the Officer, but because of the severity of his leg wound, we had to call for the assistance of the Medical Officer, who had no alternative but to amputate. To witness this gruesome and sad incident was a chilling experience. The Medical Officer poured chloroform on to a pad of cotton wool and placed it over the wounded Officer's face; he then proceeded with cutting away the badly smashed leg. Once it was done the MO passed the severed limb (boot and leg-dress intact) to a member of our party who in turn unceremoniously secreted it under some nearby rubble. The Medical Officer did say before he started, that if we did not wish to watch we could look away. We looked on, at the same time realising that the young Officer was beyond it. For him the end came quick, while for us it was move on and attend to others.

That night we secured ourselves among the ruins that once was Sidi Barrani. As the sea was close by, shore breezes added to the cold of the desert night. I vaguely recall that for some reason we did not have our greatcoats that night. Usually during operations, blankets and greatcoats remained with Company transport until it was opportune for them to be brought forward and made use of.

The usual way to fend-off the chill of the night air was to cover one's head as well as the body with the one available blanket – here I refer to times when on active operations. It was a method which seemed to generate more heat and it was also the only way one could light up and have a smoke. For the latter one cupped the cigarette in the hand to keep the glow of the cigarette from being seen; but this of course left the tell-tale stains of nicotine on the palm of the hands. It was the war-time free issue of fifty a week which started me on the habit, but in trying times it did have a comforting effect – those issued at the time were Playing Cards, V for Victory, Sweet Caporel, Cape to Cairo, or Woodbine.

Early in the morning of 11th December 1940 we moved out from Sidi Barrani to attack the position at Maktila, the scene of our October night encounter. This time we were spared a second, as on our way there word came through that Maktila had surrendered. It was a wise decision as the enemy position was completely surrounded and cut-off from their main force. Their prudence gave us a welcome respite. Because of this new development we were diverted south to attack positions at Sofafi, but again we were too late; by the time we got near to our objective, the enemy had withdrawn. From there we moved on, digging-in at several places until, finally, orders came through for us to return to base. By 16th December 1940 we were back in Wadi Gerawla (Naghamish) after having done our bit in the initial phase of the operation. Thousands of the enemy were taken POW – the support troops contained them until they were escorted back to make-shift pens in the rear area.

Our ten days' operation taught us a lot about desert warfare and, at the same time, our training had eased us into its demands. In this initial period, we executed movement over the unlimited space of the desert, one aspect which made desert operations akin to war at sea.

Space had its drawbacks – one in particular was the exposure to air attack. The only way to foil such attacks was to travel whenever possible under cover of darkness. This became recognised practice, many a time over unreconnoitered ground which usually ensured us a nightmare journey! Daytime movement could not be avoided, and it was then, when dust-clouds churned up by moving vehicles, made it easy for enemy planes to 'home-in' and pick their target.

In the early days of the Middle East war the enemy, apart from having superiority in manpower, seemed to have considerable freedom of the skies. They made high-level bombing and low-level strafing attacks a major part of their overall strategy. One aerial tactic was to shadow our movement and once we had laagered for the night they would make a fix on our position. What usually followed was intermittent bombing raids throughout the night. The appearance of the moon was a most unwelcome sight! During those raids anti-personal devices were sometimes dropped; if picked up they were capable of blowing off a hand or disabling in some other way. They generally looked harmless items, but we had been warned to be on our guard!

The desert not only made air attack easy to carry out but, because of its regularity and the far off sight of its approach, made anticipation never far from thought. It is possible this had a greater psychological impact than the waiting period prior to battle or the reaction after battle for as time wore on those who could not hide their concern were glibly described as being 'bomb happy'.

Our return to Wadi Gerawla (Naghamish) on 16th December was a welcome break. As we descended from our trucks to disperse and return to our positions, we all looked a very dirty and sand-matted lot. The positions were now seen in a different light, and we had some appreciation for the place after conditions of the previous days.

Our first move was to get rid of the dirt and grime and have a change of clothing. A change of clothing in the desert refers to the reserve items of kit which have reasonably been maintained with the limited facilities at one's disposal – i.e. sharing a limited supply of water for washing purposes.

After those eventful days it gave great relief to remove footwear and give one's feet a wash and airing. It was not unusual during operations to go for long spells without removing footwear. But lack of sleep was the one thing which had the most telling effect and, back in Wadi Gerawla that night, to make up for its loss, we got down to it as soon as we could. Complete exhaustion was a state which was rewarded with the sleep of all sleeps! It was a void which restored vigour to the tired body, to us a creature comfort which was to occur time and time again.

17

Soon after our return to Wadi Gerawla (Naghamish), a chain of events was to follow which explained the reason for our sudden departure from the scene of the fighting. On 21st of December 1940, we left by train from Gerawla railway siding and that night, after a journey of 160 miles eastwards, arrived at Amiriya Camp south of Alexandria. Our stay at the camp lasted ten days, during which time we refitted and welcomed two drafts of reinforcements. They came not from our own Regiment, but from the Leicesters and Sherwood Foresters. The 'Free British' as they came to be known, quickly became, and were proud to be, good Cameron Highlanders. Once the division was brought up to combat level, we were soon on the move again. Late on the night of 31st December 1940, the battalion found itself waiting at Amiriya railway siding for a train to take us to Port Suez. Not to be out of character with the usual Egyptian efficiency, our train arrived two hours late. To make matters worse, it happened at a sacred time in the life of most Scots – especially a Highland Regiment – HOGMANAY! The bells did not ring out for us that night. Our Pipe Major, Jackie Neil, tried his best to boost morale by playing a selection of tunes. But the cold desert night, in an isolated railway siding in the middle of nowhere, did little to enhance his chances of success – the lads were not impressed! The fortune of war had played us one of its many unexpected tricks! However, we still had something to cling to. As yet we were unaware of our final destination, so rumours – or more likely wishful thinking – kept alive the one glimmer of hope: was it to be back to India or better still the UK?

On the second day out from Port Suez onboard MV *Reina Del Pacifico*, our sealed orders were opened, and it was announced that we (the 4th Indian Division) were to link up in the Sudan with the 5th Indian Division. This put paid to wishful thinking for us old-timers – Blighty was as far away as ever!

At this stage we were not briefed, but knowing the country of destination was enough to convince us that, like North Africa, we would again be in at the beginning. This time, instead of desert, it was to be the mountainous region of Eritrea (Abyssinia): a contrast in warfare which, as it turned out, was successful. This was due in no small measure to the adaptability of the troops taking part. As the time factor will show, there was no transition period worthy of note. The thinking at the time seemed to be that there was little need for time to adapt: the operative words were, 'Get on with it'! Expedience was no doubt the driving force behind the thinking. Mussolini's Colonial Forces had been a threat to this important region for some time, and our shipping in the Red Sea was at risk. It was a situation which could not be allowed to continue for much longer.

In many ways our time onboard ship was a welcome interlude from what had been our lot in the past, and for what was to come. At the time of passage, the climate in the Red Sea was not at its warmest, but as everyone knows who has travelled in that part of the world, heat is generated there throughout the year. It makes life in a troop ship messdeck rather uncomfortable – sweat, sweat and more sweat; an ideal situation for the onset of prickly heat (miliaria). However, this time we were able to look on life afloat as a form of travel which gave us something to be thankful for. We were free for a time from sand, unpleasant smells, and flies and it gave us the opportunity to indulge in an ample supply of water.

We arrived in Port Sudan on 6th January 1941, and before we knew it we were exchanging ship for train. Our first destination was Haiya Junction and, like the next after that – Mekele Wells – both were unknown place names that were to become synonymous with the Eritrea (Abyssinia) Campaign. At Haiya Junction we spent a week under canvas, and our time was spent doing route marches and company and battalion training.

It was here, if I remember correctly, where we first saw the Fuzzy Wuzzy (Dervisher) in his natural habitat. With his bushy, matted hair, loose-robed clothing and spear, he looked a fearsome type. However they seemed friendly enough as they approached us to trade their goat's milk for our bully beef. It was only their unpleasant odour, not their appearance, that kept us distant enough for us not to get involved in barter.

Our move from Haiya Junction to Mekele Wells was made by train and truck. This brought us to a point about ten miles from Kassala on the Sudan/Eritrea Border. We were now in an area of vegetation, a pleasant change from what we had passed through. The previous landscape was no different from that of North Africa except that there were no escarpments, just flat desert terrain. This explained why we saw columns of sand spiralling upwards. Fortunately we viewed them from afar. Our arrival in Mekele Wells must have been sometime after 12th January 1941; by then we were briefed on the task which lay ahead. At Mekele Wells we bivouacked until 19th January and then moved out.

It was at Mekele Wells, or perhaps it was soon after we left the area, that we could see a dramatic change in the landscape ahead. The flat terrain of the Sudan suddenly came to an end and, in its place, loomed the towering region of Eritrea. As our approach march took us nearer this mountainous configuration, the more it seemed to throw out a threat and challenge. Some of the peaks were grotesque in shape, not unlike what one would expect to find in a lunar environment. It looked tough country and to us intruders it showed, as we were soon to find out, no mercy in testing our physical fitness.

Ahead of us, our line of advance was to take us along a series of valleys with mountain ranges on either side. Through the valleys ran the main road to link Kassala in the west with the Red Sea port of Massawa in the east. As the Campaign progressed, we were to find out just how important and vulnerable this road was. When we were in pursuit of the enemy, it allowed us mobility; but at the same time, it made us easy targets from the air and enemy mountain positions. Our main encounters with the enemy turned out to be on the rock-strewn mountain ridges, formidable objectives which initially favoured the defender.

Although it was a time of year when the river beds were dried up, there still existed in the valleys an abundance of growth. Notable were the flat-topped trees that covered much of the valleys and grew roughly to a height of twelve feet. The tree and shrub roots gave off a horrible smell which we found out whenever we had to dig-in.

In the course of our advance we were to come across the odd native village, and it was noticeable that the inhabitants were nearly all women and children. They appeared unconcerned by our passing presence, and with their unusual hair styles and topless state, went about their normal business. Their men folk were on the other side fighting in Mussolini's Native Eritrean Army. They proved to be a stubborn lot, with their meagre ration of food and water; providing they had plenty of ammunition, they could 'hole-up' and hold out for long enough – it was ideal country for these tactics.

In the region there was a variety of wildlife – gazelle, hare and various types of birds; but the one species which gave most interest and concern was the baboon. His similarity to human movement caused alarm and attracted fire. They sometimes moved among the rocks in the shadows of a moonlight night and it was then when they become a bit of a menace. In the shadows they could quite easily be taken for an enemy patrol, or a movement in force. No doubt the same experience befell those on the other side. At other times, during a quiet spell in the day, a pack would pass close by. As they did so, one would detach himself and take up a position on a prominent rock to watch the pack file by. He was usually grey round the neck and of bigger build than the others, which we took to be a sign of age. We assumed he was the leader, taking what appeared to be a roll-call.

Gun or small-arms fire sent them scurrying, and it was only during quiet spells that they ventured to pass through our lines. This was a danger time for them, as a lull was never for long and could mean them being caught in the middle of an exchange of fire. Casualties to the baboons were mostly caused by mortar and artillery fire. It was during the long drawn out battle for Keren that gave us.greater opportunity to watch the baboons at their antics.

So much for the wildlife and the physical features about the country we were about to enter; what follows is what happened to us as a unit, in the few months we were there.

After a day and a night's advance, we stopped near Jebel Mokram and waited for the order to attack Kassala and its surrounding defences. The order to attack never came; instead, we were told that the enemy had vacated this forward border (Sudan/Eritrea) position. Our source of information was from those ahead of us, the Gazelle Force. They were a motorised force, more mobile than ourselves, and consisting of the Sudan Defence Force (armoured cars), Sikhs and Skinner's Horse. Their main role, in the early days of the Campaign, was to keep contact with the enemy and at the same time inform the main advancing force. In their wake were ourselves (the 11th Brigade) and the 5th Brigade; the other Brigade in our Division, the 7th, was at this stage still in Port Sudan. In the desert, units of such strength could be spread over a wide area, whereas in Eritrea we were to find ourselves in much closer proximity with others of our Division. In fact, a lot of the time, we shared the same ground with our 5th Brigade. The other Division, the 5th Indian, was assigned to a different sector to the one assigned to the 4th Indian. Their line of advance was to our south via Tessenei and Barentu and finally linking up with the 4th Indian Division at Keren.

With nothing to hold us up at Kassala, we moved out of Jebel Mokram and pushed on. Near to Sabdarat we bivouacked for the night. Next morning, we set out in pursuit of the enemy and that day reached Wachi on the Sabdarat–Keren road. In a short period of time we had over-run some thirty-five miles of enemy territory, a distance made easier by the assistance of motor-transport. It was, however, from this point onwards that for most of the way we were required to make use of 'shank's pony' (on foot). Our transport was required elsewhere and, as we were to find out later, for an entirely different purpose. This is how it transpired – at night, with sufficient lights switched on to be noticed, a convoy of empty trucks would make their way towards the front-line. Once there, they switched their lights off and made their way back to where they had set out from. Runs like this were made on several occasions to make the enemy think that reinforcements of men and material was on its way. There were other deceptive actions carried out long before the offensive got under way. On the Eritrea–Sudan Border, wireless messages (Morse), intended for interception, were exchanged between certain defensive positions. The text of the messages was headed 'to garrison Commander', where in fact the complement in the positions referred to had only one NCO and a section of men. The artillery also used a ploy with a small number of guns. Over a selected period of time they would move their guns around and from each change of emplacement would fire of several salvos. This gave the enemy the impression that they were confronted with a number of artillery batteries.

So far, our advance into Eritrea had met with little opposition; there was some attention from the air, but nothing to speak of until we reached the area of the Sabdarat–Keren road. It was here that we were subject to a concentration of heavy aerial bombing. The battalion suffered a number of casualties – one whom I particularly remember was Sgt. T Rennie (I served with him on Boy Service); he was very badly wounded and was never to return to the battalion. It was our first experience of such low-level bombing, every detail of the under-side of the Savoia Bomber could clearly be seen. Their height and lumbering movement made them an easy target for small arms fire. But despite infuriated response, there was no sign of it having any effect – it would have been different had we had some heavy Ack-Ack support. The truth of the matter was, as a moving Infantry column, we had little defence against aerial attack. Throughout the Eritrean Campaign, air activity was below the level that we came up against in the Desert War – the type of warfare no doubt gave rise to the extent required. In mountain warfare, artillery and mortar had more penetrable capability than aerial bombing, but that is the opinion of an O/R (other rank), not an expert in the art of war!

After the disruption of the bombing raid we moved on. For several miles we had no contact with the enemy, then on the following morning, as we moved on to the edge of Keru-Gorge, he was there waiting. As a result, it took our force two days to clear him from the Gorge. One memorable incident happened here: our 25th Field Artillery and 144 Battery were charged by some 250 cavalry led by two Italian Officers mounted on white chargers.

Word soon spread throughout the brigade about the exploit of our gunners. Apparently they used open sights and at point blank range annihilated the attacking force. Perhaps research might prove that this was the only cavalry charge in the whole of the Second World War?

Up till now it had been dig-in, bivouac and pursue; but from here on we became more and more involved with the enemy. Immediately Keru-Gorge was cleared, we followed up in pursuit, but our advance was hampered by the lack of motor transport. This meant a forced march of sixteen miles and the following day a further fourteen miles. It was now towards the end of January and the temperature was beginning to rise; this added to the rigours of march and combat. As each day dawned the physical demands became greater – it is easy to remember that 30 miles' march in two days, but there were others of less distance plus the mountain ridges that had to be negotiated. If records had been kept, the overall tally of miles walked might even have surprised us!

In the last few days of January we were engaged in a series of attacks which included the lower slopes of the mountain range of Cochen and an outcrop known as 'Gibraltar'. I assume the name was given to the latter because of its similarity to the Rock. While we of the 11th Brigade were dealing with those strategic features in our drive for the town of Agordat, the 5th Brigade on our left was likewise heavily engaged on the Laquetat Ridge. After a four-day battle the town of Agordat was occupied. It was not our lot to enter the town; instead we by-passed it and made on in pursuit of the enemy.

In war one became inure to many things, but there were incidents more poignant than others which left a clear and lasting impression. During the battle for Agordat I was a member of a stretcher-party who were detailed to check-out a knocked out machine-gun post on the Cochan Ridge. Cries were heard from its direction, so it was assumed that there was still someone alive and in distress. As we clambered over into the sangar we were met with a gruesome sight. The machine-gun was a tangled heap, three of the gun crew were dead and the sole survivor lay with his badly wounded leg trapped by a rock. As we looked around we noticed right away that the four were wearing a uniform bearing prominent swastika insignias – they were Germans. This was unexpected and brought immediate comment as to the pedigree of Hitler! The remarks stirred our wounded adversary who to our great surprise, re-buked us in perfect English – 'We don't talk about your King like that, why talk about our King (Hitler) like that?' We were taken aback – we had no an-swer to his allegiance – and anyway the job in hand had to be seen to.

His command of the English language was to prove of great value. As his shattered leg was trapped by a rock, the most difficult part was getting him out and on to a stretcher. Throughout this initial stage, his response to what was asked of him was remarkable. More to his credit than to ours, we had him on a stretcher in a very short time. However the greatest trial for him was yet to come – he had to be lifted over rock-strewn ground yet at the same time had to withstand the discomfort of the angle of descent as we made our way to the valley below.

It took us a good two hours or more to get him down and considering the state of his wounds – he had more than one fracture to his shattered leg – his conduct was exemplary throughout – never a complaint! When we got him down and handed him over to be taken back the line, I'm sure that our unspoken thoughts could only be, 'Have mercy on a very brave man'! During our descent from the ridge, he told us he was one of many gun crew members whose ship was bottled-up in the Red Sea as a result of the progress of the war. When Italy entered the war, it gave people like him the opportunity to take part in hostilities by fighting alongside the Italians.

Another detail, it could have been the same day: this time it was to attend to and carry out one of our own men. He was a man I had known for a long time, by the name of MacIntosh and he came from the Nairn area in Scotland. He was a big man, so it was fortunate for us as stretcher-bearers that we had to carry him over flat ground. When we came across him, there was no blood or signs of violence, yet he could not raise an arm or a leg; he was completely paralysed. The symptoms told us where to look – on the back of his neck there was a small incision, no more than two to three inches at the most in length. It was where a piece of shrapnel had entered. He seemed unconcerned and showed no signs of having pain; he even remarked that it looked to be a Blighty one. Sad to say, he was never to see the shores of Blighty again – within an hour of us carrying him out, he was dead.

War is a time when one is continually in the grip or release of the hand of fate. What better example of that is when advancing over open ground and 'everything' is coming your way! Then there is the other element, the allocation of who draws the short straw – the given order!

During our advance on Agordat, a party of us had occasion to take cover behind some rocks. At the time we were being shelled and overhead planes were strafing. Amid all the noise, we were momentarily distracted by the nearness of a thud and eruption of earth. Whatever it was slithered to a stop a couple of feet from where we lay. When the dust settled, there it was – an unexploded artillery shell – and we quickly moved on. A similar near thing happened a week or two later but this time it was not a dud. It occurred while I was taking a shell-shocked case out of the battle area. To reach the place where I had to take him, we had to pass through some of our own artillery, who at the time were engaged in an exchange of fire. We had almost made it through their lines, when it happened: there was what seemed a momentary displacement of air, then the explosion and we were both showered with earth and stone – a shell had dropped just a yard or so behind us. It was not often when so near an exploding shell that you got away with it – it was our lucky day! The blast and the shrapnel went in the opposite direction to the way we were going.

I remember looking at my companion: he was, as he had been throughout, impassive, mute, responding only to signs. It seemed ironic that we should be so near being blown up by a shell, when the purpose of my journey was to get my shell-shocked companion away from danger and exploding shells. I quickened my step in case more were to follow, but the way stayed clear and I got my casualty safely through. I had to run the gauntlet on my return journey but I got back to my company without mishap. Like many of the casualties we stretcher-bearers attended to, here was another I was never to see again.

To use the pronoun 'we/our' in reference to the battalion, is simply a convenient way in going about setting down the chronicle of our war. To condense the overall scenario of an operation by directing attention to what goes on in an Infantry unit, reveals precisely the real nitty-gritty of war. Focusing in this way does not and is not intended to lessen the efforts and attainment of others. Suffice to mention that the others in this particular campaign were our own 4th Indian Division and the 5th Indian Division with their various support units.

The second day after our success at Agordat, we moved on, covering some fifteen miles before coming to a dried-up river bed. The bridge over it had been destroyed by the retreating enemy. Not only was the bridge blown-up, but the river bed beneath was heavily mined. It took our Indian Sappers and Miners several hours to clear a way for us to continue our advance.

It was a delay which turned out to be of vital importance to the enemy. He made use of the time to put more into the defensive ring round the town of Keren. This was something we didn't know about until we became engaged in the battle for it. One other major contribution to the defence of Keren was the creation of a road block. At a point not far from the town where the valley closed in on what was the only road into the town, a large slice of hill-side was blow on to the road, making entrance nigh impossible. It was the road block which caused no end of trouble, delay and loss of life. Had it not been for this gigantic obstacle, Keren might have fallen much sooner, instead of what turned out to be, a long drawn out seven week struggle.

By the beginning of February 1941, we had penetrated deep into Eritrean Territory and it was noticeable that ahead of us lay much higher mountain ranges. At this stage, after our success at Agordat, the Gazelle Force continued to nip at the heels of the enemy and we in their wake were making good progress. Soon we were approaching what looked a most impressive landscape – precipitous ridges and high peaks. With the bed of the valley underfoot and the high range of mountains on either side, we had now entered nature's amphitheatre. Soon we were to know that we could not remain in the arena for long, but would have to take to the high ground.

Every step was taking us nearer the assigned area for what was to be a major attack – a ridge on our left with half way down it, a railway line and tunnel. It was C Company who were first to leave the valley and get a footing on the ridge. This they did at a cost of few casualties and went on to capture the ridge. The ridge was never again to fall into the hands of the enemy, and as a mark of the battalion's achievement it was named Cameron Ridge.

While C Company was battling away on the ridge, the remainder of the battalion was down in the valley. Once C Company signalled its success, D

Company followed and took up a position on the ridge. Thereafter, by stages, the whole battalion moved onto the ridge. I remember when it came to our turn, we had to round a foothill spur and as we did so we came under heavy shell fire. We were not to be the only ones, for unknown to us at the time, it was a part of the valley which could be easily seen by the enemy. His gunners had a fixed line on it, so whenever there was any movement on this particular spot, down would come the salvos. It soon became known as Hell-Fire (Windy) Corner, a projection which during the battle for Keren, we had to round several times. I can still remember the exact words of our Company Commander, Capt. Sir Francis Head, as we made our way round it the first time. To maintain the right mood, he said in a calm way: 'Keep your distance and keep going'! Good leadership meant everything, and the battalion at the time was well favoured in that respect.

We reached the foot of the ridge and started to climb. We had to pick our way up the rock-strewn ground and once we reached the railway line, we dispersed and took up positions. As stretcher-bearers our first task was to establish the battalion's First-Aid Post; this we did at the entrance to the railway tunnel. It afforded more protection for the sick and wounded, and for the stretch-bearers of HQ Company it gave overhead protection during periods of rest and sleep. The Aid-Post remained in the entrance to the tunnel until it was moved out to a position above the railway line and below the ridge. This move took place towards the latter stages of the final phase of the battle for Keren.

In time, thanks to the Indian Sappers and Miners, the railway was used for carrying down the serious wounded and bringing up certain supplies. The vehicles used were railway flats, constructed by the Sappers and Miners. In order to carry out the operation, the flats were towed up the gradient by a fifteen cwt. truck. The return journey was solely gradient assisted and speed control depended on the improvised braking system – expedience had its dangers and there were accidents.

While HQ Company occupied positions along the railway line and the entrance to the tunnel, the remainder of the battalion took up positions above the tunnel and along the top of Cameron Ridge. Our Indian comrades, the 3/14 Punjab Regiment, pushed through from the ridge and successfully attacked one of the peaks (Brig's Peak) overlooking Cameron Ridge. The 3/14 Punjab Regiment remained on Brig's Peak until counter-attacked, and were driven off the following day. The enemy continued with his thrust but was unsuccessful with his attempt to regain Cameron Ridge. As already mentioned, the ridge was never again to fall into their hands.

The initial tenuous situation was strengthened by the arrival of the other Infantry battalion in our Brigade – the 1/6 Rajputana Rifles. They took up positions on the ridge to our left, and between us shared the responsibility of keeping the 'Line' intact.

It was only when we had time to take stock of our surroundings that we realised just how much we were territorially at a disadvantage. The valley, along which we had kept to in our advance, had now reached a height of approx. 3000 feet above sea level, and Cameron Ridge, our latest capture, rose another 2000 feet above that. Overlooking Cameron Ridge and separated by a ravine were the two awesome heights of Brig's Peak and Mount Sanchil occupied by Mussolini's elite troops – Savoy Grenadiers, Bersaglieri, Alpini and colonial units of Eritreans. They combined to put up a stiff resistance in the weeks it took to capture the key town of Keren.

Our sector, along with the high ground on our left known as Flat-top, was to remain 11th Brigade's area of operation throughout the siege. The other two brigades of the Division were also used in this sector as well as elsewhere. The 5th Indian Division was deployed on our right and was engaged against the mountain bastions of Zeban, Falestoh, Zelale (The Sphinx), Dologorodoc with its fort, and in the gorge near to the road block (already described). All the peaks named made up a vast barrier that overlooked what was known to the troops as Happy Valley. It was the same valley which turned out to be the only feasible line of advance in our sector of operations.

After the first few days on the ridge, and with our line of defence secured, it became obvious that we were in for a period of stalemate. However, I do not think it was anticipated that it would develop into such a long, drawn out struggle. Consequently, our forward companies had to adapt to a sustained state of combat with all its physical and logistic problems. To give some relief to the forward companies, a system was adopted whereby after a spell up front, each company had a turn in reserve. While in reserve, the company was given the job of carrying up food and other necessary supplies. Another link in our supply line was provided by a unit of Cypriot muleteers – they did a valiant and useful job. Many of their mules lost their lives through accident and gun-fire. Their decomposed remains only added to the stench which was already with us. It was something which got worse and worse as the days and weeks passed. Our own dead became the most disturbing of all to deal with. We could not dig down to any depth, so all we could do was build a cairn of stone over the corpse. In their death there was the uncanny movement which displaced some of the stones. This was caused by the deterioration setting in on the bloated state of the corpse.

Small sangars had to be built, as it was the only way to consolidate our positions. The rock-strewn terrain gave some cover when movement had to be made, but there was little that could be done against mortar fire. Repair work on defences and field telephone lines were carried out under cover of darkness. There was limited shut-eye for the forward companies; what respite they did get depended on the enemy being in the same frame of mind. Lying out in the open with only a steel-helmet for protection was a situation which relied on fatigue shutting out wakefulness and anxiety. Night and day there was exchange of fire in all its variety – small arms, machine-gun, artillery and mortar, while sniping went on throughout the day. The activity of one in particular, earned him the name Jimmy The Joiner. His daily *rat-a-tat-tat* went on for a very long time but eventually he fell silent! Some days were worse than others: any sign of ground movement was sure to spark-off heavy shell and mortar fire.

Sometimes there was ferocious artillery fire and, when it happened, it was not unknown for thunder and lightening to follow – nature it seemed had occasion to remind us too of its destructive power. The confined space of gorge, crevice and valley maximised the cacophony of battle. Without doubt, mortar and shell had a most devastating effect in this type of terrain. The enemy concentrated in the use of artillery (including pack artillery) and were adept at setting up their guns in positions which made it possible to range on targets and overcome certain difficulties which the land formation created. Our own twenty-five pounder and sixty medium artillery, because of their trajectory had, at times, to skim the top of a ridge to get at the target. This could be a chancy business as it only needed to be out a degree or two for things to go wrong. It was sometimes a nightmare situation for forward troops, and at Keren there were incidents when shells did not clear the ridge and as a result we had casualties. It is one of the unfortunate and sometimes unavoidable incidents which can and does happen in war.

The deadlock we were now in was much different from other engagements we had been involved in. Because of its duration, it called for greater resolve and physical effort. Each day, the battalion Aid Post had a flow of sick and wounded, giving the Medical Officer (Capt. Ferguson) and stretcher-bearers plenty to do. Here one witnessed the result of the overall cost of battle. To recover the wounded was always a difficult task, mainly because of the type of ground that had to be negotiated. For those who had to be carried by stretcher, it was an ordeal. In the case of walking-wounded, they usually found their own way back to the Aid Post. At times, wounded lay among rocks, out of sight from others; by the time they were discovered, exposure had made their condition worse and maggots had taken over in their wounds. Despite the suffering, the recovery rate of many was remarkable, while some wounds which did not look so bad turned out to be more damaging. With shell-shock, which I didn't see a lot of, they showed no reaction or expression of mood. After roughly a week on the ridge, we had an exchange of clothing and footwear, a welcome event which took place from time to time. In the field of operations, it did not take long for wear and tear to show; the worst thing of all for the Infantryman was the breaking in of new boots. A rest from the ridge came a week later when we handed over our positions to the Royal Fusiliers; and at the same time our two Indian battalions were relieved by the 4/11 Sikhs and 4/6 Rajputana Rifles. The three relieving battalions were from the 5th Indian Brigade. Under cover of darkness we moved out to a rest area some miles behind the front.

Our first day of rest after a fortnight on Cameron Ridge was taken up with cleaning and getting kit into reasonable shape. In the evening, we celebrated with the help of the soldier's convivial lubricant – a bottle of beer. Whenever there was an issue, it was one bottle per man. However, if a section had one or two non-drinkers the surplus was shared out. Surprisingly, non-drinkers and non-smokers did exist, even in a Highland Regiment. However, I would not like to say just what the percentage was. An issue of beer, cigarettes or chocolate was always a morale booster and it was also our only way of spending our money. Such luxuries were sometimes long in reaching us. It all depended on location and distance from supplies and what could be slotted in after the priorities had been given space. It was always appreciated when we got the chance to buy our own cigarettes, then the free issue became a re-serve. Mind you, although the free issue could be very harsh on the throat, we were grateful for them many a time.

A day or two after we arrived in the rest area, we came under long-range shelling so we moved out to a new site where there was more cover. From then on, time was spent in training and sport – the emphasis was on physical fitness, having in mind the demands expected in the task which lay ahead.

It was good to have to queue up again at the field-kitchen for a hot meal, a luxury compared to the repetitive monotony of bully-beef and hard biscuits up on the Ridge. At meal-times in the rest area, we still had plenty of flies to contend with but happily, in the Eritrea Sector, there was not the sand! We had, as in the desert, the same dispersal procedure to counter any sudden air attack, which meant movement was always as a small group, and at meal times we lined up at the field-kitchen in small numbers.

By now – mid February – we found that the weather was getting warmer and warmer by the day. It was all very well to appreciate this climatic change while in the rest area but it would be a different matter up at the front (on the ridge)!

While in the back area, our Padre Captain MacKinnon held a church serv-ice, the first for some time. He was a popular officer, unpretentious as befit-ting his position – he had replaced Padre Low just before we left for Eritrea. In character they were poles apart, but no doubt both had the same aim in sight: to give the troops some spiritual nourishment. In the circumstances it was a tall order, as it seemed ludicrous to expect that in our offering of prayer we should have priority over our enemy! Were we not both asking for the same – how could or would 'He' apportion it?

I recall it was Padre MacKinnon who introduced me to the game of Naval Battles. A deviation which whiled away the time during the limited periods of calm while on Cameron Ridge. It was a simple game, all that each player re-quired was a piece of paper and a pencil. On the paper was drawn a large square made up of small dots, equally spaced and in line from top to bottom and side to side. The lined dots were lettered across the top and numbered down the side. On each player's piece of paper, straight lines were drawn, created by linking up so many dots. Four dots linked was a battleship, three for a cruiser and two for a submarine. Each player agreed on the size of the fleet. To play the game, each player in turn called a letter and a number e.g. B4. The call was either a strike or a miss and so the game progressed until all that remained was one player who still had part of his naval force intact – he was the winner.

Towards the end of February 1941 we were on the move again. After a three hours' march, we were back at the front. The rest area gave us a bearable quality of life; this we now had to forfeit for the same old positions on Cameron Ridge. By now the state of the front area had reached the ultimate in discomfort. Heat, filth, the incessant activity of flies and the constant smell of excreta and death made conditions the worst we had come up against so far.

Although it now seemed ages since our baptism of fire, there still remained that unique situation to be faced – will I be favoured to appreciate a tomorrow? I have often thought since: how interesting it would have been to know the real feeling of each man as he faced the same situation over and over again, knowing full well that it had to be that someone's time would soon be up! In the secrecy of my own mind, it did not take me long to arrive at a verdict, that war was an enforced lunacy and for me, its end could not come quick enough. But it went on and on and one had to respond in unison with the 'herd', having to forget that you were also an individual!

Our supply system, the one important factor in war, seemed to work well although there had to be a strict control of water. I remember at one stage during the battle for Keren, the water was very brown in colour, similar to tea. This came about as a result of it having to be stored in two gallon tins. After a time the rust from the tins got into the water and when this happened, the effect after drinking it was like having a dose of Epsom salts. To my cost, I had to discard a perfectly good shirt – later to be reported as having been lost in action!

Rations came up nightly, most of which were carried in sand-bags. On one occasion, as the ration party passed through our position, one member (Pte. Jessiman) who I knew well, found time to let me have a good tot of rum. How he managed to have the extra rum was a mystery, for it was always strictly controlled and only occasionally issued. However in the circumstances – anyway I was not his mentor – I was pleased to accept his offer! It was a cold night for lying out so its inner warmth gave comfort and also gave me a restful couple of hours sleep, even though the shells were flying overhead. The result of my sleep left an imprint on the back of my neck from using my steel-helmet as a head rest.

The pattern of front line activity continued with the occasional diversion, such as the afternoon when we had the company of a number of baboons: this happened quite often. On this occasion they located themselves on the far side of a gully from where we lay. For a time they amused themselves, then all of a sudden they all scampered off – had they a premonition? It seemed they had, for no sooner had they left than the first salvo arrived. The enemy concentrated his fire on the area for a time until I suspect they realised it was not a party of humans.

Throughout the campaign we had aerial support in the form of Wellesley and Hardy bombers, Gladiators and Hurricane fighters. Much of their activity took place behind enemy lines (lines of communication), although there were times when the ridges held by the enemy were bombed, but it didn't seem to be that effective; mortar and artillery fire was more likely to do a greater damage.

It was not unusual for patrolling enemy fighter planes to spend time over the battle area. One morning we – or those of us in the position to see it – witnessed what was quite an amazing incident. As we watched the enemy's movements overhead, a sole Gladiator came into view – he was flying very low, making his way along Happy Valley. To our horror, it looked that the Gladiator was about to fall prey to the overhead enemy planes. No sooner had the thought entered our heads than the expected happened. One enemy Machie fighter peeled off and dived. The Gladiator, still unaware it seemed, continued on his way. Just as the enemy plane closed on him and opened fire, the Gladiator made his move. To our great surprise and shouts of joy, the Gladiator made a manoeuvre akin to a loop-the-loop and at the same time got in a telling burst of fire. The enemy unable to pull out of the dive, hit the hillside and exploded in flames. It was full credit to our pilot for his alertness and skill – just one more incident of war, which in the circumstances would go unrecognised and unsung!

We moved out of the 'line' for a second time on the night of 6/7 March 1941. The relieving battalion was again the Royal Fusiliers. While in the rest area, our Divisional Commander paid us a visit and there was also another event to cheer us up, a concert was arranged. If I remember correctly, entertainment of this sort was known as a 'go-as-you-please-concert' and it was surprising the talent that came forward. At this stage in the war, we were never favoured with visiting entertainers; this happened much later, by which time most of us were not around to enjoy the innovation.

The fleeting periods to the lighter side of life that there were, soon had to be set aside for the more serious – preparation for what was hoped to be the final assault on Keren. By 14th March we were as ready as we would ever be and, on the day, we moved to a rendezvous point. Afterwards we moved on foot past 'Hell-Fire Corner' and onto the ridge. By midnight of 14/15 March 1941, the whole battalion was in position on the assembly area ready for the attack.

The objectives of the 11th Indian Infantry Brigade were as follows: Cameron Highlanders was Mt Sanchill/Brig's Peak to Sugar Loaf inclusive; 1/6 Rajputana Rifles: Saddle to Hog's Back inclusive; and 2/5 Mahrattas (this battalion had replaced the 3/1 Punjab Regiment): Flat Top. The 5th Indian Infantry Brigade was also included in the attack and consisted of the 4/11 Sikhs, 3/1 Punjab Regiment, a Sudanese Motor Machine-Gun Unit and the 51st Palestine Commandos. The Commandos, I believe, were made up of Arabs and Jews, commanded by British Officers. The 5th Indian Division's objectives were to our right and were Mt Dologorodoc, Fort Hill, Mt Zeban and Mt Falestoh.

While the shells were whining their destructive way overhead, those of us on the ground were waiting the arrival of the zero hour: 7 a.m. Each man who was a member of the advance companies carried an orange-coloured marker on his back. This was the visual provider to let the artillery and mortar platoons know where to lay their covering fire as the advance progressed. The intention was to drop the explosives immediately ahead of the most forward troops. It was the first time we had used the method and it seemed to prove its worth – it was a time when mountain warfare called for innovation!

On the hour, the battalion advanced and immediately the enemy responded with a downpour of mortar and shell supported by machine gun and small arms fire. The area of valley which had to be crossed lay between our positions on Cameron Ridge and the high mountain range held by the enemy. It was an exposed area, in clear view of the enemy with next to nothing in the way of ground cover. Later, we were to discover that a large number of our casualties were sustained during the first 200 yards dash across this gap. During the initial stage of the attack, I was a member of the advance Aid Post, and although we were only a short distance below the brow of the adjacent ridge to Cameron Ridge, it thankfully afforded us a good bit of cover. Shell and machine-gun fire went over our heads while the occasional mortar shell dropped too near to be healthy!

For the next thirteen days the battle raged, some of the fiercest fighting of the whole campaign took place at this time – it was a costly period for the battalion. The battle went through several phases from 15th March to its final day on 28th March 1941. During the initial phase, the battalion reached their objectives, but were so depleted that, by the time they got there, they were unable to consolidate. Killed and wounded littered the path of advance and only a handful of men from B and C companies reached the summits of Brig's Peak and Mt Sanchill. Sometime between the 15th and 18th March, the 10th Brigade of the 5th Indian Division (which was in reserve), passed through our area and went forward to strengthen the gains we had made. What remained of the battalion moved back, and took over again the positions on Cameron Ridge. It was there where we stuck it out until the final shots were fired.

The arrival of the 10th Brigade, which consisted of a battalion of Garhwalis, a battalion of Baluchis and the Highland Light Infantry (HLI), made the situation more tenable. Both Garhwalis and Baluchis had a similarity in stature to that of the Gurkhas and, like them, were noted for their fighting qualities. The squat appearance of those hill-men belied their physical ability – this was illustrated as they passed through our position. I can't remember for sure which of them it was – Garhwalis or Baluchis – but it seemed no effort for them to carry a full box of .303 ammunition on their back – in the circumstances no small feat! By now we had come to recognise and admire the prowess of the Indian troops we served along side, and in sharing in their achievements, it really made us feel good to be a member of an Indian Formation.

During those particularly grim days of the final assault on Keren, there were several acts of bravery: some recognised – others went unnoticed. Our

Commanding Officer at the time was a person who expected every man to excel in the execution of his duty and, therefore, he must have had a hard time in deciding what was within and what was above and beyond the call of duty. Throughout his time as battalion commander, he appeared to hold to those guide-lines and this reflected down the line of command. However, it would be naive to think that at no time did an element of human interest come in to it!

Even after more than fifty years, two men come readily to mind who I think are not only worthy of mention but, in so doing, pay tribute to the others I have left out. One was recognised for his bravery, whilst the other was buried where he fell, forgotten except by those who knew him. There were a number of Smiths in the battalion but there was only one '37 Smith' (two digits of his regimental number). I can still see him as he waited to be attended to for a nasty wound at the joint of the arm. The front of his steel helmet was ripped by shrapnel, his cardigan which was strapped in the usual way at the back of the waist belt had been peppered with bullets and one bullet had gone through his water bottle.

He still held on to his rifle and bayonet which had been partially shattered by shrapnel. He remained unperturbed, the soothing influence of the pipe in his mouth perhaps helped. I think his presence helped us all – a truly unusual walking wounded! Later, we were to hear that he had been awarded the Distinguished Conduct Medal (DCM) for his part in the assault on Brig's Peak. He, like many others whose wounds had a lasting effect, drifted from our midst never to be seen again.

The other who like 37 Smith came from C Company was L/Cpl Delaney. Despite being wounded several times he continued to move forward until his final thrust finished in death. Like his kind, he had a great zest for life but that went in tandem with what seemed a disregard for his own life. Those who knew him and heard of his exploit, regret that he went down unnoticed/unrecognised. Perhaps it would have been different had he survived the action. The only posthumous bravery award at the time was the award of the Victoria Cross to a Havildar/Major in the Raj Rifs (Infantry) for his part in the attack on Keren. Another VC awarded was to a Lieutenant in the Royal Bombay Sapper and Miners for his good work in clearing a way through the road block – he survived the battle to receive the award.

Tradition, and the belief that there was no other regiment like your own, was the power factor behind the achievements of the individual and the battalion as a whole. But war also made one aware of the call for respect for the qualities of other regiments. We as Camerons always struck up an excellent affinity with the troops we fought alongside – none better than with our own Indian Troops in the 4th Indian Division. At different times there were the others: special mention must be given to the Royal Fusiliers, a first class 'cockney' outfit, who shared with us the hectic days during the battle for Keren. In sharing in this common bond, it gave a realistic meaning to the saying, 'We are all Jock Tamson's bairns'. This was an enlightening revelation which, alas, not too many people experience or seem aware of once war is replaced by peace!

We had our moans and groans but usually out of hearing range of the officers – an indication of the acceptance of authority. The ranker officer, that is one who had come up through the ranks, was in a position to know the minds of the other ranks. However, the structure of discipline was not just bellowed commands. I suppose one could say it was a philosophy which fed on the equality of which the majority of us were a part. As a result, it had an epidemic effect, and made it conducive for us all to accept the challenge to which our way of life was programmed to respond. In all its uncertainties, there was the one and only security in which to cling to and that was camaraderie!

As we held to our positions on Cameron Ridge from 18th March onwards, there was movement all around and the noise of battle continued unabated. The 5th Indian Division on our right was fully engaged; their objective like all others, proved to be a hard nut to crack. However, in the end it was an area of the front which turned out to be the enemy's Achilles heel. On 25th March 1941 the 5th Indian Division put in a telling attack which was bolstered by diversionary action and supportive fire from the 4th Indian Division. The cumulative action by the 4th and 5th knocked the stuffing out of the enemy and on the night of 27/28 March 1941 they started to withdraw. By the 28th, a special day for those of us who had survived, the battle for Keren was over.

After the battle a salvage operation was mounted and this included, first and foremost, a search for our dead and their burial. In groups, we were assigned an area for this painstaking work to be carried out. Before taking part in the work, I remember looking over the valley: not very far as the crow flies but, for so long, it had separated both sides and claimed many lives. It was a scene which I thought was similar to that shown in pictures of the First World War. All vegetation was stripped; the impact of HE and mortar had left their pulverised marks on the rocky terrain; and scattered bundles of humanity lay where they had succumbed. The dead had lain out ever since the final offensive began on 15th March. The heat left bodies swollen, discoloured and in an advanced state of decay. Identification discs were the only means of knowing who was Indian and who was Cameron Highlander. To dig down was impossible, so all we could do was hollow-out and build a cairn of stone over the body, leaving a mark in the shape of a make-shift cross.

The first one our party came across was the youngest of the Rennie brothers, both of whom I had served with on Boy Service. His elder brother, who I referred to earlier, was badly wounded during an aerial bombing raid on our column. Both were well known, their father and uncle having served in the regiment. One other who I wish to single out, and who was buried that morning was Cpl. Bryans of C Company, an Irishman whom I had known for a long time. A few days before the final offensive I met and got speaking to him. Some of the content of our conversation I never forgot. It was never my experience, in the army, to hear an individual talk much about their background – home life was far removed, a different world entirely! However, for some reason, Paddy on this occasion had more to say than usual. He told me how service in the British Army was not always approved of by certain people back home in his native Ireland. He even laughingly remarked, 'What am I doing here anyway, my country is neutral'! Perhaps, like many of us, he was beginning to feel the strain of the prolonged struggle, and was wondering how it was all going to end. He had, however, long since passed the test – he was a loyal Cameron Highlander and a believer in the slogan we all gloried in, 'Wha's like us? De'il the yin'! Like most of the regular soldiers, he was in his sixth year overseas and but for the war would most likely have completed his term of engagement and been back home. As he lay there curled up behind a rock, his words came back to me, giving greater poignancy to the situation – our task completed, we turned away to leave him at rest, at the spot where he fell.

By midday our group was relieved of our task and ordered back to a position to prepare for moving out. Other groups continued to scour the area and by the end of the day, all our dead were accounted for. It was a relief to get away from the stench of death – more so for having to bury those whom you knew – and there was that uncanny atmosphere which seemed to have descended over the battle-field. Our clothing by now was in a messy condition and what made it worse was the way the smell of death clung to each garment. Its presence was particularly objectionable during meal-time – along with the smell of excreta and the ever-active flies, a mushy tin of bully-beef oozing fat because of the heat, was quite a mix for the palate to come to terms with. This was an ongoing situation throughout our time on the heights of Keren and for that matter at other times.

On the second day after the collapse of Keren we knew that, for us at least, our part in the campaign was over. We were in need of reinforcements – nearly half of the complement had been killed or wounded. We who were stretcher-bearers had, surprisingly, a low casualty count. Out of a strength of twenty, one was killed and a small number wounded. It has to be remembered that we came under fire in much the same way as did the duty man, but we had no arms to reply with. Although it was a necessary job, it could be very frustrating as at times one was over-exposed – a passive target. Out of battle we carried arms, and had to take our turn on guard duties while in defensive positions or on the move.

The one stretcher-bearer who was killed at Keren had done Boy Service like most members of the Military band. He joined the battalion in 1937 and at the time of his death had been nearly four years overseas. I remember a week or so before his death, being along with him on a stretcher-party, carrying a badly wounded back from a forward position. It took us some considerable time because of distance and the precarious route we had to take to get our casualty down from the ridge. It was nothing new for us, we had done it a number of times, but it never got any easier. On this particular assignment, Frankie Neal seemed to be finding it more of an effort than usual – he was down in the dumps, very pessimistic, when would it end? We tried to cheer him up but with little effect. On hearing of his death during the final offensive, it occurred to me that perhaps at the time I refer to, he already had a premonition as to his fate. At other times, this phenomenon of war had not escaped my notice. Was it the psychic hand at work or was it just facing up to the law of average, the number factor – whose turn was it next? For me I just prayed that I would survive, I am sure I was not the only one! 'One day at a time' was the only way life could be lived. The spark remained that tomorrow, things could only get better not any worse and there was no better reward than the elation of having survived.

For the many who were killed, I write only about a few; this is not of random choice but because those I mention have in some particular way jolted my memory (this might occur again in my memory of war). However the rest, like the few mentioned, are never forgotten!

A day or two after the fall of Keren, we moved back some miles and it was there where the remnants of the battalion assembled and got itself into reasonable shape. Some of the Officers and senior NCOs visited the town of Keren but other ranks were not given the chance. I doubt if our exclusion mattered, we were more interested in what was to be our next move. For some time now rumour was that we were going back to the UK; we even had a song to express this desire, 'We are all going back to Blighty after Keren falls', sung to the tune of a well known army ditty. This wishful thinking was understandable; many of us were into our sixth year overseas and by now were well aware of the odds of ever making it back home. We hadn't long to wait to know what lay ahead.

Around the second week of April we moved out of our rest area and set out on the first stage of our journey back to Kassala. The return route by truck was via Agordat and Sabdarat, the reverse of our advance some three months earlier. At Kassala, we entrained for Port Sudan and arrived there the following day. It turned out to be just a short march from the railway station to the transit camp. At the camp, several of our sick and wounded, released from hospital, were already there. As we entered the camp, we could see a number of sailors and our men moving about in an unsteady and suspicious manner. Our regimental police set to work and rounded them all up. It was discovered that they all had more than enough to drink and it was their way of celebrating the success and the end to the campaign. To be sociable, they had invited a number of sailors from the destroyer which was in port. To add greater affinity to the occasion, some had swapped uniforms, which meant this had to be sorted out before the sailors could be handed over to their own authorities. The ship was waiting repairs after having been torpedoed in the Red Sea. A piece of tarpaulin was draped over the damage and the bodies of casualties were still entombed in the sealed-off compartment.

It also came to light that someone had thought up a plan to pretend to be the representative of the PRI, a body which looked after the battalion's social activities. They approached the army authorities in Port Sudan and asked for a quantity of beer to be made ready for the arrival of the battalion. The authorities took the request as being genuine and so a suitable number of crates of beer were delivered. However, those involved had mis-timed the battalion's arrival and so their binge was short-lived. I don't remember what punishment was given, but knowing our Commanding Officer, it's unlikely that they got away with it lightly. In wartime, punishment came under the heading of Field Punishment, but for various reasons, discretionary power could take precedent over what was normally a peace-time hard and fast ruling.

18

On the evening of the day following our arrival in Port Sudan, we embarked on the *President Doumer*, a converted peace-time luxury liner: to us it was luxury after the open life of Eritrea. The voyage back to Port Suez took four days; it was a time of mixed feelings as, early on, it was made known that our destination was North Africa and the desert.

At Port Suez, we carried out what had become a well known procedure – ship to troop-train. What lay ahead was a long, tiring train journey through the coastal route to Sidi Haneish on the Western Desert. The initial stage was via Zagazig and on to Amiriya, a well known service location some miles from Alexandria, where we had an overnight stop. Strange to relate, because of it, the battalion soiled its reputation somewhat; no doubt the Commanding Officer's wrath was vented on those who appeared before him some days later.

Ever since we had been told that it was 'back to the desert', morale had declined and NCOs and Officers were mindful that some of the likely rebellious might express their resentment at the first opportunity. How right their concern proved to be. Next morning, when we were making ready to continue our journey from Amiriya, it was discovered that a number of other ranks (O/Rs) were absent. The attraction of nearby Alexandria had been too much for them and under cover of darkness they had set out, hoping for a few carefree days. It proved that this was all they were out for, as all – except those who were apprehended on the first day – gave themselves up to the Military Police once their money had run out. Their form of protest over, they were all back in the battalion within a short time, resigned to 'face the music'!

We detrained at Sidi Haneish and from there had only a short distance to march to take up our new defensive position, known as the Baguish Box. It was here that, for the next ten days, we were kept busy digging-in, wiring and laying mines. Once this work was completed, we switched to training which went on throughout May 1941.

When we arrived in Bagush Box, the overall situation in the desert was not what was expected. When we had left for the Abyssinia Campaign, the desert fighting was fluid and in our favour. Now, in a matter of a few months, Rommel and his African Corps had arrived on the scene, taken advantage of our over-stretched lines of communication and other commitments, and as a result driven us back to the Egyptian Border. The enemy occupied Sollum, Bardia and the escarpment overlooking the Bay of Sollum. Part of the escarpment included the infamous Halfaya Pass (Hell-Fire Pass). Tobruk, however, held out and remained besieged for several months – this no doubt deterred the hand of Rommel from pushing into Egypt.

Apart from bombing and strafing, our defensive position was well out of contact with the enemy. However, desert lore had taught us that distance mattered little; a situation could change quickly, so routine security had to be strictly maintained. It was 'stand-to' at dawn and dusk with outpost positions continually at readiness.

About this time our fire-power was enhanced by the issue of several Tommy-guns. This latest addition was the first since shortly before we moved from Mena Camp to the Western Desert; then the Bren-Gun Carrier arrived on the scene and a new platoon was formed. At one time D Company was a machine-gun support company, but prior to the outbreak of war, the bren-gun replaced the machine-gun and the bren-gun was then used by every company. As a result of this change, webbing equipment also changed. Instead of the small pouches for the clips of .303 ammunition, we now had two large bren-gun magazine pouches attached to the waist belt – one on either side. For the non bren-gunner, the pouches were put to other use – e.g. carrying ammunition, grenades or shell dressings. The change also brought about more use of the khaki cloth bandolier which held fifty rounds. One other major change was the replacement of the anti-tank rifle with the two-pounder gun and subsequently with the six-pounder (shell) gun.

In the early years of the Second World War, weaponry and equipment had changed little from that which was in use in the pre-war years. Field-tactics, however, had entered a new phase: we were now part of a fast-moving war, with armour and aircraft playing a major role. Our resources, however, in those early days were limited and in no way could be compared with what was on hand in the latter part of 1942. From the start of hostilities, the Middle East Force was stretched to its limits and was to remain depleted, both in men and material up until the latter half of 1942. Nevertheless, what was asked of it and what it accomplished during that 'make or break' period, bordered on the incredible. Without this response, it's possible that the eventful Battle of El Alamein might never have found a place in the annals of war.

War historians, for the most part, take a bird's eye view of what is considered to be outstanding battles of a campaign. This is commendable, but it is a way which allows the slog of war, the uncharted course, the less sizeable encounters, to be left out, lost to the ravish of time. It is in this area of limited appraisal where the nitty-gritty takes place, and where units in the field are concerned only with their sector – their own ark of fire! It happens at battalion, brigade and divisional level, where the brevity of a 'sit rep' (situation report) so often tempers the reality! Irrespective of size and numbers involved, each action has one thing in common, it exposes the participant to an unnatural environment. It's where the individual finds himself in strange isolation, where war becomes a personal matter – is it to be death or survival? There is not only the fighting victory but there is an inner victory which must be attained – something never easy to come by!

The question of morale is the one crucial factor which governs the performance of the troops. However, this cannot be realistically assessed from a distance. I use the word 'distance' because the rank and file as I knew them were, in a sense, an entity on their own and it was where the true pulse beat was to be found. It is perhaps difficult for the uninitiated to understand – that there is an element of sham in the make-up of service discipline. Moaning and groaning was and, I assume, still is part and parcel of service life, and is usually voiced out of ear-shot of officers and senior NCOs. It is a safety valve, and along with the service brand of philosophy – do it first and complain afterwards – there arises from it, an involuntary stoicism which is a necessary characteristic to fulfil the role of a good soldier!

In the early months of 1941 as I went about my duties, I was not thinking about the motivation that kept us going. My thoughts were minimised to think only of the demands of each day. Each day was a milestone, and as each mile ticked away my receptive mind, nourished by the human machine I was part of, played a role – the input was being stored to be analysed later!

Our time in Bagush Box saw to it, that we did not miss out in having a share of the Khamsin (Sirocco) – i.e. the hot winds from the Sahara which blow across Egypt from March to May. During this time, the winds stir up more sand storms than usual and, as it turned out, Bagush Box was on several occasions clouded in sand. We were no strangers to such conditions and knew that, whenever possible, it was wise to seek cover and stay put until it passed over.

The sand storm on one particular day was not the only reason why I had to take to my one man dug-out. It was something more troublesome, as from early morning I had been very sick. As I lay waiting for the sand storm to blow itself out, my condition got worse. I hadn't the energy to remove the blown sand which in a matter of a short time half covered me. Eventually the storm abated and I managed to muster enough strength to extract myself from the half filled dug-out. I made for the Aid Post, where I reported my condition to the Medical Officer. He in turn wasted no time in having me evacuated to the Main Dressing Station (MDS). From there it was by ambulance and train and, for some reason to a naval, not military, hospital in Alexandria.

After a week in Alexandria I was moved to the 15th Scottish Military in Cairo. For the first week I was still extremely sick and did not know what my trouble was; in fact, even the Medics did not know. However all was revealed one morning, when on looking in the mirror, I noticed that the whites of my eyes had turned yellow. I mentioned my discovery to the Ward Sister whose curt reply was, 'Oh! that's all right, we know now what it is,' and at that, went off to fetch a Medical Officer. This second examination and other symptoms confirmed that I had jaundice.

My appetite had gone completely and my only desire was to drink. Now that I had been diagnosed, I was put on a strict non-fat diet and was not allowed eggs. In the case of the latter, I suspect all I was being deprived of was egg-powder. The one item in my diet which I never forgot was custard and jelly. It was the first time I had ever tasted jelly and once I was off the diet, it was to be a long time before I was to taste it again. This was not the first or only time that I found how circumstances could turn, what otherwise was a little thing, into something of significant worth.

It was my second time in hospital; the last time had been in 1938 when I contracted malaria while in the Canal Zone (Egypt). I suppose I was fortunate considering I had served quite a time overseas. This time, however, was quite a different matter – could the Eritrean Campaign be the cause of my breakdown in health? Day after day tinned corn-beef (Bully) was dished up in various form, a lot of the time it had to be eaten straight from the tin. Because of heat, eating from the tin presented a mushy mess which oozed with fat. Somehow we had to satisfy hunger but the repetitive use of Bully along with the smell of death and excreta, made eating more of an ordeal than a pleasure!

So much for what could be the cause, it was now time for the cure. It took three (or was it four?) weeks in hospital and afterwards I spent time at a convalescent camp in Nathanya, Palestine (Israel) on the shores of the Mediterranean, quite a distance from war. Here one found and enjoyed a relaxed atmosphere. After a week in camp, this pleasant interlude was interrupted by another spell in hospital. This time I fell foul of sandfly fever and was admitted to the camp hospital for a week. In the Middle East, sandfly fever was and is a common ailment and although it gives one an unpleasant few days – severe headaches and a high temperature – there are no after effects.

Once discharged from hospital, I returned to camp to continue my convalescence, a period of relaxation that went by all too quickly. One day during muster, a number of us were detailed the 'you, you and you' procedure! We were required for escort duty and had to report to the store and draw rifle and ammunition. It turned out that both rifle and ammunition was Italian; I suppose this was one way of putting to use some of the large amount of weaponry captured during the General Wavell Campaign.

The assignment came as a complete surprise and, although at this stage we had no idea what was involved, we looked forward with eager anticipation – speculation that night was rife and imaginative. It was an attitude which thrived, because many of us were expecting any day to be posted back to the Base Depot. Once that happened, it was only a short step for people like myself to be passed fit, kitted-out and returned to unit. Those of us who knew all about being up the Blue (desert) and would be returning, did not mind in the least being delayed for a time for whatever reason.

Next morning, with skeleton kit and the necessary arms, we boarded the train for Port Suez. Our journey through familiar places had little interest, but on passing through the area of our Base Depot (Fayid and Gineifa) it gave us pleasure to make in our own way; *adieu* – a soldier's farewell!

19

At Port Suez, before boarding the *Nieuw Holland*, a converted Dutch liner, we were told that already onboard were 13000 Italian POWs, and our duty was to escort them to an as yet undisclosed destination. A skeleton compliment preceded our arrival, including the officer in charge. Once we got onboard, we were briefed on our duties and after being shown our quarters, the first detail of sentries took up post.

The layout of surveillance was: double sentries at the top of each stairway leading to the lower deck where the prisoners were accommodated; single sentries had a roving commission, patrolling the vulnerable areas of the ship. The hundred-strong escort was divided into details, each detail working to a rota system and based on a twenty-four-hour cycle, with the usual period of duty: two hours on and four hours off. It was a repetitive routine from beginning to end of voyage with only marginal off-periods. However, we were compensated by having sit-down meals and the comfort of good sleeping quarters. It was not the usual mess-deck confinement but cabins and bunk-beds. After long periods of austere living it was a luxury situation giving me something to savour.

Once at sea, sealed orders were opened and we were told that our destination was Durban, South Africa. This completed the good tidings of a memorable day. As far as we knew, it was an area of Africa which was as yet unaffected by the war and the white population had an affluent, unique life style. I for one fully appreciated the prospect of getting away for a time from war and the black-out.

There were however thoughtful moments in all this elation. I had been with the battalion too long to forget about the lads back in the desert. While I was in hospital, I heard that the battalion had taken part in a three-day operation at Halfaya Pass (Hell-Fire Pass), on the Egyptian/Libyan Border and lost several killed and wounded. It was the only operation I missed during my war service with the battalion. As I was to discover later, only two days before the action, a draft of two hundred from the UK had joined the battalion. No baptism of fire could have been more traumatic. They came, in June, from the moderate climate of home to the scorching heat of the desert. That in itself was enough to contend with, let alone the inhuman conditions of war. For those of us who had had the training and long association with the desert knew they were asking an awful lot from those lads. In the early years of the war, this happened more than once, in both Eritrea and the desert – no acclimatisation, expedience demanded, and authority commanded! Some stayed the course while many died within a short time of their arrival. Killed before they had the time to really find out what a desolate place they were in – buried under its rocks and sand in relative obscurity.

In July 1941 I was far from shell and bullet but not from heat – a voyage through the Red Sea has always that to offer. In what to me was a familiar setting, one could never cease to appreciate nature's pattern – pleasing to the eye, but in consequence usually discomfort for the body. It was all there: blue skies, calm sea bordered by a ribbon of tinted horizon, and at sunset the glorious sight of a disappearing fire-ball.

We continued our voyage through calm waters until the Gulf of Aden, from then on, we were aware of the heaving motion of the ship, but this in itself did not disturb what was an otherwise pleasant voyage.

During the continual periods of sentry duty there was the occasional incident, but nothing that could not be quickly taken care of. The lower deck held a large number of prisoners, but as there was only a limited number of stairways to the lower deck, it made it easy for sentries to exercise their control. Only a set number at any one time were allowed up to visit the latrines. A strict check had to be maintained on the number in case any strayed to the out of bound areas of the ship. On one occasion I had to check on one who had taken, in our estimation, too long to return from the latrine. He was not to be seen in the latrine and as I retraced my steps, I saw him emerge from the ship's galley. I challenged him and as I approached with my rifle at the ready, he retreated into a corner and took up a crouched position. Thinking the obvious, I indicated to him to open his tunic, as he did so out dropped three or four loaves of bread. He was made to return the loaves to the ship's galley and was then escorted back to the deck below – nothing more was made of it. It was an incident which I was later to reflect on. Some twelve months on, I too was to become a prisoner-of-war – for him, he had no need to steal the bread, he was well fed and looked after; for me it was a different matter. His country's authorities were not so generous and it was the prerogative of every POW to steal from the enemy whenever he could.

Another incident, which this time I was not involved in, involved a sentry in another detail. Apparently, a number of prisoners intent on creating trouble made their way up the stairway. The sentry at the top of the stairway indicated to them to get back down. His gesture was ignored and they continued to come on in an aggressive way. At this the sentry, as a usual means of warning, rattled the bolt of his rifle but this had no effect. By now it was apparent that they were set on rushing the sentry – did they have thoughts of taking over the ship? The sentry stood his ground and at the last, had no alternative but to open fire. By good fortune, the bullets ricocheted off the structure of the ship and on their way slightly wounded one or two of the prisoners. The sentry's action had immediate result – the prisoners made a quick retreat back down the stairs to their quarters. The injured were quickly seen to, and for the rest of the voyage we had no further trouble. As expected an enquiry was held, but as there was no serious injury to anyone or damage to the ship, the whole affair was discreetly dealt with.

Most nights during periods of guard duty we were relieved of the monotony by a more placid pursuit by the prisoners – something which ever after left me with a particular liking for Italian music. After evening meal, it was nothing for them to get going with an impromptu sing-song. Their renderings of arias and contemporary Italian songs were a delight to listen to. It is possible that many had trained voices and who knows some of them might have been opera singers. I was privileged, even in time of war, to have this spiritual uplift.

With no escort, I suppose there was always the danger of meeting an armed surface raider or a submarine; the former were sighted in the Indian Ocean and reported to have done damage. I suppose there was a limit to the demand which could be met by escort vessels. Priority no doubt was given according to the importance of the cargo. It would seem in our case we were considered expendable. Despite our lone voyage, we reached our destination without mishap.

Our first indication that we were nearing our destination was when a number of lights started to pop up above the horizon. From then on, the forward movement of the ship progressively changed the horizon. Eventually an undulating mass of lighting revealed an outstretched landscape that was Durban. Black out restrictions and austerity of war were swept aside – we had arrived! It was the beginning of a period, albeit a short one, which for me at any rate, convinced me that Nirvana was to be found even in a world in turmoil.

We lay-off Durban for a time before docking. Once the gangway was down, we did not take long to hand over the prisoners to the South African authorities. We were then taken by truck to Clairwood Camp, a transit location a few miles south of Durban. In camp there were a number of formalities to be seen to, such as handing in arms and ammunition, allocation of a tent (marquee) and the drawing of bedding. Once settled in, we were issued with passes which allowed us to come and go as we wished for the next ten days. The time limit was an approximation of when the next convoy would be leaving for North Africa. As it turned out, those of us on the escort had to wait roughly three weeks for a ship.

It did not take us long on the first day to get spruced-up and checked-out at the Guard Room. Outside the main gate of the camp there were several private cars and civilians standing around. I went along with two fellow Scots and we had only gone a short distance when an elderly gentleman called us over and asked if we would care to accompany him to his home for a meal. We gladly accepted and that was the start of a friendship which, for me, was to spread to other families and which ever after was to remain something special. A lot of the contacts I made were either of Scot's descent or they had family links with the home country – my Balmoral no doubt made introduction easier!

Our host's name was Ernie Colenso who, despite a tough looking exterior, had a heart of gold and was most interesting. He had been around a bit and had known the bad as well as the good times. At the turn of the century, he had come over with the Australian Forces to fight in the Boer War. During that time he had come to know his future wife, so when hostilities ceased, instead of returning to Australia, he remained in South Africa. I cannot remember ever knowing what he or his son did, but it was apparent that both held good positions – their home had all the trappings of comfort and good living.

The first night we arrived in his house, we were introduced to his wife and son and later to his married daughter who lived just a few hundred yards along the street. My two companions and I were treated to a lovely meal. As the evening wore on and the conversation flowed, I was asked if I would care to stay with them for a spell. They only had room to put one of us up and that was to be me. It was too good an opportunity to turn down, so after making arrangements back at Camp, I stayed with the family for the next ten days.

I was treated like an only son, something as a young man I gratefully accepted. The lady of the house had a quiet unassuming manner, attention without fuss, that motherly touch, something which I had long since forgotten ever existed. For a short time a void was filled! It was a revelation which stirred in me a hankering for my own home, a place which inspired me not to let the uncertain future get me down. I was now nearing twenty-one and I was more aware of the detachment which, on the face of it, was concealed in the life I had chosen. We all had a number and that more or less was our status. However, this switch from being a number among the fodder of war, to that of a recipient of hospitality – in a country showing no outward signs of war – was a contrast to savour. It also included female company of one's own age, something due to circumstances which many like myself had been deprived of over the years.

I found at first that the effect of this was to make me feel shy and awkward in their presence. Perhaps my feelings were influenced by the fact that my experience of sex, up till then and long after, was like the dog that jumps on your leg and goes through the motions! Nevertheless, in South Africa I discovered the pleasure of being a romantic. Here was a revelation which, for me, debunked the barrack-room vulgarities I had heard and made me aware that circumstance can all too often evoke a coarseness in man's progress through early manhood. Now I knew that beauty was around as long as you thought rightly and looked in the right direction. Having said that, I am not trying to make myself out to be a paragon of virtue, far from it, but in comparing today's standards with yester-year's, I truly think many of us fitted the category 'innocent abroad'!

The ten days went all too quickly, making each day beyond that time very much a bonus. The uncertainty of our departure continued for nearly three weeks; then one afternoon, we were told to be ready for the following morning. A ship on its way north was calling in at Durban and we had to be on it.

That evening I said my farewells and early next day, we – the escort party – boarded the *Nieuw Amsterdam*.

The ship was brimming with mostly South African troops; space was soon found for our small party, and back we were to the hard reality of service life. It was the usual other ranks accommodation: mess-deck and hammocks. We were however treated to an unforgettable send-off. For a time before cast-off, we were entertained by a lady on the quayside to a medley of songs. Apart from her fine voice, she was conspicuous by her dress: she was all in white – white hat, white costume, white shoes and stockings. As the ship disengaged itself from the quay and started on its way, she followed along-side still singing until she got to the very end of the quay – the last we saw of her was her standing on the edge of the quay waving farewell.

Her presence at that time was only beginning to be known but later she became a legendary figure. To this day, she is still remembered by countless servicemen who called in at Durban during the Second World War – who could ever forget 'The Lady In White'.

Our voyage north was uneventful and at Port Suez all onboard disembarked to make their way to their various destinations. Those of us of the escort party were transported to the Base Depot at Genefa (Fayid). There we waited for orders to rejoin our own particular unit. A day or two after I arrived, I was sent for by the Sgt. Major who told me I was required for another escort job. I could hardly believe what I heard – there was no hesitancy on my part! The number in the party this time included two fellow Camerons who I knew – one was Willie Park, the other was a MacIntosh (we had a number by that name in the battalion).

It turned out for me to be a repeat procedure. Within a few days the escort party was on its way to South Africa with a ship-load of Italian POWs. The routine onboard was identical with that carried out on the previous voyage. In the evenings the prisoners were just as musical as the other ship-load and their vocal repertoire was every bit as enjoyable. The ship was the *Ile De France;* once the pride of the French Shipping Line, it was an upgrade in facilities compared with the ship on my previous voyage south.

Durban was again the destination, but the route this time had more in the way of excitement although only fleeting. Half way through our voyage, somewhere in the Mozambique Channel – the stretch of water between Madagascar and the African coast – we were told that an armed surface raider was in the vicinity. If it kept to its reported course, we would meet it about 11 p.m. that night. The prospect of a watery experience was not treated lightly. We were no strangers to lifeboat drill, but in such an emergency we knew full well that it would have to be every man for himself. The prisoners were unaware of the situation; there was no point in them knowing. If informed this would only cause panic and insurmountable difficulties. This might seem a callous decision but there was no other way. Towards the zero hour, by which time the prisoners were down for the night, we were all assembled and instructed to put on our life-jackets and loosen the laces in our boots.

The hour came and passed and nothing happened. After a while we were stood-down to resume normal duties. Evidently, after the raider had found a prey and disposed of it, he had turned away from our line of route and made off in the opposite direction. Next morning, we passed through an area of oily calm waters with some flotsam, evidence enough to convince us as to how lucky we had been.

There was one other incident during the voyage which has stuck in my memory. It happened at the time when two of us were patrolling an area of the ship and we had need to make a call at the nearest latrine. As we stood side by side doing the needful, my companion remarked, 'Have a look at this, I think I have caught a packet' (service slang for VD). My medical knowledge told me that the small festering sore on his penis was in all probability a stage of syphilis. I was not too sympathetic towards him and apart from anything else, how and where had he been to catch it? I told him I thought he was silly at not reporting sick before he came onboard. 'Oh no,' was his reply, 'I intend holding on to it and when I'm due to return north from South Africa, then I will report sick'. I lost track of him when I got to South Africa, he never came north with us and I was never to see him again.

This is one example of some of the extreme moves some were prepared to take to avoid returning to the scene of war. I think those of us who knew what it was like to face the enemy, understood better than anyone things of this nature. It is thanks to a developed wisdom which comes from spending time in an unnatural environment.

As the ship nudged its way nearer the quay side, events on the voyage were soon put behind us and we were now looking forward to getting ashore and sampling the good life of Durban. It did not take long for the South African authorities to relieve us of our prisoners and after that it was first stop Clairwood Camp, the same location as my previous visit. We checked-in and had the usual formalities to go through, then we were free to go out.

The situation was the same as my previous Durban stop-over – length of our stay depended on how long we would have to wait for the next troopship going north. Until that day, apart from a few camp chores, our time was our own and having a late pass, most of our time was spent out of camp. The mornings brought out the usual chit-chat: who you had met and all about what you did the night before. Talk about females got a good airing and this brought out the tall-stories. On the first night out, one member of our party had something to show for it. From under his pillow he pulled out a pair of lady's scanties – need I say, he was one of the few married men among us! This tended to deflate the conversation for the rest of us and cast aspersions on our so called manly ability with the fair-sex!

All my old friends were so surprised to see me back but none were more surprised than myself – I had been gifted a second wonderful interlude. The Allied servicemen who were lucky enough to stop for a time in Durban never forgot the hospitality of its people. To take but one place: the Victoria League Club in West Street, a place known to countless servicemen – here there was no such thing as a standard price for a meal. It varied according to the whim of the waitress (all voluntary workers), she fixed the price, and you could always be sure it never matched the value of the meal.

As well as getting to know more about Durban, I visited Pietermaritzburg and on the way stopped to take in the panoramic view of the Valley of the Thousand Hills. The town of Durban was an easy place to get to know and although my travels beyond it were limited, what I did see of Natal impressed me.

Now many years on, instead of being impressed I am depressed by the fact that a country so endowed should waste the intervening years in unrest and bloodshed. As a young soldier, trained for hostilities, but untrained in politics, I saw South Africa as a stable country rich in resources and beauty. There was however one thing of significance which did not escape notice and that was the type of social order between white and non-white. As guests of the dominant minority, we gladly accepted their hospitality and with an attitude of 'here today and gone tomorrow', we left any thought of the country's politics to others. Their ways were not our ways, we did not live in a mixed society so how could we know? Despite the divide, the coloured South African appeared to be quite happy with his lot. But what of the coloured population who, because of war, were in uniform; would a change from bare-feet to service boots change a society? In what has happened since it would seem to have had some bearing.

During my time in South Africa there was one annoyance to most servicemen and that was the opinion of the anti-war faction – Dr Milan openly expressed in the press his belief that Germany would win the war. They were a very small minority who were ignored by most and overwhelmed by a patriotism which was on a high throughout the war years. This showed in the people's attitude towards allied servicemen and in how their own armed forces responded to the call.

As far as I was aware most, if not all, were volunteers, many of whom were in the older age group. I recall in a later stage of the war, while in a POW Camp in Italy, seeing a grey-haired South African wearing on his battle-blouse the medal ribbons of the Boer War and the First World War – it was a good example of loyalty which impressed at least one young man! I got to know several during my captivity, and discovered that many gave up good positions in civilian life to fight in East and North Africa. The South African force consisted of coloured, Afrikaners and those of British descent. The ones of British descent were much like ourselves, whereas I found the Afrikaner more difficult to know and one who tended to keep to his own. Nevertheless, whatever the colour or difference, all did their bit in the struggle.

Time for departure arrived; our stay seemed to pass ever so quickly, a sign that showed we had enjoyed this restful and peaceful 'break'. In the morning we were told, that we would be embarking next day for North Africa and that from now on all leave into town was stopped. My two companions and myself had lady friends in Durban to whom we wanted to say our farewells, so we decided to take a risk and break camp. All went well until it came time to make our way back to camp. As we turned a corner into one of the main streets in town there coming towards us were two Military Policemen. We made a quick withdrawal back round the corner and hid ourselves in the nearest telephone-kiosk. As we crouched, we could see them approach and then pass just a few feet away from us – it was a near thing! We got back to camp without mishap and without anyone knowing we had been away. In this chancy escapade, we had talked of changing allegiance and joining the South African Forces but for me, I had to abide with the philosophy – once a Cameron always a Cameron!

Next day we joined the three-funnelled *Mauretania*, one of a convoy of ships from home, bound for North Africa. This was to be the last time I was to see the Lady In White. As we steamed away, as before there she was at the furthest most point on the quayside, singing and waving her farewells. On board, it was back to the confined space of a mess-deck in tandem with the incessant vibration of the ship's engines. This motion speeded us to our destination in a relatively fast time in what turned out to be an uneventful voyage.

20

In a matter of days after arriving in Egypt, I was back with the battalion in El Daba, a place I had known in previous times. It was here where it was possible to get in some sea bathing and feel clean and cool for the very limited time the desert allowed! Although I had been away for a good three months, it did not take me long to adjust to a way of life with which I was all too familiar.

I arrived in the battalion at a time when it was going through a schedule of training. After my leisurely time in South Africa, it seemed appropriate that I should arrive at such a time – any surplus gained was soon got rid of! Early in September 1941 training stopped, and shortly after the battalion, along with the rest of the brigade, moved out as a mobile formation.

Several days later, some 150 miles on, we arrived at our front line position of Ilwet El Qata. The area we took over was protected by mine-fields and was overlooked by a high escarpment which extended northwards to Halfaya Pass and Sollum on the coast. The latter two locations were well fortified by the enemy (Germans). Our position was flanked on the right by the Rajputana Rifles and on our left by the 2/5 Mahratta Light Infantry. Support came from the 31st Field and 27/28 Medium Artillery, as well as a number of tanks from the 8th RTR.

At this stage in the desert war, Rommel had strong defensive positions at Bardia, round Tobruk which sealed off the Allied garrison, and the Halfaya/Sollum area which we of the 11th Indian Brigade now fronted. As well as established positions, there were armoured and mobile units of both sides active in the spacious area between Tobruk and the most eastern position held by the enemy. To our rear, we had constructed defensive positions at Mersa Matruh and further east at such places as Wadi Gerawla (Naghamish), Baguish Box, El Daba and 60 miles towards Alexandria at the bottle-neck El Alamein and the Qattara Depression.

From the time we took up position at Ilwet El Qatr until October 1941 the battalion was engaged mostly in patrol work – keeping watch on the German line of defence. Foot patrols and mobile patrols sallied forth from both sides; it was a tentative time, each wondering who would make the first large scale offensive move. During this time, at least one of our foot patrols had casualties; one I remember fell foul of a booby trap. It was the type which allowed the patrol to enter an area, then the watching enemy detonated the pre-positioned explosives. Other than that, our casualties at this time were minimal – attention from the air was as usual a constant hazard and from time to time this did add to the casualty list.

We were now into November and our position was unchanged – territorially there was no gain or loss, it was a period of stale mate. We knew from past experience that it was a likely time of year for something to happen, and eventually it did. At dawn on 18th November 1941, we boarded trucks and moved out – it was the start of Operation Crusade. All of a sudden the desert stirred into activity; belching columns of sand could be seen everywhere which indicated that, not only was the 11th Indian Infantry Brigade on the move, but many other formations. In no time, it seemed, enemy aircraft arrived on the scene to peel-off and attack what was most likely a random choice of target. By furtive moves we pushed forward. It was at this stage, if I remember correctly, that we had the support of the navy. We were travelling near to the coast and as we moved forward, we could hear 16-inch shells going over to seek out enemy positions. It was our first experience of such heavy shelling – the noise was like an express train taking wings!

At that time there were two flat bottomed gun-boats, one was the *Ladybird* and the other the *Skylark*. Both were well known to us landlubbers and they did a valiant job but, as I was to hear, eventually both went down.

By evening of 18th November we had reached a position some ten miles north of the Omar Defences – we were now behind enemy lines. From then on the battalion took part in harassing moves, using a lot of desert in the process. This went on until 3rd December and then we were assigned our first big job of the operation. Our objective was a defensive position held by the enemy at Bir El Gubi, some 35 miles south of Tobruk. Our line of attack was to be from the west, which meant, having to get ourselves behind their position. To do this we had, on the night of 3rd December, to make a 50 miles journey over un-reconnoitred ground, which took us six hours. Our objective turned out to be a well-defended area, fronted with flat exposed ground.

At 7 a.m. on the morning of 4th December our artillery opened up and, about 15 minutes later preceded by Valentine Tanks, we went forward in three-tonner trucks. When it was thought we had gone far enough by transport, we debussed and went forward on foot. We soon came under concentrated fire from front and flanks – despite heavy casualties the battalion pressed on. Ultimately the power of the enemy stopped our progress and for the rest of the day we were pinned down; when night came it gave us some respite.

It was the following day, 5th December, which stands out most in my memory. I was one of four stretcher-bearers attached to C Company which at first light made a silent attack on the enemy. Perhaps the use of the word silent is a bit misleading: the only silence about it was that we went forward without the usual Artillery supporting fire. As we charged forward, we were immediately met with such intense fire that consolidation was impossible, and as a result we had to make a quick withdrawal. At noon we made a second attack; this one was just as devastating but this time, although finishing up in a pinned-down situation, we held our ground until orders were given to withdraw.

When the Company Commander, Capt. D Douglas, gave the order to withdraw, it was a case of every survivor and wounded getting out as best they could. I remember crawling some distance and then realising that the enemy, knowing what we were up to, had laid controlled salvos of shell-fire on to the area that was our only way of escape. When we got to the area, it meant making a mad dash which, thankfully, as far as I know, most if not all got through. Once back far enough to be clear of fire from the flanks, we regrouped. It was a long day and a costly one – when darkness fell there was a let-up in the exchange of fire but German flares continued to soar and fall for a long time after. This told us that there was a lot of uncertainty and movement among the Germans. Of course they were never known to move silently during the hours of darkness.

I have already mentioned that during the course of a battle there were some incredible incidents in what was an out of the ordinary environment. In casting my mind back to the Bir El Gubi encounter, I am reminded of a remark I overhead just before the attack – 'Well, I guess its about my turn next'! He was one of the first to be killed. At one phase, while we were being pinned-down, one member's response was to get up and move towards the enemy firing his Tommy-Gun – a hail of bullets soon stopped his advance. No doubt it was nerves and frustration that gave him his quick end. As we advanced in, the man on my left (Christie was his name) was very lucky. We had only advanced a short distance when he was hit. As he spun round and dropped, we stretcher-bearers went to his assistance to find, that a bullet had gone through the fleshy part of his ear – by a fraction he was spared!

In the worse situations, humour had a place, not necessarily at the time but it was open to reflection later. A good example of this occurred during the battle at Bir El Gubi. At the time we had been forced to take cover and Pte. Scivington lay just a few yards from me. As the noise of the battle raged all around, suddenly there was an ear-piercing explosion close-by. When the dust cleared, there was a shout from him that signified he had not been hit. At normal times Pte. Scivington had a bit of a stutter but on this occasion, his response had a much greater accentuation – 'What the FFFFF*** H*** (ending with the distinct H***) was that?' Whatever it was, its 'announcement' convinced us that a few more feet could have made all the difference. Forgive me Scivvy, I hope you don't mind me relating at least one light-hearted facet of war!

Bir El Gubi was a good example of what the infantryman had to take on in the Desert War. To advance over open ground where there was little if any in the way of cover, was the ultimate surrender to the hand of fate. Like lemmings we dashed forward, leaving sanity behind for it to take care of the ones who survived!

We were now into our third night without sleep and the dawning of 6th December saw us still in a precarious situation. All day we stuck to our position and then, towards evening, a large enemy armoured column could be seen coming towards us from our left flank. The flat region of desert and the aid of the daylight were the two factors which gave us the time to disengage. It was just as well that the order to break off the engagement came through as we would have been no match against such a large armoured formation. By the time we started our move, darkness had descended, and it was the early hours of 7th December before the whole brigade had completed its withdrawal. Our transport did a good job; in one move they took us back twelve miles to Bir Belchonfus, a location south of Bir El Gubi.

On 7th December 1941, the Tobruk Garrison successfully made their break-out and joined the main advancing force. For the battalion, it was a day when we were heavily bombed and machine-gunned. During the next two days, we moved from Bir Belchonfus to Acroma and then on to Marassas, a position some 15 miles west of Tobruk. Because of the heavy casualties sustained in the last few days, the brigade remained at Marassas for over a month. In that time reinforcements arrived, we reorganised and trained as well as did salvage work on the western perimeter of the Tobruk defences. Christmas and New Year 1941/42 was spent under bivouac conditions.

Not long after we arrived in Marassas, I received a parcel from my friends in South Africa – it was the first and only parcel I ever received during my time in the desert. The arrival of letters from home was always a very special occasion, made the more so because of the long delays we had to put up with – moving round the desert so much only made matters worse.

The contents of the parcel I received contained a 21st birthday gift – I had already reached my majority on 12th October 1941. It was an useful gift – a razor set, contained in a chrome plated box and a silver neck chain. Both items could have been of lasting use but the enemy had other ideas; it was to be removed from my possession. The other contents of my parcel were a cake and some crystallised fruit: the latter was a delicacy which I had never seen before. Both edibles were a delight and did not last long; my near comrades shared in this 'manna from Heaven'. It was quite a surprise for me to receive such a lovely gift. I had never before known any fuss over a birthday. In service life birthdays were glossed over; what was more important were anniversary dates. Like for me, on reaching twenty-one, I was now three years on Man Service, which meant, as a proficient soldier, I was now on the maximum pay of 4/3 a day.

The lull from combat operations did not last that long, and we were soon back to a state of readiness. During the restoration period, Rommel's forces had been pushed back to El Agheila but they did not remain there for long. Late in January 1942 Rommel made his move and, because of it, our presence was required elsewhere. A day or two after the enemy moved out of El Agheila we pushed forward via Tmimmi to Carmusa and bivouacked there for the night. Next day our force moved further west, taking up positions along a line from Maraua to Slonta (both places inclusive). It was no longer desert, we were in the Jebel Akdar, an area of rolling high-ground with reddish clay soil and a lot of greenery. It stretched roughly from the area of Martuba to Barce and thereafter sank into the desert some 40 miles from the sea.

Under the command of General Rommel, the German African Corps's forward move was no longer thought of as just a raid but as the real thing. C Company to whom I was still attached, were ordered, on 28th January 1942, to go forward and take up a position astride the road at Tecnis, a location not that far from Barce. The Company had to hold the position until the evening of the 29th – it turned out that from then onwards we were engaged in a series of rear-guard actions. It was at Tecnis or thereabouts where some of us had ready-made defensive positions in the form of natural caves – they overlooked the ground where the enemy was expected to move through. It turned out he didn't come that way, so we had to move on.

During the 30/31 January, we came under heavy shelling and increased infantry attacks. At this time every means were being used to delay the enemy: bridges were blown and roads mined. On 31st January we broke off contact with the enemy and withdrew to Slonta where we dug-in, but next morning, the 1st February, we withdrew to El Faida. Our orders for the day were to hold our position astride the road until 7.30 p.m. Throughout the day there was sporadic fire and shelling, but on the whole it was relatively quiet until late in the day – then things began to happen! It turned out that during the afternoon, with the glare of the sun to assist, the enemy had gradually edged his way forward towards our position. Just before sunset he made his move; it was not preceded by the usual artillery barrage, instead he just got up and rushed our position. In this way they quickly got in among C Company, some shouting in English to further confuse the situation.

A number of the Company were taken prisoner, among them Sgt. Gray who eventually got away during the action. His quick and enterprising response in a very tricky situation earned him a bar to his Military Medal. His captors, an Italian and German Officer, demanded that he guide them to where his platoon was positioned. He consented! As he moved forward in the direction of his platoon with an officer on either side of him, he judged his distance and when he thought he was near enough, shouted to his platoon to open fire and, at the same time, dropped to the ground. There was an immediate response by his platoon and as a result both Italian and German officers fell dead at his side and Sgt. Gray scrambled back to his men. It was two of his Corporals, Hendry and McGeachy who did the killing but I remember there was a bit of kidology bantered around the company after the event. According to McGeachy he had his rifle at first trained on Sgt. Gray but altered his aim when he dropped to the ground – was it really such a close shave as all that?

The company held out until the allotted hour (7.30 p.m.) but I can well remember that when it came near the time, word filtered through that enemy tanks had broken through. CSM Scott turned to us stretcher-bearers and told us to grab a sticky-bomb – it's the only name I knew them by! Like my fellow stretcher-bearers, I think it was the first time I ever had one in my hand. Our instructions were that, should a tank come our way, we had to get to the tank, pull the release pin, stick the bomb on the side of the tank (near the tracks), then run for cover. It sounded in theory not to be asking too much, but we were breaking new ground and what chance did we have? I am sure I was not the only one feeling apprehensive as we waited behind a knoll by the road-side. We could hear them but they didn't come our way and we were spared an encounter with hazards of an unknown dimension. In the dying period of our commitment, Cpl. Sims (fellow stretcher-bearer) and myself had to go to the assistance of one of our wounded. With shells exploding around us, we got him to safety but it was a near thing as the waiting trucks were turning over ready to go in what turned out to be a hasty withdrawal.

By early morning of the next day, 2nd February, we had covered 30 to 40 miles and arrived at Carmusa where we dug-in and engaged the enemy. It was on 2nd February or perhaps the following day that I remember seeing our mortar bombs exploding among a close formation of advancing enemy infantry. The accuracy of our mortar platoon that day played a major part in stopping the Germans' advance.

At nightfall on 2nd February, according to schedule we disengaged and withdrew to Martuba where we were again called on to carry out delaying tactics, but by now it seemed that the enemy had over-stretched himself.

In the next few days, our force moved from Martuba to Acroma, a journey over rough terrain which took six hours and finally on to Elwet El Tamar where the battalion settled for a time. The enemy by this time had reached the area of Gazala which proved, for a time, to be the ultimate of his strike. We for our part had, for the time being, done what was asked of us.

Since 18th November 1941, we had covered a lot of desert, part of the Jebel Akdar and took part in a number of engagements resulting in the loss of many comrades. In the last fortnight it had been constant moving and fighting – quite an experience! The battalion fought three notable successful rearguard actions at Maraua, El Faida and at Carmusa. There were some very near things but we always managed not to be cut off. Some daring exploits were carried out by elements of our division when cut-off, which enabled them eventually to arrive on the right side of the Line.

Towards the end of the second week of February 1942, we moved into an area which was to become part of what was to be known as the Gazala Line. A chain of defensive positions sprang to life from the coast to Alma Hamza and then swung south east for 35 miles to Bir Hacheim.

The first duty of the battalion was to construct defensive positions and lay mines: this work took approximately ten days. We were then called upon to form a mobile column and move out. For three days we manoeuvred in open desert intent on engaging the enemy. How often we did those sorties from the Gazala Line slips my memory but I do remember on one occasion making contact with the enemy, who was quick to make off. At this time the enemy was operating from the Tmimmi-Mekili area. During all the movement and combat-seeking, we were as always an easy prey from above. The attention from enemy aircraft had long since become part and parcel of the desert war and we, like other formations, suffered from it. Not only was it there in daylight but the brightness of a desert moon brought its hazards.

In the last week of February 1942 we were relieved by the Green Howards (50th TT Division) and moved back to Quarat El Hamra, better known as The Kennels. A few days later we took up defensive positions round the forward fighter airfield at Gambut, some miles west of Sollum. Guard duty at the airfield lasted 10 days, during which time we were bombed nightly; and during the day, mainly early morning and sunset, had the occasional strafing from the air. More then once we witnessed our fighter planes – Tomahawks and Kittyhawks – after returning from a patrol being machined-gunned as they touched down. The enemy fighters got in among them as they came in to land. This tactic was used by both sides at this vulnerable time. Their method of nightly bombing was to have one or two bombers circling overhead most of the night, dropping single bombs here and there over the airfield. As soon as one went away another took its place. This went on until the early hours and it seemed the intention was more to create suspense than outright damage.

One night Cpl. Sims and myself were on guard duty and this involved having to patrol round the dispersed fighter-planes. As we went on our round, we were conscious of a circling bomber overhead – the expected was not long in coming. That all too familiar and disturbing sound told us it was on its way, and as the onrushing noise grew louder and louder we knew that it was going to be a close one – just how close? Our immediate reaction was to flatten ourselves on the ground. After the impact all we had to do was dust ourselves down and continue our patrol – it was our lucky night! In the morning we surveyed the crater and discovered that where we lay was roughly a hundred yards from the explosion. It looked as if the blast and shrapnel had gone in the opposite direction from where we lay, otherwise it might have been a different outcome for both of us.

21

At the beginning of April 1942, the division was relieved and moved back from the operational area. We had been up the Blue since June 1940 so a spell back the Line was a welcome break. Our 5th Brigade moved to Palestine, the 7th Brigade to Cyprus, and we of the 11th Brigade moved to Kabrit on the Suez Canal Zone – as a division we were now in reserve. The move was no doubt a result of the lull in the fighting between March and May 1942. Both sides were re-grouping and building up for what was to come. The one who was subsequently to make the first move would most likely gain the upper hand.

During this quiet spell three new items of war arrived on the scene. They were the General Grant Tank – a vast improvement to our armour; the six-pounder anti-tank gun; and the much-acclaimed fighter plane, the Spitfire. However, despite these improvements, Rommel had still more armour and was better equipped.

At Kabrit we began a training course in combined operations which was scheduled to take three months. It included the use of landing craft and this was practised on the Great Bitter Lake – it was a period of hard training. The rumour went round that our next operational assignment was likely to be a landing somewhere on the North African coast.

A bit of a bonus came the way of the military band: we got our instruments back, but as it turned out it was only for a short time. We managed to have a few practice sessions but we were never on parade as a band. There were a number of empty places and although nothing was said, I am sure we all felt it. Three had been killed in action, including our solo cornet player, a number wounded and one taken prisoner. This limited get-together proved to be our last and I think we all had the feeling, that our days of pomp and ceremony were truly over – the practice we were having was just a comfort while it lasted.

During the desert war, whenever possible, a leave system was operated which allowed for a number of men per unit to proceed on five days furlough to either Alexandria or Cairo (you made your choice). While at Kabrit this arrangement was renewed and continued until sometime in May 1942.

Our Padre for the last 17 months (approx.), Capt. MacKinnon, left the battalion for new pastures. He had a good rapport with the rank and file and was missed by all. After showing so much devotion in the macabre situation of a front-line, he had earned himself a more peaceful parish.

Rommel started to flex his muscles once again, and after only a few weeks at Kabrit we were recalled to the desert. Our first stop was Sollum on the Egyptian/Libyan Border, then later to El Duda, a position which we took up to protect the advance base (stores) at Belhamed. In early May 1942 I was granted desert leave. It was my first but, as it was to turn out, it was also my last. Five days in Cairo turned out to be a most enjoyable time – the group of us found pleasure in every minute of our stay. The comfort of a bed, plenty of water to shower and bath, food and drink aplenty and above all the peace and leisure – it was seventh heaven! For the five days, each of us had the equivalent of thirty pounds (sterling) in piastres; at the time this was a fair amount of money. Our good credit balance was due to the long periods without wages and even when we were paid, there was little chance of spending any of it.

Early on during our leave in Cairo, we visited the 15th Scottish Hospital to look up some of the lads. One of them was L.Cpl. Davidson who I believe had some connection with my native county Morayshire; he lost a leg in one of the actions the battalion took part in. Providing we looked after him, he was granted permission to join us on our night out in Cairo. I am sure, that it was one occasion which he never forgot – we were all in the mood to leave him with a lasting memory!

On the same night, we were joined by another well known face. He was Peter Bell, one-time leading drummer in the Pipe band and also NCO I/C Boys. He was a Reservist recalled at the outbreak of war and was now a Sergeant at Middle East HQ in the Semirimis Hotel. Later in the evening, we visited the hallowed portals where he was billeted and had a commanding view of Cairo at night from the roof-top of the Hotel.

At another time a few of us Cameron Highlanders were invited to join the company of a number of Aussies – the Jocks had always a good rapport with other troops. During the particular evening, the air-raid siren sounded (it was a false alarm) and as usual whenever this happened, all transport on the street stopped until the all-clear was given. We were at the time on our way by gharry to some night spot. Rather than abide to the hold-up, the Aussies, with loud disapproval from the gharry driver, commandeered it and we all sped on our way down darkened streets until we reached our place of call. That night we all finished up in the red-light area of Sharia El Burka; most of us, I must add, were there simply to witness the ongoings which turned out to be most explicit!

I remember how we all crowded into one small room to see this Aussie give a demonstration on how it should be done – encouraging remarks filled the crowded room! On show was the one facet of character which exposed how diverse and hidden a being we humans can be! That nature in the raw is seldom mild fitted the situation and the place – Cairo! In uncertain times, the attitude 'to live for today, as to-morrow could quite easily be the last', did not mean that it was only the accepted attitude of the few; the difference lay on the individual's form of reaction. Where we did find common ground was the rapture enjoyed from comradeship and the delight of having to cope with the smooth after the rough!

Alas! Five days went all too quickly and as our little group of Cameron Highlanders boarded the desert train at Cairo Main Railway Station, we had long enough waiting time to reflect on what we were leaving behind. What came first was the food and drink: the delights of Groppis Restaurant – it was on the expensive side but worth the occasional visit. Then there was our favourite, the well known Egyptiana Restaurant on the corner of Ibrahim Pasha Street opposite Shepheards Hotel (beyond our means), where one could have fish and chips for five piastres, steak, eggs, chips and vegetables for seven piastres; and there was, of course, the Servicemen's Club in Esbekiah Gardens. The cinema was a big attraction, but the strangest discovery of all was our difficulty in getting used to the comfort of an ordinary bed. Perhaps it was the lack of contact with the ground which unsettled us – was this the legacy of outdoor living? However, I am quite sure had we had longer time in a Pension we would have soon and willingly adjusted to its comforts.

Before we settled ourselves for the long journey and the wooden seats on the train, we all made sure that our drinks were handy for us to sup as we rattled our way towards the desert and the unknown which lay ahead. By the time the drinks were finished, the hardness of the seats no longer mattered, sleep of a kind eventually took over and displaced time and distance until a sudden jolting stop told us we had, without aerial intervention, arrived at the desert rail-head. From there, motor transport carried us back to the battalion and the reality of war. During the five days in Cairo, the battalion had moved from Sollum to a defensive position at El Duda. The battalion had not been in action during my time in Cairo but its inactivity was not to last much longer. May and June 1942 turned out to be a confusing time to say the least; it was a swirl of movement and combat.

About this time, or perhaps it was earlier, I got to know Dan McCann; he was one who had volunteered for the duration. I have already written about the calibre of some of my fellow Regulars; it is now the turn of the non-Regulars. I have selected Dan because his character showed the good traits of his class.

Like any other infantry battalion in prolonged front-line service, the tide of change is ongoing and so it was that progressively more and more non-Regulars arrived to take the place of missing faces. In the early days, reinforcements came among members who had a long association with the Army and the desert and their influence was of prime importance. This nevertheless takes nothing away from the way the non-Regulars adapted to such an alien environment. They had to learn the hard way, very often given no time to adjust to climate and actual combat situations. Perhaps this is just one slant that gives one reason to think that no man, after a war, is ever the same again! Although in those days hearts were not worn on the sleeve, its more than likely that most Regulars had a silent admiration for the way the non-Regulars fitted in.

Dan came from Glasgow but I was never to know what he did in civilian life – at a guess a sedentary occupation, for his refined hands were the only indication. To us less erudite, he seemed to have had a good education and be well read. At times he could expound on matters we had very little knowledge of. He had one adversary, who will remain nameless, who thought being an old soldier he was of more worldly substance! Dan in his subtle and diplomatic way could at most times turn the tables in his own favour. He remains in my memory not so much for his verbal prowess but for his zeal – he must have gone to some lengths to get on front-line service. His physical weakness was his eyesight; whenever he had to read anything, it had to be held within an inch or two from his eyes. To conceal his weakness, he made sure to chose the right time to do his reading. How he ever managed in the first place to get through a Medical remains his secret. Most would have taken advantage of a much lesser disability but not Dan; he was his own man! Soon after, due to the changing situation, I lost touch with Dan and I was never to know for how long he duped his seniors – I hope at the end, he survived and returned to his home in Glasgow.

To the left of our position at El Duda/Belhammed were three other defensive locations which were to feature prominently in the battles to come: Bir Hakeim, Sidi Rezegh and Knightsbridge Box. Towards the end of May, about the 27th, battle broke and the enemy started his push which were to become known as the Cauldron Battles. From the outset we became involved and remained so until our final effort which ended 36 hours after the fall of Tobruk.

Apart from a defensive role, we were also part of mobile columns which went out from El Duda/Belhammed. As the days went by, the area of battle extended and it seemed to be closing in on us from all directions. Armoured formations sallied forth, and manoeuvred for position before engaging their opposites – this element of desert war could be likened to a naval battle. While all this was happening, enemy aircraft were stepping up their strafing and bombing. Ground activities developed in our area to such an extent that before we shifted our position, the distance between us and the enemy was down to a few hundred yards.

Reference to distance between Lines reminds me of the time when we had to recover a casualty from this no-man's land area. It happened that sometime during the day the gunner manning a forward artillery observation post (O/P) had been badly wounded. As it turned out, it was towards evening before we found out and by this time his call for help could be heard. As the sounds came from the direction of the enemy, we had to be careful and make sure it was coming from one of our own and not as a trap from one of the Germans. Ultimately four of us went out to investigate, by which time darkness had descended. As we cautiously made our way forward, we were momentary startled by a challenge from one of our listening posts – or was it a fighting patrol? Our quick response and their recognition allowed us to proceed. By fixing on the direction from where the moans and groans were coming from, we soon found our man. He was in a bad way: it was not only his wounds, but sun and sand had added to his distress. His condition and the near proximity of the enemy quickened our action. We wasted no time in getting him on to a stretcher and back to our side of the line. His face was obscured by the darkness but we knew by the few words he spoke that he was an Englishman. If he is still around, I wonder if he ever thinks of the four Scots who silently came on him in the dark, spoke only a few subdued words and carried him off to safety. It was jobs like this which gave one a great sense of satisfaction.

In the first week of June 1942 we moved from the Belhammed area and took up positions for the defence of Tobruk. We thought it likely that we were there to make up the numbers for a second siege of Tobruk, but that was not to be. The 11th Indian Infantry Brigade sector was south of Tobruk, and our defences stretched over a thirteen-mile perimeter. The battalion was responsible for at least three miles of the perimeter, part of which was astride the Tobruk–El Adem Road. On our right were part of the South African Forces and to our left were the two Indian battalions of the brigade. We had with us in the brigade at the time the 2/5 Mahrattas and the 2/7 Gurkha Rifles – changes did take place with Indian battalions during our time in the 11th Brigade but it did not happen that often.

As well as the outer defensive ring, of which we of the 11th Brigade were now a part, there were also defences in depth which were built during the previous seven months of siege. Since that time, a lot of those inner defences had deteriorated and were silted up with sand, evidence of how quickly the desert scene can change. As soon as we moved into our new positions, we set to work improving them and reconnaissance patrols went out. Mobile columns also went out but I can never remember the battalion having any success in engaging the enemy. Whenever we sighted him he made off, but the same can't be said for his aircraft, as they made their presence felt all too often. I recall it was at this time that I left C Company and joined B Company, where I stayed until the end of the battle for Tobruk.

The sequence of events leading up to those last fateful days had all the pending signs of ultimate disaster. During the second week of our time in the outer defences of Tobruk, word filtered through that Gazala and El Adem had been evacuated and the troops from there had joined us in the defence of Tobruk. At much the same time as this was happening, Major General Klopper of the 2nd South African Division was appointed Fortress Commander.

Mingled with all this activity was an air of cynicism which was later to prove justified. There was no intention of ever turning Tobruk into the isolated fortress it once was. It was a strategy that was kept from us at the time but even had we known, it would have made no difference, our destiny had been decided – to be the sacrificial element of a retreating Army. We already had been used in this way and, as survivors, we were becoming more aware that luck (or call it what you may) could not prevail for ever – our time was running out! Thought of such matters was put aside when on 18th June 1942, when the enemy made his first contact with Tobruk. It was the start of a battle which was to last until 21st June and for those of us in the Cameron Highlanders, a further 36 hours beyond that time.

The attack proper started on the morning of 19th June 1942 – first came the stuka dive-bombers accompanied by artillery fire (HE and Smoke), then came the tanks and infantry. I recall looking over the parapet of our position and watching the creeping artillery barrage edging its way ever closer while overhead, screeching stukas unloaded their bombs. Incidentally, in the process, two of the stukas collided with each other in mid-air. Once the artillery found the range, they pounded our positions. Salvo after salvo exploded on the parapet of our position and with it went the familiar stench of cordite along with a density of swirling sand which blotted out our view. Being below ground level and with the explosions being that odd few feet away from us, was enough to spare me and my companions – our number was not on any that day! However, we did not like being sitting ducks, so when there was a lull in the shelling, we moved to another part of the Line where we remained until the end. Nearby was Corporal Pickett and his men with their anti-tank gun – when the tanks broke through into our position, they shot up a number, how many I can't recall. Long after the action, I was told that the Corporal received a decoration for his conduct. Because of his good morning's 'shoot', we had to go out and rescue one surviving member of one tank crew. He had a deep shrapnel wound on the knee and despite the use of a tourniquet, we had considerable difficulty in stopping the bleeding. We made him comfortable and did all we could for him while he remained our prisoner.

The battalion stood its ground and repulsed more than one enemy attack but as the battle developed, there was a break through on our left flank and soon we were out of touch with all units except for the South Africans on our right flank. Later we lost touch with them also. Despite our precarious position, there was no change in our intention, which was to hold out to the bitter end. This attitude persisted even after we heard on 21st June that the garrison had capitulated.

As we continued to function as a pocket of resistance, the Germans in turn moved in on us from all sides. During the day of 21st June, they were able to mortar and machine-gun us at will! In the late afternoon, an emissary waving a white flag approached our lines. They were given safe passage and the party, one German Officer and two South African Officers were taken to our Commanding Officer. He was told that we were the only troops in the garrison still fighting and if we continued, by next morning we would all be annihilated.

For us the die was cast, we could do no more, and our Commanding Officer Lt. Col. Duncan reluctantly agreed to their demands on condition that the battalion surrendered the next day – he cunningly played for time and got away with it. During the night, all useful material and arms were destroyed, booby-traps set and guns spiked. Throughout the night we could hear from the opposing line the guttural voices of our adversary. While they let their near presence be known, some members of the battalion who were in a position to do so, slipped through the German Lines and attempted to make it to the main force which by then was rapidly withdrawing towards El Alamein. Unfortunately, few of our men got through; they were soon rounded up and one or two were badly wounded in their attempt. The only two who I ever heard made it was CSM McBride and C. Sgt. Holmes – both travelled a considerable distance and for their outstanding feat received deserved recognition.

Despite being under heavy fire throughout the battle for Tobruk, we did not appear to have suffered that many casualties – here, of course, I only refer to the Company I was with. Because of the outcome, there was no way of knowing how the battalion as a whole fared. Attack is often quoted as being the best form of defence, but the Desert War made gain costly. In most attacks we suffered more casualties than when in a defensive role.

The last wounded Cameron Highlander I went to assist before being taken prisoner was Pte. Kerr of B Company. I mention the tragic incident, not only because it was more or less my last act on the battlefield, but because Pte. Kerr left me with a lasting impression of what loyalty to the regiment really meant. I had known him a long time, for he came out with the battalion in November 1935 and here he was, in June 1942, lying badly wounded with only a very short time to live. There was not much we could do for him but one thoughtful officer (his name escapes me), was able to ease his plight by giving him a swig of whisky – a desert comfort in time of war, only for the privileged! It was one stimulant which was not advised when giving First Aid, but in this case it was a well-founded gesture of mercy. Before he slipped away, his last words were, 'Well, I suppose it's once a Cameron, always a Cameron'.

There was one other member of B Company worthy of mention who was eventually to give a spirited account of himself in an entirely different way. Pte. Agostini was of Italian stock and like his father before him, who had served in the Cameron Highlanders in the First World War, he followed suit in the Second. When taken prisoner and later handed over to the Italians he had to put up with that dreaded fear of being singled out by the detaining power because of his name, something the rest of us were spared.

Years later, I met him in civilian life and it seemed to me that his predicament in war had not soured him any; in fact it had enhanced his character. It was rather strange how we met. At the time, I was working as a counter clerk in the Post Office at Ardrossan, Ayrshire, and in the process of registering a letter I noticed that the sender's name was Agostini. My memory immediately responded to the name and when I looked up at my customer's face, everything clicked into place. Thereafter we met several times and we had many a chat about our time in the desert. I moved on a year or two later and we were never to meet again – I did, however, hear that he died at an early age.

I suppose there are many like myself who find it touching to think of the ones you soldiered alongside in peace and war and who eventually had to be left behind in the battlefield – in life they were ordinary, in death they were exalted! Their kindred spirit lives on leaving us who have survived the comfort and sadness of evocative thought. It is a legacy which, no doubt for many, has helped them to accept what turned out to be; not a bright new world, but a different world!

Unknown to me at the time, the embryo of later thinking was possibly taking shape that June morning in 1942 as I made my way towards enemy lines in what was an ordered act of surrender.

Our captors, the German Africa Korps, conducted themselves in a way which had a chivalrous touch to it. As they lay in the sand behind their weapons, they greeted us in a manner which took us by surprise. To think that for the whole of the previous day, they had been pounding us with all they had. It was an English phrase, one which seemed to be in their text-book of military training, 'Good morning Tommy, how do you do, for you the war is over!'

The remark, that the war for us was over had, for me anyhow, a significant ring to it. Yes, I thought, perhaps there was only one way to face up to our predicament. At least we were released from the daily truck with death and, possibly, captivity meant having a better chance of surviving the war. At the time, I suppose it was something to cling to but once the impact of the loss of freedom was realised, anything that one might be called on to do was better than being cooped up in a POW Camp. Alas! Irrespective of what one might think, in the end, the 'fortune of war' had, as always, its unpredictable way!

In the enemy lines we were searched for weapons, but they did not touch anything of a personal nature. We were thankful as many of us had cigarettes and chocolate, spoils which we had picked up during our rear-guard actions. In the withdrawal back to Tobruk, many dumps had to be destroyed and in the process, we had our pick! One of the dumps when detonated responded in a spectacular way; it was aerial bombs and we were not that far from it when it erupted. Near enough to be ordered to keep down and have our steel-helmets on.

Once the Germans had completed their search, what remained of the battalion formed up in columns of three. By now, days of battle had left us in an unkempt state but our main support had not deserted us – tradition and the benefit of good training. To the skirl of the pipes and with heads erect and arms swinging, we marched off into oblivion and the unknown.

Before we entered the area where prisoners were gathered, one German officer stood on his own and held his hand in salute until we had all passed. It was his way of showing respect for the way we had fought during the Battle for Tobruk. Later, we were told that same officer was none other than the desert fox himself, Field-Marshal Rommel. At the time he was a General; his elevation to Field-Marshal came the following month.

22

The demise of the battalion was something which transcended all that one ever thought could happen. No doubt it had happened before but when it happens to your unit that's a different matter. The bare reality which we now had to face was the alien environment of a POW Camp. At first we appeared to read the situation in a somewhat nonchalant way, but this I think was a cover-up for an under-lying despondency which in time, was to show in a variety of ways.

After the fighting had ceased and the adrenaline flow had time to subside and that unique 'after battle' feeling took over, it was then for me when a more balanced view of the situation took place. But what were the inner thoughts of those around me? The passing of time has taught me that in certain situations of war, words are inadequate – there is a place here for the use of a fitting analogy, 'How do you describe colour to a blind man'?

The start to the grim reality of capture began the following day when we were shepherded on to trucks, standing room only, and driven off under the control of Senussi (Libyan) Guards. Somewhat trigger happy, we were wise to contain ourselves and leave out heroics. The previous day, our captors – the Africa Korps – apologised for having to hand us over to the Italians. Later I was to understand the reason for the German's comment.

As we drove off we had no idea where we were bound. It turned out to be the first stage of a long and uncomfortable journey. The innards were jolted all the way from Tobruk to a patch of desert outside the town of Benghazi. Our stop the first day was Tmimmi where we stayed the night of 23/24 June. On 24 June we moved on to Derna and remained there for two days. In Derna we were housed among ruined buildings and were bedded down on a cement floor which made a welcome change from the sand. For the batch of prisoners I was with, our journey along the North African coast ended on 27th June when we reached an isolated spot a short distance from Benghazi – I remained there until 11th July, 1942.

It was a hastily set up enclosure with roughly assembled concertina barbed-wire fencing to contain what was a large number of prisoners. For most, if not all, the only clothes we had was what we stood up in. The extra pair of KD long trousers I managed to take with me came in very useful – in the circumstances the desert sands grew exceptionally cold after sunset. We all had a carrier of some sort, haversack or pack which contained mess-tin, toiletry and odds and ends of a personal nature. For many, their personal items did not remain in their possession for long. I for one had the razor-set and silver neck chain, my 21st birthday gifts, along with cigarettes and chocolate taken from me. When it happened, I called the Italian who searched me a b*****d. It was a word which had a similarity in sound to their own language, which meant that he understood what I thought of him. He stepped forward to strike me but I was quick enough to avoid his attempt. An Italian officer standing by stepped between us to prevent any further trouble. But in the nature of the being, they showed their authority and delight by taking all they could from me; they even had me remove my boots. For all their so-called thoroughness, I did manage to conceal a gold ring – even at this early stage, we were beginning to acquire the art of deception! My first encounter with the detaining power did not go down very well!

In the desert enclosure we were not supplied with any cover, which meant we had to pool our resources in the best way possible. This was done by splitting up into little groups: the most convenient number was four. It was an arrangement which came into being at the start and remained the mainstay of POW life. In those early stages, whatever it was, a ground sheet, a greatcoat or blanket, it went to the benefit of all within the group.

Our prime concern was to protect ourselves from the scorching heat of a North African summer. Not only was it the heat but many by this time were suffering from dysentery, reaching the uncontrollable state with blood running down the legs. We heard that several had died, but it was never to be known how many. There was no treatment available at the time, the Italians could not cope with the situation, and we ourselves could do nothing about it. The sanitation was just a hole dug in the sand and along with the general filth, it gave sustenance to a multitude of flies. There was also the lack of food, with only a meagre ration of water all of which contributed to a dire situation. Strange enough, during this period I was sick for a week, not from dysentery – something I never had – but from constipation.

In looking through the notes I made at the time, the issue of food reads as follows: from 22 to 27th June, two hard biscuits and one small tin of meat (Italian Bully) per day (at one time during the period it was all we had in two days). From 27th June to 13th July, we were given one very small brown loaf and one small tin of meat daily. At times, usually every second day, we received a small quantity of coffee (ersatz) and sugar. The coffee was said to be made from acorns. Whatever its origin, it became common practice when we reached Italy, to queue up for the residue of the coffee urns. They were, that is the coffee grains, edible, or should I say made edible, as they did help in a small way to stem the tide of hunger.

Between 22nd June and 13th July we received approximately twenty cigarettes, thereafter they were issued at irregular intervals varying in quality and quantity. From the outset, we got into a way of conserving what we had by passing one cigarette at a time round the group. Once the cigarette was smoked so far down, a pin was then stuck through the stub, by so doing a few more puffs were possible. What was then left was kept until enough tobacco was saved to make a cigarette. There was always the difficulty in finding paper to make up a roll – we could not be choosy, so long as it did not burn too quickly. Our pocket Bible made good cigarette paper, but it was one book I could not put to such use. I have still the same Bible to this day, and the traces of discoloration caused by sand and sweat is to be seen on many of the pages.

While we remained in the outskirts of Benghazi we lived in hope that a landing on the coast would be made and, with it, our freedom restored. It was all wishful thinking; the only incident to give us some cheer was when we witnessed a direct hit on what must have been an ammunition ship berthed in Benghazi harbour. Two of our bombers arrived overhead, Wellingtons I think – one peeled off, dived over the harbour and released his bombs. The scene which followed had us all transfixed. There was a terrific explosion and the whole ship lifted into the air. As it went up it split in two then plummeted downwards and out of our sight. No one could have survived such devastation. The successful bomber fired a coloured smoke signal and then linked up with the other bomber and both set off in the direction of their base. The second bomber had no need to drop any of his bombs. The mission seemed to be complete with the work of the one. At this stage, we did not see much of our Air Force but when we did, it was always a great boost to our morale.

As each day went by, the heat and conditions were making it more and more trying. For those of us who did not have dysentery, we were beginning to show and feel physical deterioration. It was at this time that I had my first desert sore, traces of which can be seen to this day. However, not many who spent a long time in the desert as I did, can say they only ever had one desert sore – I was one of the lucky ones!

Our gradual weakness – we were all in good shape when captured – and unhygienic conditions paved the way for the arrival of lice. This happened early on and all of us were infested with the beast for roughly the first nine months of captivity. Despite all attempts with our limited means, we could not rid ourselves of the pest. No one, in those early days, escaped this degrading state of being. It was at night when their presence was mostly felt, causing many to have lacerations and festering sores as a result of scratching. They multiplied and gained sustenance from our bodies which no doubt weakened us in the process.

Within a short time of our arrival in the 'pen' near Benghazi, the detaining power started to move us across to Italy – my turn came on 11th July 1942. Before we left that morning, each of us were given two large hard biscuits and a small tin of meat – this perhaps was part of the Italian Army's field ration. As it was to turn out, our two biscuits and tin of meat had to last us until late on 14th July, then we received a half-tin of soup and a piece of brown bread. This was a foretaste of the daily ration we were to receive in the camps in Italy.

When we reached Benghazi Harbour, after a march of some three miles, we were amazed to see the number of sunken ships that littered the harbour – yet as a port it still managed to function. Our ship stood out among the wrecks and as we were hurriedly herded towards the gangway, we could see on her bow, in bold print, the name *Monviso*. Our embarkation was double quick because of the constant expectation of air attack. I don't think any of us minded the hurried operation. It would be dreadful after all we had come through, to be bombed in such a situation by our own planes. Little did we know at the time, that similar bouts of fear would repeat itself time and time again during our years of captivity.

Once onboard the *Monviso* we were made to descend a perpendicular set of step-ladders to the hold below. While we made the descent, we had to hold on to our few possessions and in our condition it made it rather difficult. When all were onboard, each hold must have contained a few hundred men.

The jutting stanchions in the hold, part of the structure of the ship, restricted our space and made it impossible to have a restful position, so much so that we could not stretch our legs.

As already mentioned, several among us were suffering from dysentery but they made no allowance for their condition. Once down the hold, only two at a time were allowed to ascend the ladder and go to the latrine. We were below the water line and well aware that during the voyage if anything was to happen, we would have no chance. Our apprehension was justified, for we were to hear later that a ship ahead of us, carrying POWs, had been torpedoed. It was no surprise, for ever since the naval successes at Cape Matapan the previous year (1941), our naval Forces were very active in the eastern and central Mediterranean.

We left Benghazi with an escort of two Italian destroyers but we were soon left to go it alone. It turned out, that the crossing did not take too long but in not knowing where we were bound for and the situation we were in, made the voyage seem an eternity. It was a relief for us all when, on 13th July 1942, we tied up in Brindisi Harbour – a watery grave was not to be!

We left Brindisi that day and by stops and starts and an overnight stay somewhere between Brindisi and Bari, we finally arrived on 14th July at a transit camp outside the town of Bari. Along the way we were given a hostile reception, words of abuse were shouted and we were spat on. Some of the older people, who no doubt had memories of the First World War, showed their pity and tried to give us food and water but they were brushed aside by our guards. It was 1942 and the 'axis' were on the crest of the wave; it therefore served its purpose, to parade us through the streets in our dirty, unshaven and rather tattered state – good propaganda for the people of Italy. It was a revelation to see just how much people can change from the normal to the bizarre, all in the name of nationalism, or the assertion that their aim is for a good cause!

On the first night of our stay in Bari Transit Camp, we were shocked by the death of a fellow prisoner, who was killed by a trigger happy sentry. He had wandered too near to the main barbed-wire fence, giving the nervous sentry reason to think that he was up to something. All he was doing was looking for some privacy as he was one of the many suffering from dysentery. For some reason, the compound we were in did not have a trip-wire; this, as we were to find out later, was contrary to the rules of the Geneva Convention. All camps had to have a trip-wire round each compound, at a distance from the main fence, beyond which no man must go and there were warning signs to that effect – in Italy it was *Pericolo Di Morte* (danger of death) and in Germany it was *Achtung*. Because of a missing strand of wire, a sick man had to lose his life, one other to the list of unaccountable casualties of war!

The batch I was along with, did not remain for long in Bari. We left by train (cattle wagons) on 27th July and arrived at our final destination on the following day. Our new abode was in the country, isolated from public view, several miles south of Rome and known as Camp 54, Fara Sabina.

As we entered the camp we could see that it was in the very early stages of permanent construction. The only signs to indicate it was to be a permanent camp was the barbed-wire fencing, towers with m/c guns, searchlights and mounted lights skirting the perimeter with the only stone building, within the compound, the cook house. Our quarters were large marquee style tents with an inner and outer covering supported by fixed frames.

Inside the tents there was no flooring, just the bare ground and along either side were our two tier wooden bed-steads. On each bed was a palliasse and small bolster, both of which had to be filled with straw. This was the first thing we did and I have good reason to remember. While gathering up the straw and pushing it into the bedding I noticed, that my gold ring was missing from my finger. I searched among the straw for long enough but to no avail. It was sad that I should go and lose it in this way, especially having concealed it from the enemy for so long. I should have been more careful and noticed that even my fingers had thinned.

Italian POW Camp Money

It turned out that the building of the camp was delayed time and time again. This meant that we had to remain under canvas throughout the winter – mud under foot and cold added to our discomfort. When I left the camp several months later, everyone was still under canvas and only a little had been done towards the building of quarters.

23

The first day in Camp 54 was rather hectic as we were all paraded and made to strip off. Our clothes were taken away for fumigation. While we waited in the nude, we were dubbed with disinfectant under each arm-pit and on the private parts. At this, humour came to the fore and the coating process was aptly named the 'dot dot dash' parade! When our clothes were returned and we got dressed, we were given a hair cut – if you could call it that – which left us completely scalped. The next act we exploited – our photograph was taken in convict-like style with our POW number emblazoned on the print. There was only one expression to fit the occasion and that was a pronounced scowl. Whatever happened to them after the war? It would have been inter-esting to see the results!

The commotion of the day ended with each of us being given an injection. None of us ever found out what it was for, but it was one I'm not likely to forget. As we filed past one behind the other with the arm bent in readiness for the jab, I was completely taken aback when the Italian Medical Officer knocked my arm away and inserted the needle rather painfully into my left breast. To this day I still wonder why he should have done it in this way. Per-haps he was the kind who got some form of satisfaction in taking advantage of the defenceless. Whatever the reason we did not let it trouble us. By this time we had come to know that our adversary was out to keep us guessing, degrade and demoralise, but they would never succeed!

A day in the life of a POW in Camp 54 was measured in time by meal-times and morning/evening roll-calls. There were occasions when without warning, they would have an unscheduled roll-call. It was then, while we stood outside, rain or shine, that they would search our bed and belongings. Anything they found that could be used as a weapon or assist in one's escape was confiscated. However, we soon found ways to thwart them in their search for the prohibited. Once the search was over and we were allowed to return to our quarters, we would find everything in an untidy mess. Perhaps there were times when this action was justified but we always thought that, most of the time, it was mainly to mess us about.

It did not take long for the thought of food to obsess us and give rise to dreams of what we would have when we got back home. Conditions left no room for scruples when it came to getting a little extra food at the expense of the enemy. To scrounge for food depended on the element of chance and this was never easy to come by. Of equal difficulty was how to make whatever one had last out. This was a trial of character as well as an exercise on thrift.

The food we received from the Italians was repetitive in quantity and con-tent. The day began with morning coffee (ersatz), then at 11.30 a.m. we were given a half mess-tin of thin soup along with a small piece of cheese and 200 grams of brown bread. At 5.30 p.m., the last meal of the day was a half mess-tin of thick soup. Once a week, in place of cheese, a small piece of meat was part of the evening meal. Occasionally, we were given a tomato or an orange – in the case of the latter, nothing was wasted, even the orange peel was eaten. We were always on the look-out for anything that could safely be consumed and give the stomach the feeling of fullness.

Our meagre intake of food in the first nine months of captivity did not only debilitate but it created a strange pattern of behaviour – an infantile mentality had taken over. A lot of the time was spent in playing around with small amounts of food. Our daily 200 grams of bread was made to look a lot more by slicing it into thin pieces by the aid of an improvised cutting utensil. This of course did not stop us from finding it difficult to restrain ourselves from eating the lot at the one go – it would be very easy! If, at the end of the day, there was still a piece for the following day, then something had been achieved. You could then go to sleep with a feeling of comfort and security, knowing that, however small, you had something for tomorrow. A unique experience which only real penury can give!

Despite austere living, camaraderie did not suffer. If anything, it was strengthened – for the one who only thought of himself, he had a lonely road to travel! There is always someone, but in my experience they were very much the exception. Most of us by then knew only too well how fickle and uncertain life can be. When there was the slightest sign that someone was not getting his fair share, it was quickly spotted and downed on. I remember seeing a nasty fight over the dividing up of a small piece of cheese. At another time, when his 'oppo' was outside, I watched Taffy divide a piece of bread and spread each piece with jam (from the Red Cross) for him and his mate. In the process, he dipped into the jam and took a little extra for himself. As he did so, he looked up and noticed I had been watching him. His wry smile convinced me that he knew what I was thinking. It is strange how this stuck with me and how I found certain words in the Lord's Prayer fitted this small incident – Give us this day our daily bread and forgive us our debts as we forgive our debtors, lead us not into temptation but deliver us from evil. Taffy, if you are still around, even if you are not, I have long since come to know, that to forgive need not necessarily mean that you forget!

It did not take long for the physical strains to show, signs and symptoms were all too obvious. In those early months it was a bit of an effort to walk twice round the compound. Sleep was disturbed throughout the night, not only by lice but by having to dash every half hour or so to the latrine to pass water. The latrine was a deep pit covered by planks with a row of square slits cut out in the wood. Overhead was a flimsy wooden canopy and at night the perimeter lights cast shadows within the latrine. Occasionally, a vehement utterance might be heard which meant, that someone in the crouched position had been unnoticed and suffered the indignity of being showered by someone's hurried discharge of urine.

Because of our small intake and the type of food we were not long in developing what was called POW Tummy – in other words it was a low hung swelling! To add further discomfort I took shingles at this time – the spread went half way round the body, below the rib-cage, and lasted at least three weeks. Without any treatment it was a most uncomfortable and painful time. The after effect was a strange tingling sensation on my back near to the spine – for long after this kept recurring time and time again.

In those early days, because physical activity in the way of recreation was not possible, it made time a terrible enemy. However, in good weather we could sit out and pass the time by picking the lice from our garments. For those familiar with service underwear, the ribbed section at the bottom of the woollen vest was a favourite place for the wee beastie to nestle.

After some months in Camp 54, Red Cross parcels started to arrive. This help made a great difference to our lives, something which I'm sure made us all for ever grateful. Without this aid, how many of us might not have survived? Its worthy of thought and should not be forgotten!

There were, however, times when the supply was interrupted for quite long spells. The delays, according to the Italians, were caused by Allied bombing, but we always thought, it was an excuse, a way at getting at us by making us wait. They were adept at making promises which, it seemed, they never intended to keep – never today, always tomorrow, *sempre domani!* We were never, as it was intended, given a whole parcel. They were usually issued, one parcel between four men: on the very rare occasion it was one between two or three men. Whatever the allocation, all tinned items were punctured before issue and the bar of chocolate (per parcel) was broken into pieces. The reason for this action was to stop anyone from storing food with a view to escape. Despite a hole in each tin, it did not stop us from delaying consumption. The hole was plugged with a piece of wood; it was risky, but I never heard of anyone having tin poisoning.

It was when the bit extra from the share of a Red Cross parcel was to hand, that certain culinary delights were attempted. It made meal time more of a ritual and also helped to kill time. One popular dish was a small steamed pudding, anyway that is what we called it. It consisted of grated down biscuits, bread crumbs, raisins and whatever sweetener one had, usually condensed milk or a little melted down chocolate. A grater was required and that was made from a piece of tin which was pierced several times with a nail. Once the mix was the right consistency, it was put into a greased tin and sealed by improvised means. It was then placed in a larger tin containing a little water, placed on one's little fire and allowed to steam until the contents were dry and firm. Other hotchpotch dishes were thought up, and nature's contribution of nettles and dandelion roots were sometimes used. It was strange what was got up to in order to counter hunger. Even a prune stone was split open and the small nut inside eaten.

During my time in Camp 54, I was only once beyond the compound – it was long enough for me to return with something in the food line. I was a member of a party whose job it was to move stores into the camp from a building outside the main gate. The sentry remained outside the building while we were inside, this gave us the chance to have a look around and grab what we could. In one corner of the building was a mound of small turnips; I quickly snatched several and slipped them down both legs of my inside KD trousers. Earlier, when I knew I was going outside the camp, I had put on my KD trousers (tied at the bottom of each leg) under my battle-dress (issue through Red Cross) trousers, prepared for what chance there might be once I got outside. When the job was over and I managed to smuggle the spoils through the main gate, the small turnips were then shared among our little group. It was my permanent job within the little group to do the dividing up and to my lasting satisfaction it was never questioned.

The little group I refer to were all Cameron Highlanders, and across from where we slept was another Cameron Highlander, Norman Anderson, who I have good reason to mention. He worked in the camp cook-house and many a time he smuggled out cheese rind to divide out among us. We were most grateful for his help and it was something I never forgot.

By a quirk of fate, some forty odd years on, I recounted those days to him in a Littlewoods Store in Inverness. I recognised him at first glance but he found it difficult to place me. After a good chin-wag, we soon restored the old bond of friendship. Alas, our contact was not to last for long – already in poor health, he died some eighteen months after our first meeting. He, like many others, had much to tell about his war, his escape as a POW through the Vatican, but as so many of his kind, he kept a lot to himself.

Apart from food, the one item in every Red Cross parcel which had a very special place in our needs was the packet of tea. In normal times it has a special place in our way of life but I never knew, until I was a POW, its full stimulating power and the wonder it worked when there was no food in the stomach. Due to necessity, we used what tea we had over and over again. The way we did this was to brew-up with the tea in a little bag made from a piece of muslin or something of similar texture. We topped it up when it showed signs of getting too weak. Perhaps it was an ex-POW who was the brains behind the present day version of the tea-bag!

Early on and throughout our time as prisoners, we applied the only means whereby we could acquire the prohibited and that was by barter. The three items which served the purpose were cigarettes, soap and tea. As for cigarettes, if you restricted yourself enough and had some to spare, or were fortunate to be a non-smoker, there was always the willing sentry or civilian to do business with. Most of the time we were after bread but, also, we had a keen mind for opportunity, knowing at the same time that beggars can't be choosers. One ploy which was used often was to dry-off used tea leaves and then put them back in the original packet. With a sprinkling of good tea on top, the packet was then sealed and made to look that it had never been opened. This type of deal never failed but it could only be transacted once to a client: the next time a new one had to be found.

To barter within the camp had to be done on fair and genuine terms. In doing business outside camp, the one and only obstacle was in getting what you had out and getting the result of the deal back into camp. A search was made each time you went out and when you returned. I used a simple method which I have already mentioned, and it never failed me. Anything I wanted to conceal was slipped inside the KD trousers and placed round the bottom of each tied trouser leg. My khaki battle-dress trousers covered the KD trousers and gave the impression I had only one pair of trousers on. During a search the Italians only ever frisked as far down as the knees. There were other ways used to outwit the authorities, some more successful than others. A very uncomfortable method was to conceal something between the legs, but this was done. Some fitted false lining and pockets to jacket and trousers and space was used in footwear and headgear.

There was one item which had a great influence on many of our lives and that was the cigarette. For a long time we had to be thankful for the issue we received from the Italians. This came at irregular intervals and the quota was a mixed lot. I quote from the notes I wrote down at the time:

1942

10 Sept:	36 cigarettes	one and three-quarter packets of tobacco	
17 Sept:	38 "	"	
2 Oct:	110 "	five and a half " " "	
16 Oct	39 "	two packets of tobacco	
6 Nov:	36 "	one and three-quarter packets of tobacco	
25 Nov:	37 "	"	

1943

2 Jan	25 "	two packets of tobacco
7 Jan	25 "	
14 Jan	25 "	two packets of tobacco

After several months, English cigarettes started to arrive through the Red Cross but quite often at the whim of the detaining power we would have to wait – a trial of patience! In the case of personal parcels, although many were sent, in my experience only the odd one or two got through.

The reaction to an issue of cigarettes was remarkable, it was a terrific boost to morale. When smoke filled the air everyone joined in conversation and for a time there was no sign of the 'barbed-wire blues' (depression). Economy was a key factor and none more so than among the smoking fraternity. I have already touched on those methods, but there were of course the extremes. Like the ones who searched the ground for dog-ends or made use of dried-off used tea-leaves. I had occasion to use the latter but never stooped for dog-ends.

Apart from food and cigarettes, it was second nature to be always on the look-out for anything which could be turned to some useful purpose. A large nail for example was beaten, shaped and sharpened into a small knife. The empty tins of Red Cross parcels were our main source of material. The first things we all had to have a go at was making a knife, mug and small fire/grate for brewing up and cooking. Ingenuity was a quality of great advantage in POW life. The craftsman among us showed his skills with the limited material available and even the less-skilled were surprised to find that they too had something to offer. One member in our tent in Camp 54 made an item which created much interest from tin. It was a complete replica of the cathedral in his native home town: the roof lifted off to show altar, pews etc. in the smallest detail. Another item which was cleverly thought out were the bellows made from two klim tin lids and a piece of latex ground sheet. Klim was dried milk, part of a Canadian Red Cross parcel, a palindrome of great richness! The bellows I refer to were part of the little fire/grate. When moved up and down they created a whiff of air, enough to keep embers aglow long enough to boil up a brew of tea. This proved to be most useful as fuel was always a problem. Nevertheless, we always managed to get together enough pieces of wood to see to the cooking. It was the communal spirit which made many things possible.

It was only after Red Cross parcels arrived in the camp that there was a need for a fire. With only the bare camp rations there was nothing to cook. Much to our surprise when we started making little fires on the ground of the compound, the Italians allowed us to carry on. While I remained in Camp 54 it helped to make our days more bearable. Many a time the situation had to be exploited in order to get fuel for our fires. After curfew one evening I was party to an effort to commandeer some wood. We had to dodge the searchlights before removing a large plank of wood from the scaffolding of building work which was going on in the camp. It was a bit risky but we got back safely and managed to conceal the plank between the flaps of our tent. It was never discovered and as we chipped away a piece at a time, it remained for long our one source of fuel.

In the early months our clothes were another problem. We had to make do with the KD uniform we were captured in and, to save footwear, many like myself went barefoot, weather permitting. Eventually a supply of battledress arrived in the camp, thanks to the Red Cross. To dispose of the old (all but my KD long trousers) and put on the new, gave warmth and a bit of dignity to what had become a somewhat bedraggled lot!

The authorities put a mark of identity on the battledress before they issued them. A red patch was stitched on the back of the battle blouse and on one leg of the trousers; three eyelets punctured the blouse, just under the collar, and again on the waist-line of the trousers. In Germany their form of identity was a red stencilled triangle on the back of the battle blouse and on the front of one trouser leg.

It took time to measure just how much of an influence food had on one's outlook and thinking. The lack of food not only shrunk the stomach but it also shrunk the capacity to think. Thoughts other than about food remained dormant as long as hunger existed. For anyone with an active mind, hunger was a compensator. When food became less of a problem, the mind was more active and extended its boundaries: a situation which quite often created problems of a different kind. Physical hardship was a different matter, we had trained for it and had experienced it in different forms. I was never overwhelmed by its presence but I knew full well that it all depended on the type of frame you had been endowed with.

The desire to get into a situation where there was more food and a possible chance of escape was the prime thought in every POW's mind. In Italy it seemed that only a very limited number would ever get the opportunity. It fell to me in February 1943 when names were required to make up a working party for Northern Italy. With the airy-fairy thought of perhaps getting near to the Swiss Border, it seemed a good move, as we were also assured that we would not be involved in work connected with the enemy's war effort.

24

On 2nd February 1943 our party of some fifty British and South Africans left Camp 54 and arrived the following day at Sesto San Giovanni, a location in the outskirts of Milan. Our new quarters turned out to be much different from the camp we had left behind. It was a ground floor large room with barred windows and only one entrance; possibly it had at one time served as a warehouse. At the front of the building, a small compound for use as an exercise yard, was fenced off. It was edged with the familiar coils of barbed-wire, lights and a sentry post.

Before we began work on 5th February, we were divided up into squads. The one I joined was assigned for labouring work in the factory of AFL Falck. The factory was situated near to a main road, half a mile from where we were billeted. We clocked in and out daily just like the civilian employees. I wonder if the hours of our cheap labour are still recorded in the factory's archives?

Each day we were marched off under guard to the open area of the factory grounds where mounds of small coal/dross stood alongside conveyor belts. Our first job, which lasted 2–3 weeks, was to dig out a large hole in the ground – what it was for we never found out. After the pick and shovel work was finished, we moved on to another job. It was to move the coal/dross to another area of the factory yard. This involved shovelling it onto a conveyor belt which carried it to the new site. It was work which was to last us for the rest of our stay in Sesto San Giovanni.

Our civilian gaffer kept up a regular check on our work. He wore the Fascist Badge on the lapel of his jacket and, being a loyal member, showed all the characteristics of that horrid regime. His greatest delight was to stand where he could look down on us and repeat the only English he knew – 'no smoking, no tea'! Our policy was to exert ourselves as little as possible and act silly. When he realised this, it angered and evoked him to utter the one Italian word which became the bane of our working day – *forza, forza!*

Although we were continually watched over by a guard, we still managed somehow to barter with the civilians we worked near. It was to our advantage when we had a sentry who could be tempted. The toilet was where transactions took place; it was the only place where one could always say a call had to be made! Sometimes it did not always work, in which case a 'post-box' had to be set up within the area where we were at work. When carrying out a transaction, I stuck to the method which never failed me: the goods were concealed in the spare KD trousers I wore under my battledress trousers.

Our only weapon was to pit our wits against the enemy, civilian and sentries alike, and this was used to the utmost. Some attempts came unstuck but however serious the situation, a timely quip worked wonders. One incident which comes to mind had an excellent setting for such a response. As we were having a routine search on return from work one evening, the sentry, in addition to the usual frisk, decided to tap the headgear of one of the party. Unfortunately for him, he had two eggs concealed under his cap and the impact of the sentry's hand broke the eggs. In utter dismay he stood there with egg running down his face while the rest of us found relief in comment and laughter. As anticipated, from then on headgear was searched and what had up till then been a good place for concealment, now had to be abandoned.

The benefits of working was an extra 50 grams of bread, thicker soup and getting out beyond the barbed-wire, something which made time less of a burden. As a result we felt stronger and morale was a bit higher, but we knew within ourselves that we were only a fraction of our previous self, and time had aged us. Initially, most if not all of us, had dreams of escape but in time most of us realised that there was too much stacked against us. Such requirements – map, compass and knowledge of the countryside – were prizes possessed by few, as most of us were ignorant of our whereabouts. At most camps matters of escape were left to the discretion of a committee. Sometimes included in the 'prize' was outside contact which was very often of tremendous value. As well as those requirements, it needed a balanced capability plus a great deal of luck. There were those who took a gamble on their own but, all too often, in the end it failed.

The first one of our party to try and make a break for it was a South African by the name of Myers. I had talked with him several times and it was known that he was going to make a solo effort. It was therefore no surprise to us, when one Sunday morning he was found missing at roll-call. During the night he got out of the building somehow, cut a hole in the barbed-wire at a spot furthest away from the sentry and made good his escape.

In any escape, there was always a code of conduct among us to help the escapee in every way possible. The authorities knew this and once an escape was discovered, they took it out on the remainder of those in camp. Immediately they stepped up security measures and on the day of discovery would have the whole camp – rain or shine – standing outside while inside a search party would be going through our quarters and belongings. It usually turned out to be a long day.

As soon as an escapee was recaptured, the authorities were quick to let us know. Unfortunately for Myers, within a week of his escape we were told of his apprehension. We all felt for Myers and it was disheartening for those thinking of making a similar bid. We met two months later and then he talked of his punishment of 28 days solitary and reduced rations. I could see that it had taken a lot out of him. Soon after I lost track of him and like many others, I often wonder what became of him? He was of strong character and I am sure for him one failure was not the end.

After Myers' escape, the authorities decided to move us out. At a guess, we thought that the escape was one of the reasons for our departure and the other, the Allies had stepped up their bombing and the area we were in was likely to become a target. On 19th April 1943 we left Sesto San Giovanni and arrived the same day at Camp 62 some distance from the town of Bergamo. The sight of the distant foot hills of the Alps in a sense added a sinister twist to our predicament – freedom looked so near, so tantalising but so difficult an obstacle!

Our party, when we arrived in Camp 62, were allocated space in a room which housed quite a number of Senegalese Troops and other nationalities. The camp, as far as camps went, was an exceptional one, as it was reckoned that nearly 47 languages were spoken. It seemed remarkable that so many nationalities could be assembled in so limited a space. The French Foreign Legion, many of whom were captured at Bir Hakeim in the desert, had within their ranks, to name but a few, Italians, Germans and one Englishman who as far as I knew came from Coventry.

With such a diversity of people, some of them very hard bitten characters, it was not surprising to hear that it was classified as a punishment camp. It did not take us long to realise that it could well be the case! Although I was only in the camp from 19th April until 6th May, it was time enough to experience huge disruption caused by the many security raids and extra roll-calls. There was always someone trying to make a break for it. One who I am sure none of us ever forgot was the Frenchman who got away through an old sewer – we never heard the outcome. It was one of the more extraordinary type of breakouts, one which the camp escape network had good reason to give themselves full marks. It baffled and greatly angered the Italians, as I don't think they ever realised that it was by way of an old disused sewerage. They vented their spleen on us by having us stand outside in the rain for a considerable time, while inside the building they turned our bedding and belongings upside down.

Whatever camp one was in the Italians, when an escape took place, would always use this form of retribution, its severity depending on the Camp Commandant's attitude to such a situation. Another means which annoyed us more than anything else was when they delayed the issue of cigarettes, Red Cross food parcels or personal parcels. All the time the 'us and them' syndrome was played out – 'us' being as awkward as we could and for 'them' to make sure they got their own back, one way or another. It was a losing game but we found satisfaction in showing the belligerent side to our character.

It was with much relief that on 6th May 1943, I turned my back on Camp 62. Most of us who were in the Sesto San Giovanni work party, plus a number of others, were moved out to work on farms. I cannot remember how this came about except that it had something to do with having already been out on work. Anyway we didn't have second thoughts about getting away from the soul-destroying life of Camp 62. It has to be remembered, for any POW to get on a working party is solely to exploit the situation and do as little work as possible, be a dumb idiot at all times!

25

On the same day we left Camp 62 we arrived at our new enclosure in the small village of Milzanello. The time the journey took and the type of countryside we passed through, enabled us to work out that we were still in the Lombardia Region. Other than that, we had no other knowledge of where we were. Our accommodation was an old house which had been roughly renovated to hold us. It had three floors including the attic and barred windows laced with barbed-wire. Outside at the back of the house was a yard where we exercised. It was roughly twenty-four yards by twenty-four yards and was surrounded by a high wall topped with barbed-wire.

The attic where I slept, because of lack of headroom, only had palliasses on the floor – in the past I had been in less comfortable places! From the height of the second floor window one could see the lush greenery of the countryside and alongside the wall of the backyard ran the lane as far as the village chapel. Close by was the only road to run through the village and on which we made our way on foot to the farms where each squad worked.

On the morning of 8th May 1943, the second day of our arrival, we marched off under guard to start work at our assigned farm. The detail which I jotted down at the time reads as follows: 10 hours per day from 8th May to 10th August and 8 hours per day from 11th August to 7th September. The work we were put to was hay-making, gathering and loading tobacco leaf, clearing irrigation channels and work in the maize fields. The latter was the hardest work of all, as it involved cutting off the top part of the maize plant by wielding a small machete. It was work which went on for a number of weeks and what made it so tiring was having to reach upwards to do the cutting. The reason for cutting down the top part was to allow the sun in to ripen the cobs (corn on the cob). What was cut down was used for animal feed. Porterage on the farm was mostly done by oxen and cart, a slow, cumbersome means of transport. Occasionally a horse was used but there seemed to be few around.

It didn't matter how much one tried to skive, at the end of the day you were still tired. Despite the ever presence of a guard, I still found it a time when there was comfort for the soul. The warmth of an Italian summer, the nearness of nature, the visible space of the countryside and the attitude of the simple peasant who you worked alongside; all helped to distance war, its horror and its waste. As it was to turn out, it was four months of relief from what had gone before and for what was yet to come.

Our party was a mix of British and South Africans with the most senior member, a South African of British descent by the name of Sergeant Bernard Gill. Within a camp or working party the most senior NCO was usually nominated to take on the role of Camp Leader. His job was twofold, to see that a reasonable level of discipline was maintained and to act as a spokesman in negotiating with the detaining power on matters of welfare.

Sergeant Gill in civilian life worked on the railway and came from Bloemfontein, Orange Free State. He was older than any of the rest of us and therefore, was not only Camp Leader but was looked on as a father figure. During our time in Milzanello, we were most fortunate to have the 'old head' deal with two particularly very difficult situations. The first was when we all refused to go out to work because we suspected that for sometime, the Italians were doing us out of the extra 50 grams of bread which was due to us for working.

Our refusal infuriated the Italians so much that they immediately called in extra guards, lined us up, loaded their rifles and threatened to shoot. Knowing the Italians for their fiery temperament placed us in a difficult spot. When it seemed to us all that the only action left for us was to rush the guards, it was then that Sergeant Gill stepped forward and asked to speak to the Guard Commander. Whatever was said, much to our relief, managed to placate him and have the matter ironed out. We returned to work that day somewhat late. Had the situation been allowed to go on much longer the consequences could have turned out to be very nasty.

The second time Sergeant Gill came into his own was in a somewhat different situation, when two of our party made their escape. One of the windows overlooking the main road was chosen as the exit and, for a time, the bars had to be worked on until all were removable. As each bar was dealt with, it was put back in place and made to look intact. Once all was ready it was decided that, as Sunday was our rest day, Saturday night would be the best time for the break.

On the selected Saturday night, on the pretext of it being such a lovely evening, our Camp Leader asked for the evening roll call to be taken at a later time so as to give us a longer time in the exercise yard. Not only was his request granted, but when it came near the time to have the roll call, he pushed his luck further and managed to induce the Italian NCO I/C to put off the roll call until Sunday evening. While all this was going on and most of us were in the exercise yard, others inside the building were removing the bars in the window and lowering both escapees by knotted blankets to the road below – everything went according to plan. Both our comrades, one a South African and the other an Englishman (their names elude me) were on their way. They were now assured of at least a twenty-four hour start before the alarm was raised – all our prayers had been answered!

Sunday passed without incident until evening roll call and then it was discovered that two were missing. There was pandemonium in the Italian ranks, they were fuming and in panic. Their immediate move was to keep us under close guard while they searched the building. We had made sure that no clues were left and the bars in the window were made to look that they never had been tampered with.

They were puzzled, and what made it worse for them, they had no idea how much of a start the escapees had before their absence was discovered. We were never to know how our comrades got on, all we could hope for was that they had made it. The guards from then on were more assiduous in their duty and what little latitude had been given in the past was no longer granted. We had to pay for our deception. To think that only a week or two before the escape, they had allowed several of us on the Sunday to attend the local chapel service. I took the opportunity to go to chapel, as I had never before witnessed a Catholic service. Our change of behaviour in such a short time would no doubt come under the heading – a venial sin of war!

The chapel was filled with people from the village and surrounding farms, even some from the farms where we worked. It was interesting to see how the service was conducted and the devout response that showed up on the faces of the congregation. When at work, we got to know some of those people and in our limited knowledge of the language, much of it dialect, we discovered quite a lot. They were simple peasant folk with very little knowledge, if any, of the outside world; and of war, they didn't seem to have much grasp of what it was all about. To listen to what they had to say about their own life and still exhibit a pleasant acceptance of what it was, put our own life in a better light and left me, for one, in no doubt as to the value of our own roots!

In one respect they were not unlike ourselves (as prisoners) when it came to food; they had a limited quantity, but at the time we could say we were better off – coffee and tea was something they longed for but was out of their reach until we came on the scene. By barter they were able to sample, what to them was a luxury; other than that, their only form of liquid was milk (*latte*) or wine (*vino*). Their daily intake at mid-day (*mezzo-giorno*) was a ration of dried bread (*pane*) along with red wine. When the day's work was over, it was only then that they had their *piece de resistance*, a macaroni and vegetable soup (*minestra*).

They also had what was called *plento* which was used as a bread substitute. This was boiled ground maize which was allowed to cool and solidify. It was then sliced and eaten or, if desired, toasted before being eaten. Back home, maize in this form would be classified as poultry feed, but in our situation we were glad to get hold of it whenever possible. It was filling and very often served to keep hunger at bay. By contrast, those who adapted to the vegetarian way had the countryside as their source. They hunted around for certain growth and took it back to cook in the billet exercise yard. The civilian farm worker, on the other hand, went to what we thought was the extreme. Any small bird they caught was killed and taken home for food. Here it seemed lay the answer to why there was so few birds around.

Sunday was a day of rest and it was appreciated after a week in the fields. It was also the day when we were usually treated to a sort of re-enactment of Romeo and Juliet. Down the lane from the billet, a certain young lady made a point of posing at her window – a distant temptress if ever there was! Her actions stirred response especially from two of our men. Through the bars of the second floor window, they would ogle and throw kisses. What made this scene memorable was the fact that one of the men was one of the oldest in the working party. A married man, who made himself out to be a salvationist in civilian life, and who was alleged to have said that he never swore until he became a POW. Both men seemed to be missing something while many among us had yet to know what there was to miss! It did help to make one understand that, without having to face trial, human frailty remains an unfathomed aspect of character!

By late August 1943 we were receiving items of news about the invasion of Sicily and Southern Italy. It was all very heartening, made more so by the avoidance of questioning the authenticity of our information – it didn't take much for wishful thinking to have its way. We of course had to face the fact that a great distance separated us from the invading forces. By the first week of September 1943 there were ominous signs that something of great importance was about to happen.

On 7th September we went out to work as usual but on the morning of the 8th there was no muster and no one came near us. Mid-morning of the same day, we were told that peace had been signed between the Allied Powers and Italy. All the guards by this time had changed into civilian clothes and were leaving – we were left to fend for ourselves. Shortly afterwards, to counter receiving the joyous news, we were told that German troops were in the area – they had reacted quickly.

This was disturbing news and had us bothered, and our only aim now was to avoid the Germans and any Fascists who might be around. The latter were dangerous and were everywhere, northern Italy had more than its share, everyone was a potential. Our big problem was what was the best direction to go? It was known that northwards over the Alps to Switzerland required outside contact and a guide, while southward the River Po was an obstacle, and the Germans had early on recognised its strategic value. Whatever we did in order to succeed, luck would have to stay with us all the way and that, as always, could only be apportioned to the few.

There was no time to ponder, we had to act quickly and get away as far as possible from the village of Milzanello. With this in mind and barely any possessions, my companion – a fellow Cameron Highlander, George Sandilands

– and I set off. Keeping clear of main roads and sticking to the open country and its undergrowth, we made good headway. On the way we stopped at a peasant's house and asked for food. I have never forgotten the look of fear on the faces of the occupants of the house, both were elderly and I presume husband and wife. We explained as best we could in our limited Italian the reason for our intrusion and our needs. It turned out that they were not so much afraid of us, but what they feared most were the Germans and local Fascists. We knew that if they were caught helping escaped prisoners, they would land in jail and be treated in no uncertain manner. It was understandable that they should be so apprehensive. Hurriedly they gave us both a drink of milk and a piece of *plento*. We thanked them and wasted no time in getting clear of the house, hoping against hope that they would tell no one we had called.

Towards the end of the day we came to a vineyard where in its midst was a small hut; because of its isolation it looked just the right place for us to get under cover for the night. By now darkness was closing in and as we cautiously entered the hut, it was a relief to see that the only occupants were a few roosting hens. In order not to disturb the birds and cause a noise, we kept a distance from them. It was a smelly atmosphere but the ground was dry, so we set-to and levelled out a patch for ourselves and got down to it for the night. With nothing to cover ourselves with, we hoped that a roof over our heads would stave off the cold of the night air. It turned out to be warm enough but what we hadn't bargained for was the activity of a number of unwelcome visitors – rats! All night they kept running over us and, may I add, they were no lightweights. It was not a situation conducive for a restful night's sleep!

We were up at the crack of dawn and, our breakfast already assured, we stepped out and under the vineyard reached up and pulled a bunch of grapes. Before we left, we checked around but found that the hens had been unproductive. We hadn't been on our way very long before we realised that we were not keeping exactly to a route that would take us south. During the previous day, we had concentrated too much on not being seen and as a result our sense of direction had gone awry. On finding our mistake, we had a rethink of the situation and decided to make for the farm where I had worked. During my time there, I had found out that the farmer was anti-Fascist and had a nasty scar on his face to-show for his past activities. We realised by this time, that to get anywhere we would require help from someone and it seemed he was the likely person who might provide. It was a gamble which we thought was worth a try. Retracing our steps for some distance, we arrived in an area where two or three recognisable landmarks put us on track for our intended destination.

By the time the farm came in sight, the want of food was beginning to be felt, walking and hiding had spent our energy. I carried with me two small tins of compressed oats, but I felt I had to hold on to them as the time was not extreme enough for them to be used. It was just as well, for later on, the compressed oats was to be my only sustenance over a period of several days. Our hope rested on the farmer to satisfy our needs – we would soon know!

We hid in a field adjacent to the farm steading until darkness, then we made our way cautiously towards the farm house. Our knock at the door was answered by the farmer who hurriedly ushered us inside. He and his wife lead us along a passage to a room hidden by a wardrobe – they moved the wardrobe to reveal an entrance to a small room, we entered and were told to wait. When the farmer and his wife left, they moved the wardrobe back to cover the entrance to the room. The room had no windows and looked to be an ideal place for concealment, for the first time we felt we could relax. We hadn't long to wait for the lady of the house to arrive with soup and bread along with something of great significance – a radio. As we took food and listened in to an English wavelength we were rewarded with news, which was mostly to do with the fighting in southern Italy.

We left the comfort of the room feeling a lot better and made our way back to our hiding place in the field, to sleep and hide-up during the day. From the field we could see the movement of military vehicles on the road which passed close by. A piece of tarpaulin served us well as a cover while we remained in the field. The nightly visit to the farmer's house went on for a short time, by which time four more escapees joined us.

By now rumours were rampant, and it was alleged that the Germans were shooting recaptured POWs. It naturally left us with much doubt in our minds – would they really? After all, an isolated small number recaptured could easily be disposed of without trace. It was something to contend with, different from anything we had ever experienced.

After a few days, the farmer told us we would eventually be moved and that civilian clothes would be available – for the time being we would have to remain where we were. We accepted the arrangement without question, as we hoped that our next contacts would be the Partisans or an escape-line organisation. We felt in our position it might be better not to know too much and therefore we asked few questions

For comfort and concealment, we moved our place of sleep from the field to the hay-loft, it was much warmer and sleep came easier. The excitement of the first few days being on the loose now found a level and we resigned ourselves to a waiting game. The inactivity was not easy to cope with, but we had hope that our wait would be worth it in the end.

This was not to be, for early on the morning of 20th September 1943 our dream of liberation came abruptly to an end. The awakening rays of sunshine ended our sleep and in that moment of transition before full awakening, there was the startling guttural shouts from the yard below. We crawled to the edge of the hay loft and looked down to see four German soldiers with raised tommy-guns. They motioned us to come down, in their own words *Kommen Unten* – there was no escape. If only there had been a back door but as anyone who has ever seen an Italian farm steading will know, there is only one way down and that is by ladder from the front.

The Germans had known where to find us and this convinced us that someone had given us away. Perhaps we had our own selves to blame for not taking more care and not relying so much on others! After all, it was a time when you never knew, apart from the Germans, who your enemy was. Later I had time to think about what was a crucial time for the six of us. Did we depend too much on the farmer and his wife? Despite our let-down, I am sure we all had the same thought for the farmer and his wife, that they came out of it all right and had the good fortune to survive the war.

When the six of us got down from the loft, the Germans hounded us into an upstairs room and locked the door. My first reaction was to explore the place and I noticed an open window at the back with a drop of approximately ten feet – it seemed an easy escape route. We would never have a better opportunity; I thought at the time to 'have a go', but I needed company, I hadn't the courage to go it alone. I asked around but no one was willing to go. It was surprising how quickly morale had plummeted; the look of resignation was on everyone's face. For a long time after, I felt ill at ease with myself for not going it alone. I thought that there was a lesson to be gained from the incident and that was – never be dependent on others, be your own man! In retrospect perhaps, in the circumstances, it might be more sensible to apportion the outcome to the hand of fate!

An army vehicle arrived and whisked us away to the Police Station (*Carabiniere*) in the village of Leno. There we were taken to a courtyard at the rear of the building and there we were told to line-up in single file with our backs against a white-washed wall. I noticed at the far end of the wall there was a target (roundel) painted in red, white and blue. As we lined up and faced the front, we were told to put all our belongings in front of us and then we were searched. Once it was over with, two German guards took up positions in front of us and we were then made to remain standing for some considerable time.

During this period little was said, we were too concerned about what was going to happen to us next. Was rumour going to be proved correct, a quick execution and disposal of the bodies? It could easily be done, after all there were only half a dozen of us. By the attitude of the others, although nothing was said, I got it into my head that I was the only one having those anxious thoughts. It was fear, something which as a soldier I could only look on as a despicable intruder, although at times, I suppose, it served as a safety-valve. Was I ever going to learn that the use of sham was an adept way to obscure the element of fear!

That night as we lay on the stone floor of a dingy cell, without food or blankets, our conversation veered to what had happened in the back courtyard during the afternoon. It transpired that every one of us were thinking the same thing, that we were all for the firing-squad. Again we had fallen prey to the psychological antics of the enemy – the second trying situation in the last couple of months! These experiences seemed more traumatic after the event than at the time.

Next morning our small party marched the twenty kilometres to the railway station in the town of Brescia. As we marched, one member of the guard asked us to sing 'It's a long way to Tipperary'; we responded in the only way soldiers can – show the stiff upper lip! When we arrived at the railway station there were already a large number of POWs on the train, a train which consisted of wagons (cattle trucks). We were immediately shepherded on to a wagon and, as expected, we finished up being crammed in like cattle. It was left to ourselves to make the best of the floor space and the two broad shelves at either end of the wagon. In each corner above the shelves was a small grille, our only inlet of light and fresh air. I was fortunate to be in on time to occupy a spot on the shelf next to one of the grilles. Once we were all aboard, the door of the wagon was slammed shut and, as it turned out, the door remained that way until we arrived at our destination in Germany some four days later (24th September 1943).

It was the forenoon of 21st September when we pulled out of Brescia railway station, on what turned out to be a memorable journey. Ever since we (the six of us) were re-captured, the Germans had given us no food and this is how it remained until we arrived at the transit camp in Germany. The two small tins of compressed oats, which I have already commented on, now came to my rescue. A little at a time along with a drink of water sustained me over the next four days. I cannot remember how resources were pooled but we all managed somehow to eke out what little we had.

Even for servicemen, the call of nature within the confines of a wagon gave rise to some embarrassment. The main function was usually delayed until the hours of darkness and then the results were put to unsavoury use whenever the chance arose. I have good reason to remember, as I was next to one of the grilles and it fell to me to toss it out. Whenever the train had to stop, guards patrolled up and down outside. At one particular stop, the contents of the evening were handed up to me in a cardboard box. I had to wait until one of the guards passed close to the grille before I could make my delivery. The opportunity arrived and going by the utterance of oaths from the German guard, I must have made a direct hit. This was our way of showing resentment at being locked up for too long without any consideration for human needs.

Due to a lot of aerial bombing, our train was held up several times and at one stop there was a commotion in the next wagon to our one. The Germans, with the use of the butt of the rifle, cleared the occupants from the wagon and moved them to another because it was discovered that a floor plank had been loosened enough for bodies to squeeze through. During the various stops along the way, a number had made their escape from under the wagon. Once the alarm was raised, regrettably it foiled any further escapes. Through the grille I saw the whole incident and, among the unfortunates, I spotted an old friend who I had not seen since our escort duty to South Africa. Later in a camp in Germany I met up with him and he told me about the incident and being jabbed with the butt of a rifle and how it aggravated the wounds he had on his spine and head. His mention recalls for me his favourite comment, that the only time he had access to a mirror was when he joined the Army – he had six sisters and he was the only son. Dally Duncan came from Knightswood in Glasgow; he was a good comrade and the kind that one could never forget.

My position in the wagon, next to one of the grilles, also allowed me a glimpse of the passing countryside. It was obvious that the area leading up to the Brenner Pass had received the attention of Allied bombing. The town of Trento, where we were stopped for a time, looked to be a complete ruin. It was nightfall by the time we were on our way through the Brenner Pass and all that could be seen were the passing clouds. At one stage we were looking down on patchy cloud, and it was bitterly cold. I for one had a disturbed night, due to limited space and the cold which was made worse by the steel structure of the wagons and being near to the grille opening.

The notes I managed to keep tell me that it was 23rd September 1943 when we arrived at the Austrian Border town of Innsbruck. From then on, it was an interesting change of scenery, colourful doll-like houses shelved on high ground at different levels and dotted along the many valleys – it all looked so peaceful.

26

From Innsbruck it took us another day to reach our destination – Stalag IVB Muhlberg. Like all POW camps it was isolated, leaving us as usual in confusion as to our whereabouts. For what it was worth, we heard that the camp was 100 miles south of Berlin. When we first arrived we were put through a similar process as when we arrived in camp in Italy. All clothes were fumigated, scalps were bared of hair, finger prints were taken and a POW number along with disc was issued. Like your Army number you never forgot it; mine waswas 299855. We were also issued with battledress (thanks to the Red Cross), blouse and trousers had identification markings and lastly each of us were photographed. After all this humiliating process we were allocated sleeping quarters.

The usual thing after settling in to any new camp was to take stock of our surroundings. A single barbed-wire fenced separated us from a compound of Russian prisoners. Although the trauma of recent times had left us a bit shaken up and morose, seeing our Russian neighbours and the state they were in had a steadying influence. A reminder that there was always someone worse off than yourself! Many wore the hideous outfit of striped trousers, jacket and small cap – the same uniform which to this day is associated with the evil that went on all in the name of a 'cause'. Already our Russian fellow inmates had been selected and were treated differently. They were in a very poor state and had a glazed look in their eyes and were only able to shuffle around the compound.

During the time I was in the camp, many of the other prisoners did what they could for the Russians. It wasn't easy, as the Germans did everything they could to prevent us from helping them. However, there was one method which had the best chance of success and that was to throw the article over the fence instead of passing it through. One item for example which found its way over fairly often and that was the odd pair of socks. The Russians wore clogs without any wrapping for their feet so a pair of socks was much appreciated. Somehow at this stage in time we were not too badly off for footwear, so it was becoming of us to react in the way we did. There were other things got through to them and whatever we gave, even if it was only some *sauerkraut* or a few *dunax* cigarettes (exceptionally strong), the look on their faces told us more than any words could!

The German policy was to have as many POWs out on work, so those of us who arrived from Italy expected our stay at the camp in Muhlberg to be only for a short time. What we gathered from others was that it was a matter of chance where you finished up. I didn't have long to wait to become a victim of the 'you, you and you' procedure. The group I joined moved out on 12th October 1943, my 23rd birthday. A significant day for me in more ways than one, but circumstances saw to it that it passed off just like any other day – a day nearer to the day of all days – liberation!

After a wearisome train journey, cattle-wagon style, we arrived that evening at Arbeit Kommando (Working Party) No. 508, Stalag IVA Gruba Erika. We were now in the region of Silesia with the nearest big town Breslau (Wroclaw) some forty miles away. A short distance from the camp was a fair-sized village where many of the civilian employees at Gruba Erika lived. The camp itself had been there for some time, at least two years, as had the large number of Allied and Russian POWs who worked in the area. The Russians, most of whom I think were Ukrainians, were in a separate compound from us. Women workers from the Ukraine were also part of the labour-force and were billeted away from our camp. They did the same manual work as the men, and did it in what to us was a degrading dress – sack-cloth skirt and clogs, their feet wrapped in pieces of cloth. How they endured the life was an eye-opener to us all. Gruba Erika was a large surface coal-mine and because of the work coal dust was everywhere, creating a drabness to the landscape and an atmosphere, which was no place for the depressed – an affliction which we all knew about at some time or other.

As soon as our group arrived in the camp our new comrades welcomed us and, naturally, wanted to know where we had come from and what news we had as to the progress of the war. Many of them came from the Northeast of England, the Ashington, Northumberland area and in civilian life had been coal-miners – they proved to be a good bunch to be along with. There was also a mix of others – Australians, New Zealanders, Poles (captured when Poland was overrun), Scots, Welsh and several from various parts of England. Apart from the Poles, all had been captured either in France (1940) or

Greece and Crete (1941). The camp had a British Medical Officer, Capt. Ferguson – it was the first time I had been in the same camp as an officer. The nature of the work and the size of the working party must have been the reason for a Medical Officer's presence.

Our group arrived on a Saturday, and because Sunday was a rest day we had a day's respite before starting work. The mine stretched over a wide area and to get to our work place involved a train journey followed by a varying distance to walk. Our travel by rail wagon during the winter months was a cold and miserable experience. The interior sides of the wagon had to be avoided because the frost made the metal sides adhesive to touch.

On our first day, we were allocated to one of the many groups of workers who were scattered over the wide working area of the mine. My job was to do with the construction of a new piece of machinery known as a Bridge-Bagger. I assisted a German civilian on a drilling machine which made holes for the riveters. It was a job I remained on throughout the time that I worked outside in the mine.

The new Bridge-Bagger, when completed, would take the place of the existing one. It was a massive machine and was central to the operation of surface coal-mining. Its function was to remove top soil enough to expose the seams of coal which lay at various depths below ground level. By the use of their revolving buckets, the soil was dug out, then dumped on a conveyor on the bridge structure of the machine which ultimately disposed of it to the rear of the huge trench it made. In order for the Bridge-Bagger to carry out this work it ran on rails which were located at either end of the machine, spanning a large area of ground.

Once the coal seams were exposed, smaller machines moved in to cut the coal and load it onto railway wagons which plied to and fro from the site of operation. As the whole thing was a moving process, many of the POWs were used for shifting and re-laying rail tracks. A few worked on the electrical side but nearly all were given to labouring. As far as I am aware, no one worked underground.

In the winter months, it was out in the morning in the dark and back in the evening in the dark. Before leaving camp in the morning, the number of heads were counted and each guard was responsible for his charge throughout the working day until return to camp. In camp, there was roll call each evening and twice on Sundays. At work we were never without some form of surveillance. If a guard was not around, there was always a civilian foreman, supported by a Nazi Badge on his lapel, ever ready to exert his authority. Many a time my drilling machine civilian partner would be chatting away quite the thing but as soon as the foreman appeared, he would dry-up. To bear witness to a regime (Fascism/Nazism) which governed by fear was one thing no POW ever forgot!

After a day's work, most of us had little to do except rest up for the following day. Saturday evening and Sunday gave us time to relax, see to our needs and stroke off another week on the calendar. There were those who had talent to express in some form or other and this we all benefited from. One feature of camp life was the occasional Saturday night dance (less the female partners) or a concert. A few instrumentalists got together and regularly treated us to some enjoyable music. It was amazing the ingenuity which went into the making of stage props and costumes, all made from bits and pieces which somehow found there way into the camp. We had a small hall with a stage and it was here where recreational indoor activities took place.

In Gruba Erika, as in every other camp, there were a number of characters who stood out because of their attitude and sense of humour. It was good to have them around as it influenced the staying power of us all. There are two who still have a special place in my memory, more so, because of the difference in character and because one of them I was to meet many years later. Captain Ferguson, our Medical Officer, in his pursuit of caring for others, did not in any way deter him from showing his dislike for the Germans. His definition of the pedigree of a German was very often expressed in unrefined words. On one occasion, he borrowed a private's battle-blouse and joined our party; we were attending the nearby POW hospital for treatment. His masquerade enabled him to meet some of his fellow Medical Officers who worked in the hospital. By all the signs it looked to have been a most convivial meeting. When the time came for us to return to camp, it was obvious to us all that he had been too well treated – POW home brew was noted for its potency! As a result of his intake, another fellow prisoner and I had the difficult task of keeping a hold on him and restraining him all the way back to camp – he was threatening to make a foolish move towards the guard. By good luck our German guard was more understanding than most, otherwise things could have been difficult for us all.

When we got him into his room at camp, he was still as pugnacious as ever. Before the drink got the better of him and sleep took over, he hurled a chair at his room window just as a German guard passed by. Again luck was with us; the inside set of bars to his room window stopped any damage being done and the passing guard was unaware of the intent. Not long after the incident, he was moved to another camp and in his place came Captain Burns, a New Zealander.

The other fellow prisoner I relate to featured in a strange happening many years later. While on holiday in Yugoslavia, a chance remark to a fellow holiday-maker put me in touch with Charlie Judge, an old friend of Gruba Erika days. We eventually arranged a meeting and, along with our wives, we had a marvellous week together in Charlie's native town of Newbiggin-by-the-Sea. We intended having a second get together but, in the interim, his unstable health gave way and he died before I had the time to see him again. Come what may, Charlie as a POW never seemed to loose his jovial approach to the daily grind of that life, in his spare time, he played the accordion in the camp's small orchestra come dance band.

He was one of the stalwarts of our generation and even in declining years, he still displayed that common trait among his kind of a ready camaraderie

German POW Camp money

and a sense of humour. Our renewed friendship was not for long, but while it lasted it enriched a period of my life.

While I was in Gruba Erika I experienced for the first time a regular issue of Red Cross food parcels. This no doubt was because we were a large working party and the Germans were better organised than the Italians. It was still the usual allocation of one parcel having to be divided up. However, we had long since realised that without that extra food from the Red Cross our situation would have been entirely different. It is possible that our state of health would have deteriorated to the level of the Russian prisoners. Our German daily ration consisted of black bread, soup/sauerkraut and a piece of ersatz cheese which gave off a disgusting smell – it was said to be made from fish. Sometimes there was an issue of *wurst*, a form of sausage which we had no idea what it was made from. For us all, our ration of black bread was the mainstay of our daily intake; you had to acquire a taste for it, but it did serve the purpose!

It was while at Gruba Erika that the 'old timers' warned us newcomers about a certain German officer from the Propaganda Department who made a periodic visit, but especially whenever there was a new intake. He spoke perfect English, knew a lot about Britain and his method was to get talking to anyone who was prepared to talk. It was dangerous to do so as he was a very astute person and wanted to know all about you and if you had any political views. If, as a result of a conversation, he thought he had someone who could be worked on, his report would sanction that the person be moved to a special camp, known to us as a Propaganda Camp. In these camps, conditions and treatment were far and away better than at the ordinary camp or working party.

Once in the special camp the inmates went through a process of brainwashing and according to its influence they either joined the German Free

Corps or returned to a camp with worse conditions than the one they came out of. It was alleged that they succeeded with some but personally I never knew of anyone who turned in this way. All fellow prisoners I was with, whatever the temptation, stuck firmly to their allegiance. I did see the German Propaganda Officer once but it was a brief encounter. We had just returned from a day's work when he appeared at our room door. As he made to come in, he was stopped short by two words, all occupants in one voice – 'F*** off'. With that retort, he turned on his heels with a parting salutation, 'Good evening gentlemen'!

In January 1944, the opportunity to get away from working for the enemy came my way. Medical Orderlies were required for the Camp Medical Room, so I applied to the Medical Officer and because of my First Aid training, I was accepted. I soon settled to my change of work and, as it was for the needs of fellow prisoners, it gave to an otherwise drab and aimless existence a sense of purpose.

The demands of the work varied from accidents at work to major and minor ailments – the medical staff was under the supervision of the camp Medical Officer. The rigours of the life exposed weakness, some suffered a great deal, while others had much to be thankful for in having greater staying power. I think it was good for us all to be mindful of our position compared to that of the Russian prisoners. Unlike us, they had no assistance from the Red Cross and no doubt this was the reason why they had a greater number on the sick-list. They attended our Medical Room for treatment and, to assist us in our work, we had one Russian who spoke perfect English. He was one of three interpreters, the other two were a Pole and an Australian – the Pole spoke English and German, and the Australian French and German. While most prisoners had a smattering of one or two of the different languages, a recognised interpreter was an essential member of any camp.

It was a very sad day for us all when the life of our Russian interpreter came to a very tragic end. Early one morning, he was found hanging from a beam behind the hall stage. He was a very intelligent man and got along well with those of us who had contact with him. What made the whole unfortunate incident a lot more unbearable was the attitude of the Germans. For reasons best known to themselves and despite all protestations, they left him hanging for all to see, from 6 a.m. to 4 p.m. in the afternoon. He was then taken down and unceremoniously placed in a roughly made wooden coffin and taken away. I, like a number of others who were in the camp at the time, witnessed the whole unsavoury event. We saw something which proved that, in an unnatural environment, behaviour sometimes goes beyond the realms of explanation and understanding. Throughout those years, it was a phenomenon which cast its shadow over the minds of us all!

From January 1944 until the end of June 1944, I carried out the duties of Camp Medical Orderly; the work was mainly in the mornings and when the men returned from work in the evenings. It was sometime during this period when, for the first time, I found myself in the trough of depression. The

157

Barbed-Wire Blues, another name for it, was the scourge of the life of a POW. Once it got to you, its disturbing factors were not easy to shrug off. Some withdrew into themselves while others kept up a front which concealed how they really felt. My turn had come and like everyone else I had to deal with this 'alien' as best I could. I suppose the trauma of war and privation had caught up with me at last! One never thought at the time the marks it was to leave; it aged us and made us different in many ways!

However, as so often happens, when one door closes another opens, or as I prefer to put it, someone is watching over you! I feel this is what happened to me that July day in 1944. There was a need for more Nursing Orderlies in the POW Sanatorium which was just up the road from our camp. On hearing of this, I approached the camp Medical Officer and told him of my interest and could he do anything for me. He spoke to the right people and his word did the rest. I was taken on and took up duty as a Nursing Orderly on 3rd July 1944.

27

Reserve Lazarett Elsterhorst Stalag IVA was the Sanatorium for allied POWs suffering from TB – it was made up of several single-storey barrack blocks, each divided into wards. Separate from the wards was the staff accommodation and buildings which housed operating theatre, X-ray department, mortuary and cook-house. I don't know when it first opened, but according to what I was told, it had been a hospital since early on in the war. It was run, as far as was possible, on similar lines to any other medical establishment. There was one significant difference: it was controlled and set-up in the same way as any other POW Camp – barbed-wire fence, emplacements at each corner of the perimeter, search-lights, standard lights, sentries, daily roll call and curfew between 9 p.m. and 8 a.m.

The patients were a mix of many nationalities, all members of the Allied Forces who, during captivity, fell victim to tuberculosis. Very often, because of late diagnosis, by the time they were admitted to hospital they were already in an advanced state. This was due to the attitude of the Germans; they were not concerned so much about the health of a prisoner, but of how much work they could get out of him. It was expressed by our own Medical Officers that if treatment for many had been given earlier, the mortality rate in hospital and later would not have been so high.

From early July 1944 until liberated some nine months later, I worked as a nursing orderly for patients who had pulmonary and miliary tuberculosis. Although the risk factor was ever present, at no time did we orderlies wear face-masks while at work in the wards. Our only protection was hygiene and careful handling of bed-patients – most of the time it was simply a case of common sense. When giving a patient close attention, you had to watch that he did not breathe or cough into your face and that his sputum bottle was secure and covered. As a precaution, one had a hand always ready to turn the patient's face away from your own. This usually only happened when you were giving the patient some form of attention – i.e. washing/bed-bath or attending to bed sores. The latter was the bane of the very ill, and many a time they gave us cause for concern. It was pitiful to see the extent of some of the sores and how the natural healing process was no longer there to assist. Many a time all we could do was to contain the damage already done.

During the time I worked in the Sanatorium there was only one nursing orderly who contracted tuberculosis. Looking through my service pay book, which I still have, I note that the details of the work I did at the Sanatorium are recorded – thankfully, I have never had cause to use this information.

I suppose as we went about our work, we had a dormant fear of infection. The patients I feel understood but we could not drop our guard, as there was always the possibility that one might want to share his trouble with you! Whenever a sputum bottle was knocked over, it was sometimes difficult to know whether it was done intentionally or by accident. We had the odd one or two difficult ones but, by and large, they appreciated what was done for them. The best way to come to terms with a difficult situation was to remind oneself that, unlike our patients, we were not dogged by the sentence they were under; we had only to put-up with being a prisoner-of-war. They will always remain for me men of spirit, showing resolve of a special order. One who epitomised those qualities was Corporal (equiv. rank) Wazik of the Polish Army – there were many more besides, but he is one who fills a special place in my memory.

I had on one occasion to take Wazik by wheeled stretcher to the X-ray department for a screening. Major Wallace (his home town was Liverpool) one of the Medical Officers, was making one of his periodic checks on the condition of Wazik's chest. During the course of the examination, Major Wallace called me over so that I could see the extent of the damage that had been done. As he pointed out in detail on the X-ray screen and explained the implications, it seemed incredible that Wazik should still be alive. One lung was blacked-out and completely out of use, the other lung, apart from a small area of the upper lobe, was in a similar state. All that was keeping him alive was a part of lung, roughly half the size of a normal size clenched fist. It flicked up and down apace of his short rapid breathing. In this condition he held out for a further two months, in which time he was often heard to remark in his limited English – 'Me no die in Germany, me die in Poland'. In the end the 'will' was not enough, and like others, he was buried in the cemetery just a short distance along the road from the hospital.

Even though death was always a frequent spoiler, it was never easy when you were told by the Medical Officer that one of your patients had only so long to live – they were never far out with their estimated time. It was uncanny how they were able to put a death or survival tag on each patient.

During my time in Elsterhorst there were two repatriations, one in September 1944 and the other in January 1945. Both times I assisted in the loading of the Hospital Train. There were guards everywhere and the security was as tight as it ever could be. Nevertheless, it did not stop one from having the dream idea of sneaking onboard and making it back home. There was an excuse for the fantasy but I am quite sure that none of us would want to change places with our unfortunate comrades. Their future looked to be more precarious than ours; too many were already condemned.

One patient who went on the train was David Phimister; I mention David because I served with him in the Cameron Highlanders. After the war when I tried to trace him, I discovered that he had died two years after he got back home. The only other Cameron Highlander I was to come across while at the Sanatorium was John Gallacher, who came from the Inverness area and like myself was working as a nursing orderly. While at Elsterhorst he suffered a nasty accident. It all came about as a result of the nightly curfew, a restriction which allowed no one to be outside any of the buildings; if caught by the search-lights you ran the risk of being shot. Anyway, John, on duty one night, decided to take a chance and made a dash for one of the open windows in the barrack block opposite. He wanted to contact the night orderly in that block. However, what he did not realise was that the window he picked was above an unprotected step way leading to a boiler room below. He fell about ten feet onto the concrete below, damaging his pelvis and fracturing one of his legs. Because each barrack block usually had one night orderly, John lay for some time before he was discovered. Instead of looking after patients he became one himself and it took a long time for him to recover from his injuries.

John and I were two of a very small number of nursing orderlies who came from infantry units, most of the medical staff were members of the RAMC and there were a few from the RASC. The staff consisted mainly of British and Australians, with a few French, Poles, and Yugoslavians. Our senior Medical Officer was Lt. Col. Bull, a New Zealander, and his medical officers were a mix of British and Australians with one or two French. We had two members of staff – there might have been more – who were originally members of a Friends (Quakers) Ambulance Unit and were captured either in Greece or Crete.

Our Padre, Capt. Fraser, was the one who figured prominently in the arrangement of recreation and entertainment and of course the spiritual needs of both patients and staff. He had the flair to help lift the gloom from those who were down, and he was popular with the rank and file. Many a game of football we shared with him in our off duty time. After the war he resumed his ministry in the town of Nairn and was later to move to another parish in the Dundee area (Monifieth). I had the pleasure after the war of visiting and meeting him and his family at his home in Nairn. It was very sad to hear of his early death in 1962.

As attention to patients was a 24 hour job, nursing orderlies worked on a shift system. Day duty involved seeing to the needs of the bed patients and giving medication, which sometimes included giving injections. There were also the daily chores of making beds and cleaning the wards. Time slipped by quickly as there was always plenty to do. Night shift, on the other hand, was usually less demanding, time was monitored by the hourly walk round the wards to see that each patient was all right. When you had seriously ill cases in your charge, the night could be difficult, as it was usually then when the very ill were at their worst. If something cropped up which you were not too sure how to handle, there was always the NCO I/C to contact who was a recognised trained medical man – he slept in the barrack block. When on night shift it was better to be busy, for a quiet night made it a long night!

It was a distressing experience to see a tuberculous patient in the throws of death, made the more tragic by the circumstances we were all in. I often thought to myself, I've been through the rigours of war just like him, perhaps more, perhaps less, but here I am and there he lies. He was a healthy and fit young man not so long ago, now he is reduced to a wreck, eaten away by what was a merciless invader. When the disease eventually reached the unbridled stage, then the last bastion, the will to live gave in – an undeserved end!

However, all was not loss; amazingly we had a great deal of success, all due in the main to the good work of the Medical Officers and the dedicated efforts of all the staff. Apart from the need for rest for both bed patients and up patients there were, at the time, two main forms of treatment – streptomycin had not yet arrived on the scene.

Known as Pneumothorax, this was one way to collapse and rest the lung by the use of air. What appeared to be a simple device was used to carry out this form of treatment. It consisted of two glass cylinders, each half filled with a clear liquid and fixed side by side to a box style container, which was upright when it was in use. When not in use, it could be closed like a suitcase. From the cylinders was an extension of rubber tubing and connected to its end was a large hypodermic needle. The Medical Officer inserted the needle between the ribs at a specific spot, then by manipulation of the cylinders he controlled a flow of air into the patient's pleural cavity. Over a course of time a level of air pressure was maintained in the chest wall, enough to keep the lung at the required position to give it rest and allow the diseased part to heal. All patients were monitored at regular intervals, with X-ray screening being the essential part of the process. Adhesions in the costal arch were sometimes present and had to be cut to allow the lung to continue its collapse. In some difficult cases when there were adhesions, a rib or two might have to be removed.

The other method, which likewise was to collapse the lung, was known as the Phrenic Crush. To get at the phrenic nerve, it was necessary for a small incision to be made in the area of the collar bone and on the same side as the affected lung. Once access was made, the nerve was crushed which put the related side of the diaphragm temporary out of action. Instead of the diaphragm making its usual flattening out and upward movement, it now remained in the upward position, putting pressure on the lung and preventing it from moving in its usual way. Again this was a way of resting the diseased tissue and giving it the chance to heal.

Both methods were used in the treatment of pulmonary tuberculosis. In the case of the miliary type, it was a far more complicated disease that was a different matter. It was most dangerous because the tubercle bacillus was not localised like in the case of pulmonary; there was no knowing where and how far it would spread. I have no knowledge of how many progressed – if that's the right assumption – from pulmonary to miliary. What I do remember is that miliary claimed nearly all of those we lost. To show the extent of work that was done, we had one patient who had a kidney successfully removed. It seemed that in a medical sense, captivity did not restrict: if anything, it looked to have gained from what went on.

It was up to nursing orderlies to get to know as much as possible about the theory of the disease, but that was as far as it went. The intricacies, which no doubt were many, were a matter for the Medical Officers. There was an excellent rapport between Medical Officers and orderlies, an important factor in our fight against the disease. The situation we were in, broke down the barrier of rank. The Medical Officer's attitude was more akin to that of the family doctor.

I find it surprising that I can still recall some of the limited knowledge I gained during my time as a nursing orderly. This I make accountable to one particular mentor; he was the NCO i/c of the wards where I worked. Reg Penton was a corporal in the Australian Army Medical Corps and in civilian life was a male-nurse. He was good to work with and, to those who were keen to know, he was always willing to pass on his wide range of medical knowledge. Even the Medical Officers allowed him a latitude which far exceeded that of his rank. They knew that his capabilities deserved it. His work rate was prodigious and he showed all the finest qualities of a man devoted to his work. My later thoughts raised the question, what recognition, if any, did men like Reg (and others) get? In my reference to others, I take as an example a fellow Scot by the name of Davie Talbot. He was a member of one of the Corps (RASC or RAMC) who was captured early in the war and had been a member of the Sanatorium staff for quite some time. Much of his work was in the morgue and it included assisting at post-mortems. The wearing of a rubber apron was a sombre feature of his attire as he went about his work. I thought then and I still think now, that in those circumstances, it was a job which called for someone of special character.

There is one other Australian I have cause to remember, but for a different reason. I first met Ivan Chapman in Gruba Erika Stalag IVA where he was one of the recognised interpreters. He moved on to the Sanatorium at Elsterhorst to do admin. work and it was while he was there, that his word helped me to be moved from Gruba Erika to Elsterhorst. Ivan was a medical student before the war, but on his return home after the war decided not to continue with his studies. I had a letter from him not long after he got back home and by then he had found employment with the Australian Broadcasting Commission. Our good intentions to keep in touch petered out, but for all that he – to use the Aussie lingo – will always be remembered as a good cobber!

For myself, I was most grateful in many ways for the opportunity to work as a nursing orderly in Reserve Lazarett Elsterhorst. I gained much from the men I worked alongside and from the patients I looked after. It was rewarding work and seemed to lessen the stigma, if that is the right word to use, of being a prisoner of war. In looking after others, it helped to divert that introvert leaning which tended to find greater scope in the environment of a prison camp. The Sanatorium atmosphere gave one, to a certain extent, the feeling that you were back in service and contributing to the war effort.

Apart from those important considerations, Elsterhorst had something extra to offer which was paramount in the life of a POW – you did not have the same uncertainty of where your next bite of food was coming from. I no longer had to forage and scrounge! A steady flow of Red Cross parcels came the way of the Sanatorium and along with the German rations, our cooks saw to it that by POW standards we didn't do too badly. As to its quality – for the patients, the best was deservedly given. The food situation remained like this until the last few months of the war and then things became difficult. Because of the general disruption on road and rail, supplies became a big problem.

The Christmas of 1944 was, for me, the only one since 1939 that had any measure of what the celebration was all about. Conditions in the Sanatorium at Elsterhorst allowed this to happen. Preparations were ably carried out by Padre Fraser and his committee, whose improvisation on the required trappings were a masterpiece. Mass and Holy Communion were held on Christmas Eve and Christmas morning. At midday the patients had Christmas dinner and those of us on the staff not on duty had dinner in the evening at 5.30 p.m. Despite the deceptive menu card, we all appreciated the cook's magnificent effort.

From Boxing Day until Friday 29th December, there was a show each evening of the pantomime 'Harem Scarem' with Padre Fraser a leading light in the production. The bed patients were the first to see the show at 2.30 in the afternoon of 26th and 27th December. In addition to the pantomime, for those of us on the staff there was a football competition; and for some of the patients, an arts and crafts exhibition. Throughout the whole of the Festive week there were the usual duties which had to be carried out, but no dispensation was given by the Germans – the curfew which commenced each evening at 2100 hours remained unchanged.

By comparison, the two previous Festive Seasons, particularly the 1942 one, had given us little uplift from our impoverished situation. We did however appreciate the arrival, on time, of a consignment of Red Cross parcels. In each was a small Huntly and Palmer's Xmas Cake, and Festive greeting labels were fixed on some of the items. This thoughtful gesture touched many of our hearts, but as usual parcels had to be shared – during the first eighteen months of POW life we never had a whole parcel to ourselves. The distribution varied: one parcel between four, three or two and the issue was seldom if ever on a weekly cycle, supplies were erratic.

The Festive Season was a time of year when a celebration drink was missed, especially at Hogmanay by the Scots among us. However, the inventive mind of POWs got to work and we produced a potent substitute, known as 'POW Hooch'. This illicit activity was not easily set-up as the equipment, ingredients and the one necessary item – yeast – had to be smuggled from outside into the camp. The larger camps were better favoured than small working camps (Arbeits Kommando), as they had a greater choice of where to distil and hide the product. However, security was never easy within a camp whatever the size, mainly because of the smell the brew gave off during distilling.

A fitting motto for those of us who served in the POW Sanatorium, Germany

I first heard about Hooch when I arrived in Germany, but it was not until I arrived in Reserve Lazarett Elsterhorst that I tasted it and saw how it was processed. The hospital, with its dispersed barrack blocks, offered advantages. There was easier access to ingredients and equipment, with a choice of where to carry out the process. Our own security made sure that only certain people did the distilling and knew where the end product was kept.

Distilling equipment consisted of a few simple utensils – a container for soaking and boiling the ingredients; a small basin or suitable receptacle for holding a quantity of cold water; and finally a length of rubber tubing. Most of the ingredients were saved over a period of time from Red Cross parcels; but there were odd items, such as potato peelings and dried bananas. The latter were a bit of a mystery, where did they come from? Anything with a sugary/starchy content served the purpose.

The process was simple once the ingredients, aided by a quantity of yeast, were left to soak for sometime: it then fermented and was ready for distilling. The container with its fermented contents was then sealed off (by improvised means). One end of the tube was already in place inside the container, fixed in a way that kept it above the liquid level of the fermented contents. The tube in this position acted as an outlet for the vapour which the fermented contents gave off during the time it was being boiled. Part of the remaining tubing was submerged in cold water and it was at this stage when the vapour reached the submerged tube, that a change from vapour to spirit took place. The spirit then slowly passed through the remaining piece of rubber tubing to drip into a small container from where it was put into a bottle. It was a slow process, with the end product's degree of proof confirmed by how easily it ignited at the touch of a lighted match! Afterwards it was watered down to go further in the sharing and also to lessen shock to the palate!

Not only did we have a source of Hooch in the Sanatorium but there was also a hidden radio. For security reasons the radio's location was known to only two or three of the staff. When news was received over the radio, it was jotted down as a bulletin, circulated to just a few and the paper was then destroyed – thereafter word of mouth did the rest. Nothing could be of greater value than to know what was going on in the outside world. It was a situation which ended when we moved from Elsterhorst, leaving us with only camp rumours to get on with.

As far as I can remember, the Germans did not bother us too much, they let us get on with the work of looking after the sick. German doctors visited the wards but other ranks kept clear. They were only there for guard duty and administration. Not long after I arrived in Elsterhorst, the German soldiers (*Wehrmacht*) changed their usual military salute to that of the Nazi way, an upward extended arm – *Heil Hitler!* We discovered soon after that the change was made because of the attempt made on Hitler's life. This was their way of showing that there still remained throughout the German Armed Forces an allegiance to the Fuhrer. About this time, very heartening war news was getting through to us; it was all very exciting and hopes were high that our days of captivity would soon be over. The Germans too seemed to be showing a less arrogant attitude towards us, so all in all morale was on a high.

It turned out that the last repatriation, in January 1945, got away just in time, for by the middle of February, the eastern front was moving dangerously close. Distant gunfire was a signal that it was time for us to move out.

28

To move a hospital and its patients at short notice, especially under the circumstances, called for a huge effort on everyone's part. However, it was done, and by 18th February 1945 we were on our way by train, heading for somewhere that would distance us from the advancing Russians. Because of German security, we did not know until towards the end of the journey where we were bound for. It took us six days to cover a journey which in normal times would only have taken two days at the most. Time and time again, we were shunted into railway sidings to allow military trains to pass, and there was also Allied Air Force activity to further our delay.

As it turned out, we were into the last few months of a period of incessant bombing and strafing by the Allies. Shortly before we left Elsterhorst, the Americans in their 'Flying Fort' bombers made a daylight raid on a factory not that far from where we were. Here was an example of German decentralisation of industry and the extent of Allied aerial activity. It reached a stage when we hoped that we would not be moved. But that wasn't to be, and although we were within earshot of bombing during the move, our luck held and we arrived safely at our destination.

During the journey we did everything possible for the patients, but conditions made it extremely difficult. The bed patients, most of whom were in a bad way, suffered by having to lie on stretchers in cattle-wagons with the floor of the wagon covered in straw. For the sitting patients, they could at least do things for themselves, which left the nursing orderly with more time to devote to the lying patients. I had one very ill patient in my charge. He was Sudanese and was not expected to last long. The jolting of the train was more than he could stand and because of his bowel condition, it was necessary for me to give him an enema. I attended to him as best I could, but it was distressing to see him go through such a harrowing time – relief came some days later when he passed away.

After all this time, my memory only gives a faint reflection of the journey. Perhaps it was because of apprehension, the monotony of the journey and the frustration in not being able to carry out properly the care which the patients required. There was one comforting thought – had the repatriation not got away the previous month, there would have been many more who would have had to suffer the same ordeal.

On 24th February 1945 we arrived at our destination, Reserve Lazarett H57 Hohenstein-Ernstthl Stalag IVF. It was a large, rambling building with outhouses and a few ground floor barrack blocks, all of which were enclosed by barbed-wire fencing. In appearance, the main building looked to have been, at one time, a land owner's country residence. It was situated close to a main road which, we discovered, was part of the one time famous motor cycle racing track known as the Saxon Circle. The village of Hohenstein-Ernstthl lay approximately 4 kilometres from the hospital and some 18 kilometres further on, near the Czechoslovakian border, was the town of Chemnitz. We were also not that far from an *autobahn* intersection which turned out to be a most informative landmark. Most days it was used as a rendezvous by large formations of American Flying Forts. We were now into a phase of the war when 1000 bomber raids were not uncommon. Once the bombers arrived over the intersection, they would split up into smaller formations to go in different directions to their allotted targets.

Reserve Lazarett H57 Hohanstein–Ernstthal Stalag IVF already functioned as a general hospital and therefore, when we arrived, it was necessary for our patients to be isolated. We took over a number of wards and remained on our own until liberation. It did not take long to get back to the routine of the Elsterhorst days, but there was one telling difference – our food supply had become a problem. Because of the now general disruption of road and rail, supplies were not getting through. It was now up to those of us on the staff to tighten our belts so that the patients got what nourishment there was. It was back to square one, having to resort to the wiles of the hungry. I was fortunate to have help from a fellow Scot, Andrew Bell of the RSFs – his daily work took him outside the confines of the camp. When he returned from his stint, true to the ethics of a POW, he did not return empty handed. Somehow he always managed to get through the gate with a boiling of potatoes, which was later shared out among our little group. The word 'manna' had often crossed my mind, again was a time! This was to be the last of an era, when acts of genuine sharing was the norm – the one great good to come out of war and privation.

The advance of the Allies from east and west, plus the day and night bombing, had a devastating effect on everything. From the time we moved into Reserve Lazarett H57 Hohenstein–Ernstthl Stalag IVF, not a night or a day passed without hearing the might of the Allied air forces at work – we were in the right area to attract such attention. It was the Americans by day and the RAF by night – daylight was high altitude bombing and at night we had close experience of how the RAF did it! When Chemnitz was the target, which was very often, the RAF would fly low over our camp. Even a snow storm on one occasion did not stop their presence.

As time wore on, February into March, the hospital was taking in more and more patients. In one day alone, a batch of prisoners arrived all suffering from frostbite. They had been on a long march, making their way from east to west to escape the consequence of being caught up in the Russian advance.

The severe winter weather had taken its toll and their condition was well advanced by the time they reached hospital.

They were given a ward to themselves because of the type of treatment they received, and it also localised the smell which frostbite gives off. It was the first time I had seen it but the smell was familiar – decaying human flesh. All were confined to bed and those with frost-bitten feet, which was nearly all of them, lay with their feet uncovered. This was to allow the injury to dry and also to monitor the reaction temperate conditions had on the affected part. Fingers and ears were the other extremities which suffered. Despite the men's distress, their appreciation for being rescued and given cover, hid any rankle they might have had.

Again one was seeing another distressing sight – to think, after years of captivity, they had to suffer in this way, which for several would mean having to lose at least part of a limb. The mention of this type of disability reminds me of one unforgettable character in the hospital. He was an American air crew member and had both legs amputated while in captivity. I never knew his background or when he arrived in Hohenstein–Ernstthl but he could not have been a prisoner for long, otherwise he would have joined the January 1945 repatriation. What made him so well known, apart from his disability, was the way he got around the camp compound. Whenever he wanted to go from one place to another, he mounted the back of the first passer-by and pointed where to go.

Towards the end of March 1945, as well as intense air activity, there was on the ground every indication that very soon we would be in the path of the retreating German forces. The now regular appearance of our fighter planes strafing nearby roads, was a sign which told us that a lot of transport must be on the move and that the front line could not be that far off. People as well as transport were on the move – one unforgettable incident took place when a party of young women passed close by our camp. It was just a week or two before our liberation. The young women ranged in age between sixteen and early thirties and all were in a pitiful state, hardly able to walk, trying to assist each other and at the same time crying for mercy.

We assumed that they were Jewish, and by their condition looked to have been on the road for some time. Their escort, SS Guards, both men and women, had no scruples on how they went about keeping their prisoners on the move. It was the women SS who were applying the brutal touch – hitting the young women with their leather whips across the back of the neck and the small of the back. Our immediate response to all this were shouts of abuse – words unfit for the parlour! As expected, it made no difference, they continued to behave in their inhuman way. We were told later that the young women ended up in the woods further along the road, where automatic weapons and grenades sent them to their rest.

Moving to Hohnstein–Ernstthl had lifted a shutter on a situation which had gone on for a long time. In the past, the frustration for most of us had been not knowing where we really were or where we were going. Camps were located in out of the way places, leaving one in a world which stopped at the barbed-wire fence. Now it was different: we were in an area of landmarks, where all around things seemed to be happening – we had at last found our bearings!

I had another unpleasant duty to do towards the end of my captivity, which came about as a result of an American bomber crashing not far from the camp. The plane in its out-of-control dive just missed the main hospital building before hitting the ground and exploding in a pillar of smoke and fire. On its way down, we only saw one member of the crew bale out, but to our horror, his parachute did not open and he hit the ground near to where the plane crashed. We could only assume that the remainder of the crew perished in the plane. Once the crew member's body was recovered, it was taken to the hospital mortuary where another nursing orderly and myself prepared the body for burial.

He was a very young man and what surprised me most of all was his appearance – he was all in one piece! It was somewhat naive of me to think he should have been any other way. It was the thought of him hitting the ground with such force that made me think on such lines. He had the telling marks on his body of a large shrapnel wound on the thigh and bullet wounds on the chest (entry and exit). The wounds made it likely that death came before he had time to pull the rip-cord of his parachute. As we progressed with the work of preparing the body, it became noticeable that discoloration and swelling was setting in, signs of severe internal damage and multiple fractures. Once our work was complete, we left for others to accord him the respect he deserved.

A day or two after this exciting but tragic event, we were to hear once again the familiar sound of shells passing overhead – an exchange of fire. This told us that we must now be between two fronts and, although the sound of shell fire was music to our ears, we were all a bit edgy. After all, we had run a good race and with the finishing tape now in sight, we all wanted to make it! The shelling continued to pass overhead and luckily for us it remained at long range.

Unfortunately not all were to reach the finishing line. The most tragic incidents – made doubly so as both victims were well known – were yet to come. On 13th April 1945, the penultimate to our day of liberation, three nursing orderlies and an ambulance driven by a German, went out to collect wounded from the fighting which had taken place nearby. On the way out, they were caught in crossfire and one of our nursing orderlies was badly wounded and died soon after.

We all grieved the passing of this popular Australian who had served the TB patients a long time and had been a POW for four years. Shortly after, I can't remember if it was the same day or early next morning, we lost one of our English TB patients. I had known him since Gruba Erika (Stalag IVA) days and it was very sad that he had come so far and had to give in at the end. It was ironic that the last few months of captivity was tinged with much sorrow – it added to the pressure of those latter days!

I now turn to the closing notes from my diary: '14th April 1945, at last the long awaited day has arrived, at 0855 hours this morning advanced units of the 3rd American Army arrived at the gates of Reserve Lazarett H57 Hohenstein-Ernstthl Stalag IVF. Greeted with loud cheers, they hoisted their flag, the stars and stripes. It signalled their arrival and our liberation. Words cannot express one's feelings on this great occasion.'

29

For years the day of liberation had never been out of our thoughts and now it was here, everything about it seemed unreal. We would soon be on the road to normality, a transition period, which in time was to uncover many problems; but for today, it was for us to try and take in the full significance of our position – freedom at last!

Our liberators did not hang around for long and left us to get on with our work, we still had patients to attend to. They in turn seemed, for the time being at least, to be in little need of treatment – the special prescription of the day had done wonders. A day or two after liberation our work in the wards came to an end – a fleet of American ambulances arrived to take away the patients. Before the hand-over could get under way, the American medics, themselves already with masks on, asked us to put a mask on each of our patients. Once this was done, they then set about loading the ambulances. We assisted them with the stretcher cases, and I remember their look of amazement when they noticed that we went about our work handling·TB patients without the use of a mask. When we told them that we had been doing this for a very long time, they just looked at us. I wonder what they were thinking?

The hand over did not take long and with all our good wishes, they were on their way. So ended an exclusive relationship between medical staff and patients. Its form was something which none of us would ever again experience. With our responsibilities shed, our first thought was when would it be our turn? We had a further ten days to wait, during which time we were well looked after by the Americans. Perhaps they looked after us too well – there was plenty of food and our natural reaction after the penury of the past was to eat more than there was a need to. This tended to disrupt the digestive system – for some more than others.

Our days of hunger and scarcity of food were over, but we had yet to experience what it was really like to be free. As we waited for transport to take us away, time seemed to stand still and it was an impatient period for us all. I gained some relief when, along with two fellow Scots, we broke camp and made our way down to the village of Hohenstein–Ernstthl. Perhaps it was a bit foolhardy of us to venture outside the camp, but with no restrictions, there seemed no call for restraint which I suppose blinded us to the element of risk. It transpired that armed irregular bands of Hitler Youth were roving the countryside, no doubt a nuisance to the rear elements of the advancing Allies. In our travels, we saw none and if we had, we would not have stood around for long!

As the three of us walked through the village, we encountered no signs of hostility; if anything they were quite friendly, and seemed every bit as pleased as we were that the war was about over. A good example of their attitude towards us came about as we were leaving the village on our way back to camp. At a house on the fringe of the village, three young women were leaning out of a window. As we passed, we shouted up to them in our limited German and asked if we could have something to drink. It was as good an excuse as any: good enough to grant us an invitation to come inside.

They had little to offer, but it did not matter, we were interested in the young women – as young men and ex-POWs, we had been starved of more than just food! The family consisted of the three daughters and their mother and, like nearly all German families, there was no man around. All were doing their bit for the Fatherland. Their appearance and the furnishings of the house indicated that they were of good standing.

They made us most welcome and eventually the mother disappeared, to leave each of us to chat up one of the daughters. My limited German seemed sufficient to make an impression on one of them. As it turned out, she was the only married one of the three and had not heard from her husband in two years. He was serving on the Russian front and because of his silence, she did not know whether he was dead or alive but she feared the worst. She conveyed to me that she had given up hope of ever seeing him again and, perhaps, this could well explain her way of response to my company!

When I returned the next day, she told me if I was to return the following evening I could sleep with her. How could I resist such a tempting offer? Here was a young married women of respectable stock, stripped down to the innate because of war and there was I, being given the chance to experience the natural pleasures of an aspect of life which, up till now, I knew very little about. I always wanted, when the time came, to realise from my belief that there was a sublime and finer side to it all. But how in these circumstances would I react when the time did come? This I hoped to discover when I returned the following day, but alas there was not to be a next time. When I got back to camp that night, we were told that we were moving out early next morning!

It was the news we had been waiting for, and what had been on my mind a short time before was now forgotten. I had long since recognised the part the hand of fate had played in one's life. It was at it again, altering the course and leaving speculation to conjure up what might have happened!

After breakfast on the morning of 26th April 1945, we set off on the first leg of our journey home. The Americans were sparing with the number of trucks they arrived with, which meant that we had to make the best of the limited space. It was no hardship, we were used to uncomfortable journeys anyway, and this of all times was no time to belly ache: it was our day of triumph.

As we passed through the main gate of the hospital (Hohenstein–Ernstthl Stalag IVF), there was a release of emotion. Further on, as we rounded the first bend in the road, we were given a last glimpse of the now deserted camp. It was no longer a place of oppression, but only a lonely edifice, a symbol which now marked the end of an epoch. An epoch which no doubt would find its place in history but would also leave us to rid ourselves of the memory of those wasted years – would that ever be possible?

Once we joined the autobahn, we drove in a westerly direction. At no time did we ask what the day's schedule was – as long as the driver had his foot down and was going in what we guessed to be the right direction; that was all that mattered. The road was in good condition and was being used a lot by the American Forces. Because of heavy growth on either side, we only had a patchy look of passing countryside, a limited view of what the ravages of war had left behind.

We made good headway and after two or three stops, we arrived that afternoon in what was left of the town of Erfurt. It turned out that Erfurt was as far as we were to journey by truck and we were to remain there for the next fortnight. Our quarters, on the outskirts of town, had previously been occupied by German Artillery. It had been extensively bombed and only a few large barrack blocks remained habitable. Already a large number of ex-POWs had congregated and it looked as if the barracks were being used as a collecting point for those POWs liberated within the vicinity of Erfurt.

The Americans (members of General Patton's 3rd Army) were still in charge and continued to see to our needs. Our only complaint was that they kept us in the dark as to when we were to be moved out of Germany. Naturally, we wanted to get home as quickly as possible but realised that to move such a large number of men would take quite some organising. Day after day for the first week, there was a steady flow of arrivals but it was to take time before there was any outward movement. However when it did start, they wasted no time in getting us away.

While we waited, we were left very much to ourselves, which gave us the impression that the Americans were fairly easy going. Perhaps they felt we deserved kid-glove treatment, for there were no restrictions and they did not stop us from visiting the town. We took advantage of this and got to know some of the locals. It was too early in time to know about fraternisation and its perils.

It was in Erfurt where we saw the full destructive power of aerial bombing. Not one building was intact, the town was a complete ruin with the population, living in cellars or whatever vestige of shelter they could find. It was a situation, as time was to reveal, typical of the havoc and chaos throughout towns and cities in Germany. Later, in our flight from Erfurt to Brussels, we were to have a more impressive sighting from the air. This showed the incredible extent of the damage inflicted on the country – a reflection of the instability of man's sanity!

On one visit to Erfurt, two companions and myself got talking to an American who was standing guard over a partially damaged building. He told us that behind the door where he stood was a cellar full of the finest champagne, all of which had been taken over by the Germans when they occupied France. We had his permission to enter the cellar and have our fill and once we had finished, we could carry away as many bottles as we wished.

It was our lucky day: as we entered the cellar, the sight that met our eyes was incredible – the four sides of the cellar were stacked full from floor to ceiling. We found some empty boxes to sit on, made ourselves comfortable and drank for the first time the so called nectar of the rich. After drinking several toasts to our liberation, we decided to move on. With eight bottles concealed on our person – sobriety at this stage prevailed, I still remember the exact number – we left the cellar.

Once back outside, we found ourselves in the middle of a hostile crowd of civilians. We did not hang around to find out what the demonstration was all about – most likely it had something to do with the distribution of food. As we made to get away from the crowd, there was a sudden noise of screeching brakes and before we knew it, four jeeps appeared and out jumped several American Military Police with drawn truncheons. Their immediate reaction made it clear that they were not particular who caught the end of their weapons. They went into the crowd striking out in all directions. This spurred us on to a quicker pace and despite the weight of the champagne, we made our get-away without mishap and with all bottles intact.

We spent the evening in Erfurt arriving back in barracks without a bottle to show for our day's good fortune – proof of how convivial the evening turned out to be. It was my last outing in Germany – perhaps it was not such a bad way to take leave of a country which had contributed so much to a dismal period of one's life. There was the consolation of having partaken of a high quality champagne, something which I was unlikely ever to savour again.

Our somewhat flippant behaviour did not blind me to what was going on. My stay in Erfurt was long enough to convince me of the desperate plight of the German people. The arrival of the Occupying Forces changed overnight the attitude of the Germans, who no longer exhibited the face of the 'master race'. There seemed nothing that most of them would not do for such luxuries as coffee, chocolate, cigarettes and toiletries.

By now, I had come round to think that it was better to learn from such behaviour than to be critical of it. If placed in a similar situation, how many of us would have reacted in much the same way? When we live in a kind world, there is no demand to come to grips with the unknown self. If anything, it is then when a less virtuous side is likely to show!

On 12th May 1945, we left Erfurt on the second leg of our journey home. This time our method of transport was different. After a short journey by truck, we arrived at a nearby airstrip. Without much ado, we were numbered off, mustered into groups and then assigned to one of the many American Dakota planes lined up ready for take-off. Before boarding the plane many of us were a bit apprehensive having not flown before. However, going on the casual way the American crewmen went about their business, was perhaps their way of saying, Have confidence in us, we will get you there. It worked for me, for once we were airborne, I was quite taken with the sensation of flying. With a fair amount of broken cloud and flying at not too high an altitude, we were able to see areas of landscape. It was interesting from a height to see the form war destruction took on. Our time in the air did not seem long and as we touched-down at Brussels Airport, I for one had a feeling of satisfaction at having completed a first!

After a smooth transfer from plane to truck, we were whisked away to billets in the outskirts of the city. The Americans at this stage had completed their mission and we were now in the hands of the British. From then on, it was noticeable the change in how we were handled.

Once settled in our billets, we were mustered for the one parade all servicemen look forward to – pay parade. This was our first one in a very long time and expectation was high, but as it was to turn out, we felt we were let down. Each man was handed out four pounds and ten shillings in Belgian francs and one English ten shilling note: the latter was for when we arrived in the UK. We did not know at the time, but the authorities did not think it wise to give us too much money so soon after liberation – our opportunity to squander was only delayed!

After pay parade we were free to leave the billets and visit Brussels. It so happened that in the course of that day I met up with three Cameron Highlanders who I had not seen since our capture. With our francs in our pockets, we set out to enjoy a night in the city. At first we took in some of the sights and then had refreshments. To this day, I can still see the four of us, sitting round a cafe table, each with a glass of beer; and in the centre of the table, a bowl containing 28 hard boiled eggs – seven for each of us. It was an order which had unanimous approval, as it was years since we had last tasted a real egg – the cost also suited our pockets! With our remaining few francs we managed to have another beer, which we lingered over before making our way back to billets.

In a way, our night out was the start of a re-learning process, which in time would rid us of one oddity which captivity had taxed us with – an erratic sense of value. To think, only a few days before, I was drinking the best of champagne yet now a hard boiled egg was being thought of as a luxury.

Next morning, with all our francs spent, it left us no other option but to remain in billets – it was 13th May. But again my lucky number hadn't failed me, for it turned out that it was to be our last day of waiting. On the forenoon of the following day, 14th May, we debussed at Brussels Airport and boarded an RAF Dakota for our last leg of our journey to the UK.

Throughout the flight, the pilot and crew were most helpful and kept us informed of the route we were taking. Before our run in to land at Aylesbury, Bucks, the pilot altered course slightly to give us a sight of some of the prominent landmarks of London. It was quite an experience for a landlubber to see London from above; but before that, what gave us the greatest thrill, a dream come true – seeing for the first time the white cliffs of Dover. As we flew close by the prominent landmark, each of us had our own silent thoughts which I'm sure could only be the paramount one of all – at long last, we had made it!

On board the plane there were men I had been along with since the day I arrived in Elsterhorst (Stalag IVA) and now we had come to the 'parting of the ways'. In retrospect, I think of those last few days as an anticlimax to a period of time that none of us would ever forget – it finished in such a casual way! We seemed to be in a hurry to get away from restrictions and to feel free, to find our own individuality in a private way.

It was a phase in our lives when we were all on a high, with the expectation that freedom would take care of everything. I soon discovered and as I suspect others did, that ahead lay a lengthy, complex transition period.

Home-coming has a special place in my memory, but I have not forgotten the mixed emotions I had at the time. Like any returning son, I was given love and attention from parents and family. But despite this comfort, I felt ill at ease because my response was not what I thought it should be. I did not expect, and I was not prepared for, the distance which seemed to have come between us. However, in time, I could see that it was what the absent years had done, and that I was no longer the boy turning to his parents, but a grown man.

Other peculiarities made their presence felt in those unsettling years. I remember feeling out of place in new company, a sense of isolation even though people were around and there was impatience – e.g. unable to stand in a bus queue or to remain indoors for any length of time. What was the most disturbing of all was the way one's memory responded – happenings the day before were very often shut out.

For a time I found solace in the company of fellow ex-POWs, for we understood each other and the meeting place, the pub, was where we found escape! However, in time I came to realise that to shut out reality in this way was no solution – it was a challenge which had to be taken on! The word counselling was unheard of and anyway, by and large, we were a generation that tended to keep things to ourselves and not shelve the burden onto others. Initiative directed me to do something about regaining the equilibrium and in the process took up pelmanism and various Skerry's correspondence courses.

After a long period of furlough in 1945, I reported to a camp in Otley Yorkshire where, as an ex-POW, I went through a schedule of physical and mental tests and, at the end of it, was given a medical grading. Like many others I was downgraded and therefore unfit to return to my own Infantry Unit. Instead I was posted to the Royal Engineers Postal Service at Nottingham where I saw out the remainder of my time.

In October 1947, with my Demob suit in its cardboard box, I passed through the barrack gates for the last time. I had known nothing else but service life and its camaraderie, and now I was venturing into the unknown.

Like the good Cameron Highlander I always tried to be, I took heart from the stirring words of our Chieftain, Cameron of Lochiel, that 'Whatever men dare they can do'!